# PAPER
# BOY

PAPER
BOY

# PAPER BOY

## THE MEMOIRS OF
## STUART KEATE

Clarke, Irwin & Company Limited, Toronto/Vancouver

Canadian Cataloguing in Publication Data

Keate, Stuart, 1913-
   Paper Boy
Includes index.
ISBN 0-7720-1300-4


1.  Keate, Stuart, 1913-     2.  Publishers and publishing-
British Columbia-Vancouver-Biography. 3.   Canadian
newspapers (English)-History.* I.   Title.

Z483.K42A3        071'.11'340924        C80-094712-6

©1980 by Clarke, Irwin & Company Limited

ISBN 0-7720-1300-4

1 2 3 4 5  W 84 83 82 81 80

# Acknowledgement

In a prefatory note to their book *The Brethren*, authors Bob Woodward and Scott Armstrong acknowledged with gratitude the assistance of some thirty-three colleagues who had participated in the "research, editing, reporting and writing" of the book.

That statistic struck a chill in my heart; obviously, I had gone about things in the wrong way. For I had undertaken on my own the task of sifting through a lifetime's accumulation of memoranda, letters, news-clips and books. It was a self-imposed assignment which took, off and on, five years to complete.

To be sure, many friends rallied round, offering encouragement and support. I was especially fortunate to have a wife who was, and is, a "walking memory bank" — the kind of person who can recall precise conversations of twenty-five years ago, together with a description of clothes worn, drinks consumed, and arguments joined.

My former secretaries Elsie Edwards, Hilda Weston and Dianne Kleinsorge helped trace some elusive quotes and typed the manuscript; Shirley Mooney, head of the Pacific Press library, generously made available its superb resources; Marilyn Stusiak of the *Sun* put together the index; and photographers Bill Halkett of Victoria and Charlie Warner of Vancouver were enthusiastic in their pursuit of relevant pictures.

Finally I want to thank Paul Nanton, a director of Clarke Irwin, now in Victoria. Paul saw a tiny item in the press about the work-in-progress and wrote to ask if he could read a chapter or two. I am much indebted to him for his interest and encouragement.

For Letha, Richard and Kathryn
... companions along the way

# Foreword

On a certain sunny Sunday afternoon in May of 1935 I was whiling away my time on the practice green of the old Quilchena golf course in Vancouver. The next morning I was due to start as a staff sports writer at the Vancouver *Province*, at a salary of $20 a week, and to celebrate the occasion I had bought a new suit at Tip Top Tailors — $22.50, with two pairs of pants.

Suddenly the afternoon calm was rent by a terrible crash, followed by the gunning of a car engine and what sounded like human moans. I dropped my putter and started to run in the direction of the sound. I placed it at Thirty-third Avenue and West Boulevard, directly behind Quilchena's first green, so I knew the distance exactly: the first hole was 392 yards long.

The sight that greeted my eyes at the busy intersection was not pleasant. The bodies of two elderly people sprawled haphazardly on the road, their old car splayed and battered. The second car had obviously fled the scene. It was a tableau that cried out for a news picture. But where to find a camera?

I remembered that a school chum, Charles Guy, lived just a couple of blocks away and started to run for his home. Luckily, he was in. "Charlie," I gasped, "Have you got a camera?"

"Only a Box Brownie," he replied.

"Give it to me," I said. He handed me one of the little black boxes, a sort of precursor of the Instamatic, and I started to run again, back to the scene of the crash. I was no photographer. But I figured that if I played the percentages, exhausting the film, I might just capture one shot which was usable.

Back at the office, I handed the camera to the photographic department and went off to check the accident with the police. The story got better: the car which had barrelled east on Thirty-third Avenue and run the stop sign had been stolen by two boys. The police had since apprehended them.

Thus it came to pass, on my first day as a "professional" journalist (albeit in a different department) that the *Province* rolled off the presses with an on-the-spot account of the tragedy: a front-page picture of the wrecked car and its victims, a story and a by-line.

Somebody Up There, I reflected, had decided that I should be a newspaperman.

# Chapter 1

"All life is 11-5 against"

— *Damon Runyon*

Stephen Leacock said it better than anyone: if he had known beforehand what a beautiful city Vancouver was, he would have arranged to have been born there.

As a native son, I find it hard to quarrel with that assessment. There was, to begin with, the magnificent natural setting of snow-capped mountains, forest and sea. The climate was temperate; if it rained 58 inches a year, it was still better than the gelid blasts of the prairies and East. Vancouver's fine harbour bustled with cargoes of lumber, mineral, grain and salmon, and in 1913, the year of my birth, the raw young city, perhaps 100,000 in population, was moving confidently towards its destiny as one of the great seaports of the world.

It was a boy's idyll. The bungalow my father and mother built in 1911, four years after they came west from Michigan on their honeymoon, had only a few vacant lots between itself and the sea. Few could foresee that our Point Grey Road, on the outskirts of the city in the middle-class district of Kitsilano, would half a century later command prices of $2,000 a front foot and, with one of the most majestic views in Canada, evolve as luxury property. Sidewalks then were of rough planks and the road, more often than not, thick gumbo.

Within fifty yards of our house, from an outcropping called "the ledge", we caught flounder, sea trout and the occasional salmon. Smelt ran in such thousands that they could, when trapped by ebbing tides, be scooped onto the beach by hand. It was possible to swim in the ocean four months a year. The air was rich with the fragrance of wet logs, salmon roe and rain forest.

Our pleasant little cottage was heated by coal, which was delivered in sacks to a basement bin and thereafter shovelled into a sheet-metal furnace by the Keate brothers for an allowance of twenty-five cents a week. Food was kept cool in a wooden ice-box on the back porch. On hot summer days the arrival of the iceman was a cause for celebration. With easy grace, he clamped a twenty-five-pound block of ice with tongs, swung it onto a leather saddle on his shoulder and made for the back of the house. As soon as he was out of sight, neighbourhood miscreants (including me) materialized from every alley, descended on the tail-gate of his truck with ice-picks, and chipped away "icicles" which seemed to taste as good as ice cream.

Delivery service, almost unknown today, was a commonplace thing. A cheery Chinese named Wong offered fresh Lulu Island lettuce and other vegetables from his horse-drawn truck. Grocery stores delivered daily. Laundry, dry-cleaning, bakeries, drug stores (and doctors!) responded promptly to calls. A Sunday-morning telephone order for a Seattle newspaper, a cigar and a pint of ice cream was not too small to be honoured.

The tradesmen were well-known to householders, often on a first-name basis, and respected as members of "the neighbourhood family". At Christmas time, gifts were exchanged — dolls, a box of ginger, even a delicate Oriental fan. For years we employed a clean-up man named George, who had suffered brain damage. George was a little strange, but in spite of his infirmity he enjoyed the total trust of my mother, who gave her permission for George to take us to the Rex Theatre on a Saturday afternoon, and to buy us a doughnut after the show.

William Lewis Keate, my father, was described in newspaper obituaries in 1942 as a "pioneer timber-broker". Another way of saying it was that he was a Ten-per-center. He bought and sold logs and timber-lands. This brought him a good, at times even prosperous, living.

He was a member of the Jericho Golf Club at the end of Point Grey Road, of the Shaughnessy Heights Club on the hill, and the downtown Terminal City Club. He bought a new Buick phaeton every two or three years, complete with celluloid curtains, a canvas top which could be wrestled down in slightly less than a day, and a tiny vase for the display of bunches of sweet peas. It was a Sunday treat to be driven to Stanley Park and have the family picture taken in the hollow of an old tree; or, even more exciting, to cross the border into the State of Washington and have lunch at the Chuckanut Shell.

So the Keate family of four boys and a girl, of which I was the "middle child", was raised, if not in affluence, then at least in comfort. For pin-money we could sell beer-bottles — of which we seemed to have an inordinate supply — or deliver the *Province*, which came up to our sub-station at four o'clock each afternoon, smelling better than home-baked bread. Sanny, the old Greek grocer, would also pay us five cents for delivering a carton of eggs during the noon recess from school, but this was on the canny (and altogether correct) assumption that we would promptly re-invest our reward in one of his Lowney's Caramel bars.

Our public school, General Gordon, was just six blocks away, and it was in many ways unique. Among its graduates were the renowned Canadian diplomats Norman Robertson and Hugh Keenleyside. If it appeared a little militaristic, it also had access to touring writers and poets from the extremely thin ranks of Can. Lit. On one occasion we were visited by Sir Charles G. D. Roberts, who read a few of his poems and then gave us a short lecture on how to behave if confronted in the wilderness by a bear. Apparently the thing to do was to pretend that you were a tree. Freeze. Don't move. This intelligence baffled me at the time, as it did later in life when I encountered three wilderness bears. Two ran. The third couldn't, as he was trapped on a small island in Sproat Lake.

Our school principal, Major H. B. King, was recently returned from World War I and insisted on forming a Cadet Corps, complete with khaki uniforms, brass buttons and puttees. The school's janitor, a lumbering South African, taught cricket and installed huge fish-nets for the practice of bowling. In the basement there was a rifle-range. To add to this colonial ambience, walls of the school were festooned with pictures of Edward, Prince of Wales, in the uniform he had worn on visits to the front.

The hub of our little community, however, was not the school,

3

but St. Mark's Anglican Church, where the redoubtable Rev. Arthur H. Sovereign held sway. There were bean-feeds in the church basement, minstrel shows, hikes up Grouse Mountain, and an annual "Gym Display" where we tumbled on mats to the tune of "Barney Google and His Goo-Goo Googly Eyes".

My father was a people's warden at St. Mark's. It was his duty to see that the collection ended up where it should and generally attend to the seating and well-being of parishioners. On one notable occasion he and his colleagues stoked the furnace to such intensity that an elderly widow succumbed to heat prostration. What to do? The Rev. Sovereign confessed that he kept a bottle of brandy at his home, half a block away, for just such emergencies. A minion was dispatched. When he returned, the widow had come around a bit and was fluttering her eyelids.

"Hell," my father said, "she's all right. Let's throw some holy water in her face and drink the brandy." Which, while a little unorthodox, was what was done.

"Louie", as my father was widely known, had his frailties and they cost his family a good deal of anguish. But it was almost impossible not to like him. He was generous to the point of folly; his weaknesses were devoid of animus and caused him as much grief as those who suffered from them.

He was, by any standards, a handsome man with a mane of white hair and a Roman nose which gave him the mien of a senator. He affected a cane and was given to wearing stylish tweeds, which he had cut in England and gave him an air more British than North American. He used tobacco in all its forms (including "snoose" and "Old Chum"); was partial to oysters, savoury and other gourmet delights; and consumed strong waters with joyous abandon.

His problem was that he was a "bat" drinker. For seven or eight months of the year he toed a very precarious line, abjuring drink altogether. Then he would take off, hole up in a hotel, club, or some nearby city, and drink himself into a state of senselessness for weeks at a time.

Strange events flowed from these aberrations. On one occasion a taxi-driver knocked on the front door of our house to announce that he had a present for me. He opened the back door of his cab and out bounded a beautiful hunting dog, which my father had acquired after a beer-parlour conversation with a noted dog breeder. (As was inevitable with a "country" dog, the poor beast was run down and killed by city traffic in a week.) On another, we turned up at our summer cottage on Vancouver Island to be greeted at the door by a well-known bartender and his current *inamorata*. "Your dad said I could have the place for a little holiday," he explained.

Inevitably, Louie's domestic and business life suffered. In spite of threats, cajoling and endless tears, my mother would always take him back, dry him out, and put him together again. As we boys grew older and came to understand the problem, we became directly involved in the salvage operations — buying foul-smelling chemicals which were reputed to stifle the desire for booze; chipping ice for the ice-packs; and on one occasion, wiping the blood from his face after he had wrapped his car around a Granville Street lamp-standard.

For some reason, we could never stay angry with him. He was our pal. He boxed with us after supper, drove us to our ball games and our swimming meets, entertained us by "chording" on the piano while he sang about "The young Salvation Army lassie . . . who went to the Big City to Seek Employment . . . and rashly broke her Tambourine. . . . " He lectured us on the evils of the Conservative Party, whose members he described as "Fellows who spell Jesus Christ with a small 'j' ". Once he paid my brother Jeff and me twenty-five cents each to stand in front of Tory headquarters and sing a parody which he had written, entitled "They ain't a-gonna reign no mo', no mo' . . . "

His occasional disappearances, therefore, provoked more tears than anger. The pity was that they often occurred when my father was in the midst of important business deals, with the result that his family led a feast-or-famine existence, surviving during the lean periods on credit.

The word "deal" was of peculiar significance in the Keate household. "Be quiet tonight, boys," my mother would admonish. "Your father has a deal on." Sometimes these negotiations lasted for weeks or even months. If they turned out successfully, there were new wardrobes for everyone and the bills got paid. If they collapsed, belts were tightened and we knew it was only a matter of time before Louie would disappear for another protracted joust with the grape.

I remember being enormously cheered once when my father

sold some Rockefeller timber on Barkley Sound, in the Port Alberni area. The buyers were the Bloedel people and they paid $1 million.

"Isn't that great?" I said to my mother, when she relayed the good news. "Now Dad will have $100,000 for his commission."

My mother smiled wanly. "Yes, it's great," she replied, "except that he owes $94,000."

But in spite of these wild fluctuations, my father was able to provide a good education for each of his five children. When my brother Jeff was warned that he would never succeed in school because he drew funny pictures in the margins of his text-books, Louie sent him off to the Chicago Academy of Fine Art and thus started him off on a highly-successful career as a panel cartoonist. My sister Marcia, who had an inclination for the stage, was packed off to Missouri to study under Maude Adams. An older brother, Bill, prospered in the logging business; he was joined by a younger brother (Ed) who later made a name for himself as an entrepreneur in real estate, free-lance writing, a restaurant and a travel agency.

I was sent to the University of British Columbia — a good place to be during a depression. But even in the "bottom year" of 1933, my father was able to provide me with $300 so that I could visit the Eastern seaboard chapters of Psi Upsilon fraternity and attempt to persuade them to establish a branch on the UBC campus.

The mission was a success — and as a grace note, New York Fraternity headquarters invited my father to be initiated as a senior member at ceremonies in the old Hotel Vancouver in 1935.

This, in turn, led to Louie being invited to address the annual dinner of the fraternity at the Jericho Golf Club. On this occasion, Louie appeared a mere ten minutes before dinner was scheduled. Drinks, which had been delayed until his arrival, were served in jig time and the atmosphere of congeniality mounted. I watched with trepidation from across the room as the Guest Speaker began to throw them back. His tolerance was somewhere between one and two drinks, so when I observed him heading for the dining-table with a drink in his hand, and further observed that there was wine on the table, I sensed disaster. All the signs were there: Louie's face was flushed, his hand a bit unsteady; most frightening

6

of all, an occasional tear was stealing down his cheek, which meant that he was on the threshold of a "crying jag".

With extravagant praise, the chairman of the dinner announced: "And now we give you our featured speaker of the evening, Louie Keate!"

Louie braced himself on the arms of his chair, staggered to his feet, and began wiping tears from his eyes with his table napkin. With trembling chin, he surveyed his audience of young fraternity nobs. Then he spoke:

"Boysh," he said, "alwaysh be genn'lmens."

Then he sat down.

For a moment, there was a stunned silence. Then the brothers, realizing that they had just been delivered of a four-word speech, lasting about five seconds, burst into cheers and laughter, followed by a standing ovation.

In many ways, the university seemed detached from the dreadful privations of the ouside world. Tuition fees for the 1,500 students then on the UBC campus were $135 a year. Meals could be had in the cafeteria for thirty-five cents. Gasoline cost a quarter a gallon. Seniors attending the Saturday night dance at The Commodore brought with them an eighty-five-cent mickey of Silver Fizz gin. On one memorable New Year's Eve, I hired a five-piece Mart Kenney orchestra for the staggering sum of $36.

There were rugby matches with Victoria College, tours of the interior of BC with the Players' Club, golf excursions to the University of Washington in Seattle, a hazing of freshmen so outrageous it had to be stopped. There was also a brisk trading of pins with Delta Gammas and Kappas; if these interludes led irrevocably to matrimony, it was agreed that a young couple could manage nicely on an income of $150 a month.

A noted academic once observed that "Education is what you have left over when you leave school." If that is true, it seems to me that the most valuable training I received at UBC stemmed from extra-curricular activities. The campus newspaper, *The Ubyssey*, taught me how to write a news story and make up pages. The Players' Club taught me how to stand in front of 1,000 people without flinching. Golf, basketball and swimming kept me in reasonable shape. The fraternity taught me how to drink beer. The Students' Council introduced me to politics.

As a result, my grades were neglected. It took me five years to pass freshman trigonometry and algebra. The only academic triumph I enjoyed was in, of all things, Shakespeare, when the renowned Dr. Garnet Sedgwick gave me 98 per cent on an essay purporting to show how the language of Othello and Iago illuminated their respective characters.

"I don't believe it," said Sedgwick, as he read out the results and found my name at the top of the list. But the fact of the matter was that we had Shakespeare in our house, and read it.

We also had music. In the beginning, it emanated from a wind-up Victrola, playing records as thick as manhole covers. Later we graduated to an Orthophonic, with something called Red Seal records (Richard Crooks and Jascha Heifetz), and a radio component which inaugurated our lifelong love-affair with Fred Allen. On Friday nights the entire family decamped to a box in the old Orpheum vaudeville house and on one glorious occasion a performer who could sing both coloratura *and* mezzo came back to our house and regaled us with gems from *No, No Nanette*.

Good days; and, in spite of the miseries being visited on the rest of the world, relatively happy ones. When in June of 1935 I graduated, the 125 of us being presented for our degrees marched into the women's gymnasium to the strains of "Pomp and Circumstance". A few potted palms festooned the platform where the Premier of British Columbia, The Hon. T. Dufferin Patullo, was to deliver the Convocation address.

His message to the fresh-faced hopefuls in front of him was one of unrelieved gloom. Prospects in Canada were bleak; the economy was in dreadful shape; the banking system was all wrong; unemployment was rampant; there were no jobs to be had.

And I sat there, thinking: *what is this guy talking about? Next week I am going down to join the staff of the Vancouver Daily Province at the princely salary of $20 a week.*

# Chapter 2

"Go back to that goddam son-of-a-bitch and
tell him with my compliments that a Herald
reporter kisses no man's arse."

— *H. L. Mencken*

About the only avenue to the downtown Vancouver press in the
mid-1930s was *The Ubyssey*. There was not then, nor is there
today, a School of Journalism at UBC The rare jobs that opened
up in that bleak era were usually decided on the basis of nepotism:
an editor had a son, or a nephew, or an in-law.

Lacking such a cachet, my own credentials were not strong. I
could claim three terms as an editor of *The Ubyssey* plus two
summers on downtown dailies. The first of these, at the now-
defunct *News-Herald*, had paid me exactly $7.50 for five months'
work as a sports writer; the second, at the Daily *Province*, had
catapulted me to green-cheque (as opposed to regular, or blue
cheque) status at $11 a week.

Obviously, the fascination of newspapering was not in the pay.
Nor did it stem from any desire to reform the world. Investigative
reporting of the Woodward and Bernstein genre was largely
unknown in earlier days. What journalism offered was a somewhat
raffish, below-the-salt job which was blithely referred to as "a
game". It did not glorify itself as a "profession" even though some
of its practitioners *professed* a fondness for the craft. There was
no formal training. Indeed, when as a cub reporter I approached
the *Province*'s city editor Aubrey Roberts and asked him where
I could learn the business he replied: "Read the *New Yorker*" —
which wasn't bad advice at that.

What seemed to be needed was an insatiable curiosity — which Robertson Davies later described as "altruistic nosiness" — and a relentless urge to bellow the news to the world. That I possessed both these qualities in strong measure had been made obvious to me at the tender age of ten. On the evening of September 14, 1923 I was listening to a radio broadcast of the heavyweight boxing championship between Jack Dempsey and Luis Firpo, "The Wild Bull of the Pampas". When Firpo knocked Dempsey out of the ring I dashed into nearby Granville Street and stopped the first car I could find. "What's up, son?" asked the driver. "Firpo has just knocked out Dempsey and won the heavyweight championship of the world," I cried. Which, in retrospect, was an authentic harbinger of the career to come: I was not only first with the news, but had it totally wrong.

The *News-Herald* had been started in the early 1930s not so much to espouse brave new concepts as to provide jobs for a few unemployed newsmen. Its founder was an inventive Irishman named Pat Kelly, whose initiative was recognized by *Time* magazine (itself only a decade old) with a story, a picture of Kelly, and the caption: "He found his press in a junk-pile." In addition to his baling-wire press, Kelly somehow managed to scrounge a rabbit's warren of small offices on Pender Street, furnished it with a few beaten-up typewriters and some orange crates (for seats) and arranged a "pony service" telephone link-up with United Press in Portland for a pauper's ration of International news.

The sheer audacity of starting a Depression daily, together with admiration for the impoverished journalists who were challenging the *Province* and the *Sun*, created a sympathetic climate for the fledgling morning newspaper. Senior staffers were rewarded with a few dollars (the editor was reputed to pay himself a whopping $40 a week) and some dubious shares in the enterprise. They also benefitted from "due bills", a form of barter in which the newspaper would trade advertising space for hotel accommodation, railway transportation, theatre passes, liquor, and even food. College students and other summer trainees were paid off in passes on buses, to the theatre, sports events, and service-club lunches.

Over the years, the *News-Herald* attracted some remarkable talent. Its first office boy was Jack Scott, later star columnist of the Vancouver *Sun* and foreign correspondent for the Toronto *Star*. Its editorial page editor for many years was Burton Lewis who, as correspondent for the Toronto *Telegram*, had scooped the world on the United States' 1933 decision to quit the gold standard.

No one would suggest that the *News-Herald* was a major Canadian newspaper. But the fact is that the people of Vancouver *liked* it. Perhaps because it lacked international contacts, and depth, it was not a threat. It reported the news succinctly and was readily forgiven its various lapses and shortcomings. Working there taught me a lesson: a newspaper with character and personality could command a relentless loyalty. Character would embrace such things as courage, decency and a sense of humour. If, in addition, the newspaper happened to be an underdog, reader loyalty remained unshakeable. (This was remarkably proven thirty years later in the stunning success of the Toronto *Sun*.)

Circulation of the *News-Herald* grew slowly to a peak of 40,000, but at best it remained a marginal financial operation, depending on "flyers" (advertising inserts for the food chains and department stores) to stay alive. Later the advent of the war, and subsequent rationing of newsprint, resulted in complicated backstage manoeuvring which saw the paper change hands three times in less than a decade.

My first by-line in a metropolitan daily came in 1933 with the *News-Herald*. It resulted from a sports editor's dislike of golf. The editor, Himie Koshevoy, was a gentle, gnome-like character who would have looked perfectly at home in a rock-garden, with water streaming from his mouth. He was also celebrated as the town's most avid punster. Why had he been kicked out of his campus fraternity? "Because," said Himie, dead-pan, "I refused to pay my Jews."

While dedicated to wrestling, boxing, lacrosse and other vigorous sports, Himie was firmly of the opinion that people who played golf were roughly in the same category as those who built sailing ships in bottles or frequented the outdoor checker board at Stanley Park. For that reason, he flatly refused to cover the Vancouver City Junior Golf Championship at the Burquitlam Country Club. Besides, he argued, it was fifteen miles away and hence well beyond the circulation reach of the *News-Herald*.

When I remonstrated with him, he responded: "You going?"

11

"I'm playing," I said.

"Okay," he replied. "Give me a fast 300 words for Monday morning."

I remember treating that obscure story as though it rivalled Lindbergh's conquest of the Atlantic. Hammering an old Underwood in my bedroom on a late Sunday afternoon, I wrote and re-wrote the piece six times. I tabulated the scores in order: first nine, gross, handicap, nett.

But next day, there it was, exactly as I had written it, with a 10-point black line on top: "By Stu Keate." I stared at it until my eyes were glazed. I was hooked.

The piece obviously caught the attention of Robert Truscott ("Bob") Elson, recently come to the sports desk of the *Province* from the Winnipeg *Tribune* with the express mandate of raising *Province* sports coverage to the standards of the Vancouver *Sun*.

Elson was a fanatic about Canadian football, track and field and box lacrosse. Like Koshevoy, he knew nothing about golf but he was shrewd enough to realize its importance to the tycoons who played the game and, often enough, also happened to be large advertisers. He began clipping golf items from a number of British newspapers and publishing them in the Saturday *Province*.

On a drive back to Vancouver from Harrison Hot Springs, where we had been covering a hydroplane regatta for our respective newspapers, Elson asked me what I thought of his new column.

"It's no good," I said.

"Why not?"

"Because it's too far removed. There are dozens of items going on in Vancouver every week that would be more interesting than that second-hand British stuff. Local names, gossip."

"Do you think you could do any better?"

"I know I could."

"You're on," Elson said.

Thus, while still an undergraduate and a summer trainee in the newspaper business, I became a sports columnist with my own space and by-line. But, far more important, I had discovered in Bob Elson a guide, mentor and friend who was to become a major influence in my career.

Of the three dailies publishing before the war, in Vancouver, the *Province* was far and away the most profitable and therefore the most secure. (The *Sun* at that time lived from week to week; it was reported that the publisher, R. J. Cromie, would visit the teller's cage regularly for his walking around money, dropping an IOU into the till.) What every young reporter was seeking in those harsh and impecunious days was a toe-hold. Like indentured students of law, medicine and chartered accountancy, they accepted the fact that it would be years before they could obtain a passable salary. Thus the invitation I received in 1935 to join the *Province* felt somewhat akin to being nominated for a Rhodes Scholarship.

Staid, stodgy and eminently respectable, the *Province* was in the 1930s regarded as the leading daily newspaper west of Toronto. It viewed events with quiet objectivity, rarely raised its voice, and generally reflected the conservative stance of the Establishment.

It was also excessively timid toward advertisers. This was borne in upon me when, doing a spell as movie critic of the paper, I covered the weekly "Thursday Night Preview" at the old Kerrisdale theatre. One week they screened a Dorothy Lamour epic which was simply rotten. In my review, I said so. The first edition was scarcely off the press when Larry Bearg, regional manager of Famous Players, stormed into the newsroom with steam coming out of his ears. The city editor of the *Province*, working from a press kit, re-wrote my critique (without seeing the movie) to proclaim in a later edition that Lamour had starred in one of the greatest films to grace local screens.

To a young reporter, it was a world of fascination and delight. I was enchanted to discover that newspapermen were granted front-row seats, at no cost, at baseball games, wrestling, movie houses and circuses. When reporters were offered books for review, they were permitted to keep the books and thus started building a library. On Saturday nights, they could count on a pair of tickets to the Mart Kenney dinner-dance in the old Spanish Grill, in return for which they would gather guest-lists from the various tables and turn them over to the lady known as the Social Editor. Very quickly the reporter discovered that the phrase "the power of the press" reached down to some extraordinarily mundane levels. He found himself being treated deferentially by head waiters, promoters and press agents.

The chance to watch Bob Elson in action was an extra attraction.

I think it could be argued that Elson turned out to be the most successful Canadian journalist of our times. Twenty years after his Vancouver sports editorship he emerged as general manager of *Life* magazine, which at its highest point reached a record circulation of 8 million copies a week.

It was evident, even in those early days, that Elson was *sui generis*. He was the most consummate newsman I ever met: totally dedicated, totally honest, a fighter; a sports fan whose idea of a perfect Sunday afternoon was to invite a few university professors to his home for tea and the *Ring Cycle*. Each day when he left the office he packed with him a bulging armful of newspapers from around the world, which he read avidly.

His lean, rangy frame contained a high-tension bloodstream and the bounce of an athlete. He was much given to wearing double-breasted grey suits and blue silk ties, which he invariably wore at half-mast. His jaw looked as though it had been fashioned from Brillo. As a long-distance track runner, he lacked the innate speed of many of his contemporaries but doggedly wore them down and frequently beat them to the tape by the length of his determined jaw.

His rages were legendary. On one occasion, he leaped over the railing by his desk like the man in the Enos ad. hurdling a tennis net, to scream at an errant reporter: "You're fired!"

He was a nail biter and an enthusiastic consumer (literally) of newsprint. Hallowed to this day in the corridors of the *Province* is the story of the time Elson burst screaming into the composing room in search of a front-page headline which had gone missing at the last moment.

The composing room foreman, Jack Matthews, listened patiently to the harangue and then said softly: "Bob, put your hand in your mouth."

Elson did, and sheepishly removed the remnants of the missing headline. He had been chewing it.

Elson's volcanic eruptions at the *Province* struck terror into the hearts of some subordinates, one of whom expressed his disapproval of the boss by urinating in Elson's typewriter during the wan hours of the lobster shift.

To be sure, Elson could be excused his tantrums: he presided over one of the wildest zoos ever gathered in one cage. His soccer writer, Austin Delany, was a dedicated Communist; his racing

14

handicapper was a lovable alcoholic named Johnny Park, who spent his time on the night shift playing high-stakes bridge with a doctor, a wrestling promoter, and the lower mainland's leading pimp.

But greater than all these was an Old Country soccer expert and cricket devotee named Charles Ramsbottom Foster. Charlie was renowned at the *Province* as the only man on the premises who could do four things at once — he was observed one day in the men's can eating sandwiches, smoking a foul-smelling pipe, tending to his call of nature, and reading proof on the sports pages!

Charlie's method of covering the old Wednesday soccer matches at Cambie Street Grounds was simplicity itself. He simply started with the kick-off and thereafter gave a stenographic report on each movement of the ball. This made for accuracy, since Charlie's short-hand notes were impeccable, but also blew up these minor skirmishes into dispatches rivalling the length of a budget report from Ottawa.

Exasperated by this practice, Elson advised Foster that in future he would accept only copy typewritten on one piece of paper. Craftily, Foster set about confounding this ukase. Setting the margin of his machine to its outer limits, he typed in single space and pasted the "takes" together so that they met the requirements of "a single piece of paper".

Elson's reaction on receiving the first of these submissions was entirely predictable. Howling with rage, he picked up the copy, opened a window above Cambie Street, and shouted: "Look, Charlie, look! I warned you! Out it goes!" And he let the offensive story drift down on the startled pedestrians below, who were even more baffled when the portly Foster dashed into the streets to recover his masterpiece.

At one stage Elson was lured away from the *Province* for a brief term as editor of the *News-Herald*. While there he converted the morning paper to a tabloid and added to his growing legend as a mover of men. Alumni of the *News-Herald* like to tell the story of the night Elson barged into the office and demanded to know of city editor Scott the identity of a tall, red-headed young reporter standing at the file desk, idly riffling through the pages of a paper.

"His name is Pierre Berton," said Scott.

"What's he doing?" demanded Elson.

"He's reading the comics, sir," replied Scott.

"We can't afford to have reporters standing around reading the comics," barked Elson. "Fire him!"

The irate editor retired to his cubicle-office and examined the first edition of the newspaper. On the front page was a feature which he read with mounting interest and enthusiasm.

"Great!" he exclaimed, waving the paper over his head and descending on the city editor. "Who wrote that piece?"

"Pierre Berton, sir," replied Scott.

"Give him a raise!" ordered Elson.

"I can't, sir," said Scott.

"Why not?"

"Because you just fired him."

"Well, hire him back again," said Elson, with just the right note of exasperation and reproach for his subordinate.

Elson's rages were short-lived, usually dissolving after the paper had successfully been put to bed, and invariably followed by profuse apologies. I was myself the victim of a dreadful tongue-lashing one morning when I turned up for work at the *Province* ten minutes past the starting-time of 7 a.m.

"Goddamn you!" Elson barked, "Don't you know what time we start around here? Now listen, you lazy, good-for-nothing bastard, if you're late again I'm going to take you and kick your ass out of here. Now get to work, you sonofabitch."

I was crestfallen to have stopped such a blast from a man I revered. But I shouldn't have worried too much. Ten minutes after the paper went to press Elson approached me, placed a friendly arm around my shoulder, and said: "Stu, I don't want you think there was anything *personal* in what I said."

It is strange that Elson, a friend who hired me three times during my career, is also the only man to have fired me. It came about in a hilarious way, when a group of Vancouver sports writers crossed the Gulf to Victoria to cover a golf tournament.

Working late, I wrote my story and column. The next duty was to join my compatriots and head for the midnight boat, which would debouch us in Vancouver the following morning, in time for the early shift. One of my colleagues, alas, had become en-amoured of an Amazonian woman golfer who was reputed to be as wild in the boudoir as she was off the tee. When I knocked

16

on his hotel door to summon him to the boat, there was no immediate reply. I knocked again. After a few moments, a hoarse voice came over the transom:

"Go away and come back in half an hour."

I waited as long as I could and then dashed for the boat — just in time to see the gangplank being hauled up.

When I straggled into the *Province* office the next day, Elson was in a singular state of agitation. "You're fired!" he bellowed. "Git!"

I was stunned. Sadly, I made my way home. Two hours later, the telephone rang. It was Elson

"Stu," he said, "I blew my top. Forget it."

"Bob," I replied, "you were too tough on me. I want to think this thing through."

Although it was gratifying to know that Bob's "firing" was a spur-of-the-moment thing, I sensed that the time had come to make a change. I went to my bedroom and started packing my bag.

# Chapter 3

"A newspaper office is a haven for salaried eccentrics."

— *Lord Thomson of Fleet*

In Vancouver I had been making $22.50 a week, working eighteen hours a day and, incidently, loving every minute of it. But I felt that, in order to broaden my horizons, I ought to head East to Toronto, which was then, as now, the communications centre of Canada and the place to go if you wanted to make a name for yourself.

As a city Toronto was Cleveland North — flat, uninviting and decidedly pokey, with its street cars clanking down the main streets. But Joseph Atkinson had recently installed the *Star* in a grand skyscraper on King Street and, with a circulation approaching 400,000 copies a day, it was the clear leader in Canada.

My assault on the *Star*'s imposing brass doors would be not entirely unarmed. In my pocket was a wire from Andy Lytle, the former Vancouver *Sun* sports editor now employed as columnist on the Toronto *Star*, which read: "Come at once. Bring scrapbook. Have job for you."

My mother, who was going through a bad period with my father, was distraught but understanding. It was the practice of the CPR in those days to provide free transportation to journalists who were "between jobs", so, through the kind intercession of my friend Travers Coleman, I boarded the 7 p.m. Continental train one summer night and headed east.

On arrival in Toronto, I found that I could get a room in the

Psi Upsilon Fraternity house on St. George Street for $25 a month, breakfast and supper included. Since this was less than a fifteen-minute walk away from the *Star* office, it looked like an ideal arrangement.

It developed, however, that friend Lytle was not exactly precise when he wired: "Have job for you." What he really meant, he told me (after overcoming his initial astonishment when I walked into his office) was that he could arrange a job *interview* with the legendary managing editor of the *Star*, Harry C. Hindmarsh.

"Don't worry about it," he said. "I've spoken to Hindmarsh about you. Just run down the hall and speak to his secretary."

That worthy turned out to be a lean, dark young man named Jack Karr, later to achieve some renown as public relations director of the Stratford Festival. Karr regarded me with icy hauteur when I explained my mission.

"Mr. Hindmarsh is terribly busy," he said. "I'll try, but I can't guarantee he'll see you."

"When?" I asked.

Karr thought for a moment. "Oh, I would guess in about three weeks," he replied. My heart sank. I knew very few people in Toronto. I had no money. I could cover a month's rent but beyond that had only a few dollars.

But then I got lucky. As I was walking disconsolately to the elevator a man approached me and said: "Stu — nice to see you. What are you doing here?" His name was Tom Wheeler, and he was a man of some influence at the *Star*, with dual responsibility for the *Star Weekly* and the Toronto *Star* Syndicate. I had met him just a couple of months before, when he had come to Vancouver to sell some syndicate material, and we had shared a fine game of golf on the old Jericho links. I explained to Wheeler about the "job" that wasn't quite a job and about the interview with Hindmarsh which might — or might not — come off three weeks hence.

"It's all right, don't worry," Wheeler said. "Hindmarsh will see you. In the meantime, why don't you do some pieces for the *Star Weekly*? I'll pay you $35 for a half page, about 1,000 words."

I accepted this life-line gratefully. The articles produced, to be sure, would never qualify for a Pulitzer prize. About women who wrestled in mud. Baseball umpires backstage — "The Pariahs of the Diamond." An interview with a teen-age Negro singer, Phyllis

19

Marshall. But the $35 a week, to me, represented almost unimaginable riches.

At the end of three weeks, the Great Day arrived. Mr. Hindmarsh, who was reputed to subsist on a diet of old razor-blades and hemlock, would see me. I found him, a great bear of a man, hunched over some papers on his desk. For what seemed an eternity, he did not speak. Finally, he glowered at me over thick glasses and said one word:

"Well?"

I began to talk — if not to babble — about what a great paper the *Star* was; how every young journalist in Canada hoped one day to work there; how I had come 3,000 miles for the express purpose of talking to him about a job.

At the end of ten minutes, I thought I detected a faint grin at the corners of Hindmarsh's mouth. I could imagine him saying to himself: *I've listened to some con men in my day, but this kid beats them all.*

"Are you married?" he asked.

I had been warned in advance to expect that question. It was not only that Hindmarsh took a benign interest in the private lives of his employees; it was a fact that he had two unmarried daughters and was said to be constantly on the look-out for eligible suitors.

"No, sir," I replied.

"How much money did you earn on the Coast?"

I gulped and said: "$35 a week, sir." Which was true, if you added to my basic salary the $10 a week I got for a basketball broadcast and a few dollars free-lancing.

"That's a lot of money," Hindmarsh observed. "But we'll take a chance on you. I'll notify the business office to start you at $35. Report in the morning to Mr. Brown."

Thus began one of the wildest, most unpredictable — and most educative — interludes in my entire journalistic life. Enterprising, hard-hitting and cocky, the *Star* rarely let the facts get in the way of a good story. Its philosophy was simple: spend money to get the news. To the exasperation of its rivals, it had mastered the "mass attack" technique of covering a story. When the famed Honeymoon Bridge was carried away by ice on the Niagara River, no less than twelve of us were there to record the event.

Politically, the *Star* was strident in support of the Liberal party.

On the eve of the 1949 federal election its readers were astonished to be confronted with a front-page headline crying:

KEEP CANADA BRITISH
DESTROY DREW'S HOUDE
GOD SAVE THE KING!

However, support by the *Star* became something of a kiss of death. When provincial Liberal leader Walter Thompson felt the smothering embrace of the paper, and was roundly rebuffed by the voters he issued a public statement begging the *Star* to leave him alone and support someone else.

With its vast circulation edge over the *Telegram* and the *Globe*, and with a vibrant, hyper-thyroid newsroom, the *Star* should have been a happy shop. But its electricity was of the kind that usually accompanies a storm. The building was raddled with office politics. No appointment was too small to escape notice and analysis by house critics. The women's sports writer, Alexandrine Gibb, was reputed to have a direct pipeline to the executive suite and was accorded an influence which, in my neophyte's view, was vastly overrated. You did your job with Hindmarsh and you were okay.

After six months of general reporting and a bit of editing on the news-desk, I was assigned to a new venture — an office which would develop feature stories for both the daily *and* the *Weekly*. This, as things turned out, was carnival journalism at its worst and referred to in the corridors as "The Nuts Department".

Nutty it undoubtedly was; but it also harboured some splendid talent. Greg Clark was a senior contributor, as was Fred Griffin, a handsome Irishman generally conceded to be the paper's most gifted reporter. Ken Clark, a rumpled, pipe-smoking cherub, had come up from the no-advertising-newspaper *PM* in New York to join the staff.

The boss was Ken Edey, widely acknowledged to be one of Hindmarsh's "bright young boys"; a brilliant editor who spoke softly and had the look of a handsome gangster. He was the first editor I met who could instruct in the value of re-writing. "Not good enough," he murmured of one of my early submissions. "Try it again, this way..." To a young reporter, accustomed to shovelling raw copy into the paper to meet a deadline, Edey's injunctions on a more thoughtful approach were invaluable.

Before long, I found myself sharing an editorial cell with Gordon Sinclair, already a legend around the *Star* for having been fired, and re-hired, more often than any man in history. His fame as a foreign correspondent and as author of the gaudy "Footloose in India" saga had propelled him to the dizzying financial heights of $65 a week, and he was inclined to look with condescension on rookie reporters of lesser affluence.

One day, however, in a benign mood, he tilted his hat back on his forehead, leaned back in his chair, and said to me:

"Kid, you want to get ahead on this paper?"

"Sure," I said.

"Then go out and get yourself a story on snakes."

"On *what*?" I demanded.

"Snakes," he repeated. "Snakes and gorillas. The old man is queer for snakes and gorillas. Get a good yarn and you're a cinch for page 1."

Not long after, I was thumbing a suburban weekly when I saw a one-paragraph item to the effect that the Sunnyside amusement park in Toronto was about to acquire a new rattlesnake.

"Hey, Sinc," I cried, "look at this."

Sinclair took the paper and began to read. A curious light came into his eyes. For a few moments he stared at the ceiling. Then, with mounting enthusiasm, he began to speak.

"Tell you what we're going to do," he said. "This is the age of the picture magazine, right? *Life* magazine — tremendous success. We're going to tell this story in pictures."

"What story?" I asked.

"We're going to hire three models," he replied. "A blonde, a brunette and a red-head. Then we're going to hire a male model and dress him up in one of those white doctor's coats. He'll have a stethoscope around his neck and he'll carry one of those blood-pressure machines. We'll take him down to Sunnyside with the three girls. He'll put the blood-pressure machine on the blonde's arm. Then we'll have the guy who handles the snake jab it at the blonde. First, the blonde. Then, the brunette and the red-head. You watch; the blonde will jump.

"For the first time in history, we're gonna measure the FEAR QUOTIENT of women. Think of it! That snake will drive them crazy! Fantastic!"

I sat there in awe and wonderment. Without setting foot out

of his office, Sinclair had created one of the great sociological stories of our time. So this was how Big City journalists operated? I am sorry to report that the experiment never reached fruition. Sinclair was called to more important duties, and all talk of snakes was soon completely overshadowed by Tommy Lytle's success with gorillas. Tommy, the son of Andy and a superb feature writer, had spotted an item about an animal trainer in Chicago who claimed that he had taught a pet gorilla to understand English and was quite capable of carrying on an intelligent conversation with him. It was Tommy's glorious conceit to hook up a three-way telephone call between gorilla, trainer, and himself. There subsequently appeared in the *Star* a sober report of this dialogue, in which the responses of the gorilla read like the bottom line of an eye chart.

It was obvious that the Nuts Department could not last long, and it didn't. Whenever this bizarre assembly of trained seals produced a lively feature, the daily paper would grab it, pleading urgency; the *Weekly* was suffering. In a retrenchment program, the *Star Weekly* fired one of its writers. A friend met him on King Street and asked him how it was going. "Terrible," he said. "I think Hindmarsh must have lost one of his gorillas; I don't think the paper will come out next week."

As it happened, an even stranger assignment awaited me. One day the mighty Hindmarsh invited me into his office and disclosed that he had just been made president of the suburban Oakville golf course.

"Our trouble is, we haven't got enough members," he told me. "I want you to detach yourself from the newsroom for a month and rustle up some new members. It's a great little golf course and a spectacular buy — just $15 a year. Half an hour from Toronto."

"Have you any idea where I might begin?" I asked.

"Certainly," he said. "Just walk up and down Bay Street — go into the banks and brokerage houses, sign up the young fellows who are keen on golf. We'll back you up with a little publicity. Write some stories. Take some pictures." *Translation: the paper is yours, kid.*

The softening-up process began immediately. We hired some models who trooped out to Oakville in the 1938 equivalent of hot pants, posed at the pins in spiked-heel shoes, and clutched niblicks in the sandtraps with the ferocity of Frank Buck dissecting a water buffalo. The local professional, a gentle soul rejoicing in the name of Leslie Louth, was clearly bemused, particularly when he read the eight-column caption under the pictures: "GIRLS LIKE THIS WILL PLAY GOLF AT OAKVILLE THIS SUMMER."

The budding financial genii of Bay Street were not responsive to my overtures. At the end of a week, I hadn't sold a single membership. But then I had an inspiration. There were on the staff of the *Star* a number of shrewd characters to whom membership in the Oakville Golf Club, under the aegis of H. C. Hindmarsh, would represent life-time tenure.

The first one I approached was a portly (and snobbish) Englishman named Claude Pascoe, who was reputed to be something of a Hindmarsh worshipper. He signed on the spot. After him came Peter MacRitchie, a man who calculated the odds. Then came John Heron, managing editor, who went on to create the Royal Bank Monthly Letter. After him, a pleasant young reporter named Ab Fallon, who later married one of the Hindmarsh daughters.

As word got around, men who wouldn't know a two-iron from a set of hair tongs were seeking me out, begging admission to this exclusive club. At the end of three weeks, I had sold nineteen new memberships. Eighteen of them were from the *Star*'s newsroom.

In retrospect it all seems wonderful fun — joyous, giddy and of little consequence. But there were lessons to be learned as well. One of them was to avoid hero-worship. I confess I was thrilled when the *Star* sent me out to the Canadian National Exhibition to interview Tom Mix. He had been my boyhood idol, a straight-shootin' cowboy who enshrined all the earthy plains virtues. I found him behind a tent, burnishing the silverwork on the bridle of his horse, Tony. Attendance had been poor at his show that afternoon. Mix was in a sullen and liverish mood and either refused to answer my questions or grunted a monosyllabic reply. I began to realize that heroes can be sons-of-bitches, too.

To cap a thoroughly depressing day, I accepted an invitation for a good-night beer with the show's press agent, a flamboyant Texan who affected a straw hat and red bow tie. We were scarcely settled in his suite in the King Edward Hotel when the barker sat down beside me on the sofa and placed his hand on my leg,

24

murmuring obscenities. At precisely that moment, there was a knock on the door. I ran to open it — and kept on running.

In fact I was finding Toronto as a whole an unattractive place. The humidity was frightful and aggravated one of the worst summers of hay fever in my life. For hours I lay on my bed at the Psi U house, compulsively sneezing, sweating and blinking. The city, if not hostile, seemed unfriendly. It was also puritanical. It was impossible to buy a newspaper at the corner store on a Sunday; cigarettes were prohibited from sale. When I picked up my friend Bob Harcourt, at his Bloor Street apartment, to play golf on the Sabbath, church-goers fixed us with disapproving stares as we loaded our clubs into the rumble seat of my jazzy little Ford roadster.

I remember one night, sitting alone at the back of a street car as it clanked its way down King Street. The sidewalks were almost deserted. But I was entranced with a beautiful sunset, which seemed to accentuate my aching loneliness. I thought to myself: "What the hell am I doing in this crummy town when I could be back with my family and friends in Vancouver?"

Succour arrived in the person of Bob Elson, visiting Toronto on Southam business. We went to the Royal Alex Theatre to see Orson Welles and his Mercury Theatre in a modern-dress version of *Julius Caesar*. Later, over coffee, Elson urged me to come back to Vancouver and rejoin the *Province*.

"We'll pay you $42.50 a week," he said. "And what's more, we'll pay your way home."

The salary was just about double what I'd left, eighteen months before. But there was a more compelling reason for making the move. At a Saturday afternoon tea-dance at Hart House, I had met a Vancouver expatriate named Letha Meilicke, who was studying physical education at Margaret Eaton school, an adjunct of the University of Toronto. She was wearing a blue velvet suit, with a bonnet to match, and I fell for her with a resounding thud.

Within the stern limits of Margaret Eaton curfews, we courted. Cheese sandwiches at Murray's. A bit of golf. A tour of the *Star's* offices. A visit to a farm where I was investigating the dubious theory that cows gave more milk when serenaded by Muzak.

At the end of her school term, Letha went back to Vancouver. As soon after as decently possible, I followed — but not until I had cleared my decks with Mr. Hindmarsh.

"Why are you leaving?" he asked.

"Mr. Hindmarsh," I replied, "I'm going to get married."

"Tell me about her," he said.

I told him.

"Good," he said. "You're just the right age. Good luck to you."

Letha and I were married in July 1939. Six weeks later we were awakened by the cry of a newsboy on Granville Street, hawking an Extra. There was a war on.

# Chapter 4

"Preserve us from the dangers of the sea,
and from the violence of the enemy..."

— *Book of Common Prayer*

To be a sports editor in the years 1939-1940 was to live in an unreal world. Red Smith of the *Herald-Tribune* described the milieu — accurately — as "the toy department". While heroic men were straggling off the beaches of Dunkirk, while London was being pasted from the air and France was falling, it seemed incongruous to sit around Vancouver writing about grown men in funny suits, playing child's games.

To be sure, there had first been the "phoney war", and even now only a small percentage of Canadian troops were actively engaged. But already three Air Force friends had been killed in training accidents; two had been torpedoed and drowned in the Atlantic. Furthermore, some of the pre-war volunteers had begun drifting home on their first, brief leaves, or to sell War Bonds. A few dropped by the *Province* to regale us with feats of dramatic derring-do in the skies over France. One of them, a well-known fisherman named Pitt Clayton, was already "gonged up" with the DFC and Bar. I remember my sense of outrage — duly translated into a column — when he told me that he had exhausted his funds and was having difficulty raising the money to get back overseas, and into action.

By comparison, my own work seemed the ultimate in futility. It was not only the sheer *unimportance* of it that was galling. There was a mounting sense of boredom with the endlessly repetitive cycle of sports events: hockey and basketball in the winter, golf and tennis in the spring, baseball in the summer. After two circuits, I wanted to get off.

Accordingly, in 1941 I went down to the Royal Vancouver Yacht Club to face an officer selection board for the Royal Canadian Naval Volunteer Reserve. I was interviewed by a panel of four senior officers, and turned down. Although no formal explanation was given, I was told later that I was considered (at twenty-nine) to be "too old". What they were looking for, it was said, were bright young fellows just out of university who could step into a training course unencumbered by home or family ties.

However, as a second string to my bow I had applied to the Department of Naval Information in Ottawa and in 1942 received from them a telephone call which should have, but didn't, raise some doubts about their professional savvy.

"We're studying your application," the civilian in charge told me. "Can you write captions?"

"I can write captions," I replied.

"Good!" said Ottawa. "Report to *HMCS Discovery*, get sworn in, and get down here as fast you can."

In a matter of days I had passed the physical and been handed a commission as Acting Sub-Lieutenant (Special Branch). I remember being puzzled when the officer in charge said: "Now get yourself a uniform." In some vague way, I had imagined that uniforms were issued, along with gas-masks and ditty-bags.

"How do I get one?" I asked.

The officer looked at me with something close to pity. "Go down to the store and *buy* one," he replied.

So I debarked for the estimable Tip Top Tailors and after some minor adjustments emerged onto the streets of Vancouver, considerably embarrassed, as a full-fledged officer of His Majesty's Navy.

I was away three years. In retrospect, it occurred to me that there were three kinds of wars being fought:

First, the dreadful war of sorrow and pain, of bombings and torpedoings, of cripplings and maiming, from which 40,000 Canadians never returned.

Second, the "enjoyable war" of little men in safe berths, far behind the lines. ("I hope it never ends," one confided to me one night in Newfoundland. "I was getting $35 a week on civvy street and now I'm making $350 a month.")

Third, the "spectators' war" of men who volunteered to do a job, went cheerfully where they were told to go, did what they had to do, were *in* action but only infrequently *of* it. It is in this latter category I place myself, an opinion corroborated by the captain of my last ship, who signed me off at the end of the war with the formal judgement: "This officer did his best in unfamiliar surroundings."

Perfect. It *was* unfamiliar — and if I had to do it all over again, I wouldn't. I went from one of the most free-wheeling, undisciplined vocations in the world to a service hoary with tradition, where everything was done "by numbers". I served, in effect, as a naval war correspondent. I should have gone as a civilian war correspondent, free of the rigidities of naval protocol and at-times-ridiculous censorship. I quickly learned that I was press agent for a service that wouldn't talk.

I also learned to stay out of Ottawa, where chaos abounded. The information department was presided over by an amiable toper and a stylish-stout female who kept top-secret signals in an open drawer, along with her lipstick, finger-nail polish, bobby pins and old stockings. The astonishing fact was that the town was thickly populated with naval officers, 3,000 miles removed from the action, who actually believed they were running the war.

Nowhere was this more apparent than in the radio division of Naval Information, where Commander (VR) William Strange was charged with the responsibility of sinking a German U-boat every Thursday night on the CBC. His show was called *Fighting Navy*, and in order to get into the proper mood for these factually-based salty dramas, Cmdr. Strange had equipped his office with ship's bells, ropes, lifebelts and Wrens, who provided something called "mug-up". Irreverent newcomers to the department, like the actor Austin Willis, secretly referred to it as *"HMCS Static"*.

The bizarre nature of this operation, which seemed to me straight out of Gilbert and Sullivan ("they never, never, never ... got out to sea") finally began to pall. With more audacity than good sense, I challenged Cmdr. Strange about the efficacy of the entire naval information program. Strange, who looked and acted like Charles Laughton in his role as the Captain of *HMS Bounty*, eyed me coldly for a moment and then began to pace his quarter-deck, hands firmly clasped behind his back.

"Stu, old boy," he said (and I quote him exactly), "as long as I am in command here, you shall do as I direct. Otherwise, old boy, we shall simply have to ABANDON SHIP!"

Which is precisely what I did. A friendly operations officer got me a posting to a newly-commissioned fleet of Fairmiles, which were known as submarine-chasers but were more successful in post-war life as luxury yachts. It was an inauspicious beginning: we chuffed down the St. Lawrence from Quebec City but got lost in the fog off Halifax harbour. This, in turn, led to a pleasant few days on a minesweeper, running between Halifax and St. John's, Newfoundland, and soon thereafter to a really good posting. I was assigned to write some pieces about Canada's new Tribal class destroyers, largest ships in the burgeoning fleet of the Canadian navy, and took passage for Scapa Flow in *HMCS Iroquois*.

Of the various ships I had encountered, this one was populated with the sternest captain and the merriest crew. The month was March and the year 1943, when the U-boat war was at its peak in the North Atlantic. The harsh realities of that war were borne in on us when, two days out of Newfoundland and zig-zagging through heavy seas, two men were washed overboard. The captain did not stop the ship to look for them.

The image of those two men in the icy waters, watching their ship steaming away at twenty-two knots, haunted me for months. There was some grumbling on the mess-decks. But the captain posed a chilling question: which was more valuable, a $7 million destroyer or the lives of two men? (There were reported to be twenty-three U-boats along the route.)

From Scapa, I was sent down to London to join the staff of the Canadian Naval Mission Overseas, arriving just in time for the "Baby Blitz". (To paraphrase Mr. Churchill: "Some baby! Some blitz!") It is hard to conceive of a better introduction to that superb city. Its infinite capacity to absorb punishment had united the "clippie" on the bus and the dowager duchess in an indomitable spirit of camaraderie. In spite of the ferocious assaults, the sun continued to shine, the grass to grow and the flowers to bloom. The orators of Hyde Park maintained their cheerfully malevolent attacks on the Prime Minister, Mr. Gandhi, the British

30

Empire and the King himself, while bobbies grinned and let them say their piece.

In spite of the black-out, theatres flourished. We ate spaghetti at "Mother Massey's", drank Scotch at the Haymarket Club, went punting at Maidenhead, and roared at the music-hall ribaldries of Max Miller.

It was the beginning of some lifelong journalistic friendships. Bruce West was at Canada House before taking up a successful career with the *Globe and Mail*. Andy O'Brien was roving around in behalf of the Montreal *Standard*. Ralph Allen had been released from Conn Smythe's "sports battery" to become an outstanding combat correspondent for the *Globe and Mail*. With Scott Young, I sat on the banks of the Thames at noon-hour, smoking cheap cigars and philosophizing about the Canadian Press, for whom he was working in London.

In the fall of 1943 I was summoned to the offices of my immediate superior, a peacetime insurance salesman with all the gentle instincts of a piranha. Slapping a wall map with a pointer, and with a thin, sadistic smile, he said: "The U-boat war is heating up in the Bay of Biscay. Ottawa advises there's room in a Canadian corvette for one man. You or me?"

And then, answering his own question, he pointed a finger and said the single word: "You."

Accordingly, I found myself on board *HMCS Calgary*, one of the whackiest ships in the Canadian fleet. Her captain was a Kingston stockbroker named Henry ("Hank") Hill, who affected a golden earring and was fond of saying "The balloon's going up tonight!" Somewhat to my surprise, the *Calgary* did not head for the Bay of Biscay. Instead, it was assigned to a North Atlantic convoy group and steamed off in the opposite direction.

"Hank" Hill's philosophy of fighting the war at sea was simple, and pervaded with a mordant humour. Whenever a "blip" occurred on the ship's radar — whether from a passing pod of whales, an abandoned lifeboat or an itinerant log — "Hank" would throw depth-charges. The result was that the *Calgary* farted west on a barrage of scummy explosions, all of them self-induced. There were doubtless U-boats in the area; from time to time bits and pieces of debris floated to the surface, but only an optimist would classify these as "kills".

Nevertheless, these ear-shattering forays carried with them a valuable lesson. The compelling groan of the Action-stations klaxon, followed by the thunder of depth-charges, made sleep difficult. I was berthed in the Sick Bay, presided over by a "tiffy" who had been a Calgary undertaker in peacetime and was even more lugubrious than the captain. He assured me nightly that I should be prepared to meet my Maker. These doleful ministrations got to me; I was haunted by visions of a torpedo crashing into the centre of our munitions storage. But after three or four sleepless nights I became tired. The conquest of fear, I discovered, lay in boredom. I suspect that thousands of other men in uniform came to the same philosophy: so what? After that, I slept.

While the *Calgary* reported that it had fired many rounds of "shots in anger", its only real peril occurred when the engines broke down and the poor tub wallowed in mid-Atlantic behind the rest of the convoy. Captain Hill thought that the engines could be repaired at sea. Another officer, Lieut. Jack Fraser of Victoria, felt differently and told the captain so, in vigorous terms. A permanent-force officer would have regarded these protests as insupportable impertinence. But "Hank" Hill was a volunteer and a peacetime yachtsman. He listened to Fraser and finally signalled for a couple of rescue tugs, which came out and towed the *Calgary*, ignominiously, into St. John's harbour.

There followed ten months of amiable shore duty in the place sailors call "Newfiejohn". As the staging point for Atlantic convoys, the ancient port was bursting with activity. Freighters with their bows blown off rode at anchor, mute testimony to the battles beyond the gates. From time to time, giant icebergs blocked the narrow neck of St. John's harbour. But, for all its rocky isolation, St. John's was a haven. Men in from U-boat actions headed invariably for "The Crow's Nest", an attic eyrie on Water Street, where plates of bacon and eggs, a roaring fire and cheap drinks inspired the spinning of salty dips and rousing, ribald choruses.

When it became apparent that I was going to stay ashore for a few months, my wife boarded a Lockheed Lodestar in Vancouver with our year-old son Richard, who had been born three months after I went into the service. It took her plane exactly a week to touch down at Gander airport. What was normally a two-day flight was extended to seven by intense fog. We boarded with Newfoundland families and came to love them for their honesty, their simplicity, and for their lilting accents, especially memorable when they recounted the sad sagas of the sea.

As an information officer, I had one distinct advantage over my colleagues who had been lawyers or accountants or salesmen in civilian life. Their careers were suspended for the duration. I was not only able, but was commanded, to continue my craft. Newspaper and magazine markets back home were eager for copy. Travel restrictions and censorship made it difficult for them to generate eye-witness reports, but, by clearing with headquarters in Ottawa, I had at least a chance to get out some stories "through channels".

*Liberty*, a mass-circulation magazine, published my account of an anti-submarine action led by Lieut. Barry O'Brien of Ottawa. Unhappily, this national debut was marred by the fact that the action sequences in the story were printed upside down. (O'Brien, who went on to peacetime fame as president of the Ottawa Roughriders, was kind enough to tell me that he liked it better that way.) This, in turn, led to two pieces in *Maclean's* magazine and an invitation from *Time* magazine in New York to seek a discharge from the Navy and try out with them.

I turned this down because of an exciting posting from Ottawa: I was to take a bit of leave and then head for the Mediterranean to join *HMCS Uganda*, which was bound for the war in the Pacific. This was a distinct honour, for *Uganda* was Canada's first cruiser and the largest ship in our fleet. Originally a Royal Navy vessel, she had been bombed off Italy, limped across the Atlantic for repairs in Charleston, and been recommissioned as senior ship of the Royal Canadian Navy.

I caught up with her in Alexandria and reported at once to the commanding officer, Captain E. Rollo Mainguy of Duncan, BC. A stylish man and the perfect picture of a senior naval officer, Capt. Mainguy had already made a name for himself as Capt. "D" (of destroyers) in Newfoundland.

"Hullo," he said, with flinty eye. "What are you here for?"

"I'm from naval information," I said. "Ottawa sent me here to write some stories about your ship."

"Nonsense," he said. "I'm short a man in radar, in the Action Information Centre. You can stand a watch there."

After a few days in Egypt, during which we managed to inspect both the battlefields of El Alamein and the belly-dancers of Cairo, we steamed off through the Suez, dropped off a few soldiers and a deckload of lumber at the Cocos Islands, called at Freemantle and fetched up at Sydney, where the Captain led an assault on a local club and where, as the first Canadian ship to call in Australia, *Uganda* attracted considerable press attention.

With a more or less hand-picked crew (including a young gunnery officer named Lieut. John Robarts, later to become premier of Ontario), *Uganda* joined the British Pacific Fleet north of the Philippines on April 8, and for nearly a month did her routine job of screening battleships and carriers, bombarding remote Japanese islands and supporting air strikes against Okinawa.

Then, on April 28, Capt. Mainguy received a disturbing signal from home: Ottawa had decided that all service in the Pacific — navy, army and air force — would be voluntary. Did *Uganda* volunteer to continue what she was doing now?

The query infuriated the ship's company — both permanent force career officers and men who had volunteered for wartime service only. When they joined, they had agreed to serve anywhere in the world. Now, after several months of tropical heat, Spam and dehydrated turnips, they were in a sour and militant mood.

Then came the letters from the wives. Ottawa's decision had been debated in the House of Commons and was duly reported. The defence minister had stated that *Uganda's* sailors would be given thirty days' leave and, if they so elected, be replaced by young recruits. Three-quarters of *Uganda's* crew had fought in other ships; many had done three years or more in the Battle of the Atlantic. "Come home," their wives and girl friends wrote, "and let some kid take your place."

Immediately, the ship became a sea-going Hyde Park. Messdeck lawyers blossomed fore and aft in a tense and disputatious atmosphere. On May 7, the exasperated Capt. Mainguy outlined conditions of leave, proposed returning home in the fall and declared in an address over the ship's loud-hailer system: "Anybody who signs that declaration (that he wouldn't volunteer) is a quitter and I wouldn't want to be in his shoes for anything."

That afternoon the crew voted. Result: 605 for going home, 300 for sticking it out. The embarrassment to Canada as a nation was obvious. Here she was, the first Canadian ship to serve in the

Pacific, *voting herself out of the war.* Ringed around her were such famous British battle-wagons as the *King George V, Anson* and *Howe*; the aircraft carriers *Formidable, Illustrious* and *Indomitable*; and from New Zealand, the cruisers *Achilles* (one of the heroes of the Battle of the River Plate) and *Exeter.*

On May 8, news of Germany's surrender was received and it appeared that Japan's own demise was not far off. But within twenty-four hours, five Japanese kamikaze planes dived on the British Pacific Fleet, scoring direct hits on two carriers. *Uganda* cut loose with its full artillery but hit nothing.

In an address to the crew on May 26, Capt. Mainguy told his men that Royal Navy admirals now recommended that, with a new British cruiser arriving in a few weeks, *Uganda* should return to Canada for leave and recommissioning. But July came and *Uganda* was still there, abuzz with wild rumours, awash in bitterness and discontent. There was a certain caustic resignation in the slogan: "Home for Christmas". On July 16th her crew got a bit of a lift when the British fleet linked up with Admiral "Bull" Halsey's American armada. This conjunction of 125 fighting ships was one of the most awesome displays of seapower in naval history.

The Japanese capability for retaliation, meanwhile, seemed to have disappeared. When Admiral Halsey put his fleet within sixteen air minutes off Tokyo Bay, gave them his course and position and challenged them to come out and fight, there was no response. Within a week Allied battleships were standing just a few miles off Japan's shores, lobbing in 1,400 tons of shells in less than an hour.

By July 27, with replacements en route, it became evident that the British Pacific Fleet could fight its war without *Uganda.* When Commander-in-Chief Admiral Sir Bruce Fraser recommended that we return to Canada to recruit a new crew, the captain of a British carrier sent a signal: "I feel we are losing an old friend. Good-bye and good luck."

In reply, Capt. Mainguy somewhat pointedly messaged: "Thank you. Is there anything we can bring you on our return?"

Back came the signal: "Six pairs of silk stockings for a woman with small feet."

Next day the *Uganda* headed home.

On August 7 she received word of a new bomb which had

been dropped on Japan and had wrought such havoc that re-connaisance pictures were unavailable. On August 10 she arrived in Esquimalt, BC, where she was met by twenty-three reporters and photographers anxious for details of what had been described in the Canadian press as a "mutiny". But their stories that day were shunted aside by the more momentous news that Tojo had quit.

After 130 consecutive days at sea, we were ripe for leave. In Vancouver, where I rejoined my family, it had been announced that the end of the war would be signalled by the ringing of bells and sounding of air-raid sirens. We were lying on the sands of Locarno beach on a warm August day when the jubilant signals boomed across English Bay. I rolled over in the sand and thought to myself: *What could be tidier? Here I am, back in my own home town, and the war is over.*

I could envision the dialogue of later years:

"Daddy, what did you do in the war?"

"Children, you should be proud. Your daddy served in the only ship in history to vote itself out of a war."

# Chapter 5

"Newspapers — history in a hurry."

— *Matthew Arnold*

I was anxious to get back to work and for the first time had begun to think seriously about the purpose and meaning of life; of getting out of the "toy department" of journalism and taking an interest in politics. I asked myself what I intended to do in the years ahead.

It was all very neat and tidy, in a way. I could not see a future that did not include Vancouver, which I loved, and a few executives of Southam's had whispered, benignly, that they "had plans for me". I liked the company and felt that there was the possibility, if not the certitude, of a reasonable career with them.

Accordingly in September of 1945 I presented myself at the Cambie Street offices of W. L. ("Biff") MacTavish, editor of the *Province*. I was still in uniform and boasting the extra half-stripe on my sleeve which was described as a "discharge promotion" — actually, a bonus to improve rehabilitation gratuities and veterans' benefits.

MacTavish greeted me warmly: "Good to have you back, Stu," he said, shaking hands. "Take off your coat and go to work."

"Fine, Mr. MacTavish," I said, "but what about the dough?"

"I'm sorry about that," he replied, "but I can't do anything for you right away. Wages are frozen. We'll pay you what you got when you went away."

That was $60 a week, a pretty good salary by *Province* standards in 1942. But I felt I was entitled to more. I was, I felt, more mature, certainly a lot more travelled and experienced, and I had a family to look after. I reached into my pocket and produced a telegram which I had just received from Bob Elson in New York, where he had gone as the first Canadian editor of *Time* magazine. It read: "Vice President Eric Hodgins very anxious to have you go to New York at *Time*'s expense to meet him and other executives at your earliest convenience preferably between 17th and 22nd."

MacTavish reacted strongly. "Oh, for God's sakes, Stu," he said, "don't have anything to do with those people. They're all crazy. I've just come back from the organizing conference of the UN in San Francisco. *Time* had thirty-two men there, all running around like chickens with their heads off. Stay away from them."

"But what have I got to lose?" I argued. "This isn't exactly a job offer. Bob has just invited me to New York to talk to them."

"Okay," said MacTavish. "But keep your chin tucked in."

A few days later we flew off to New York. Elson was in high spirits, and enjoying his job. When *Time* was planning a Canadian edition, he had been invited up from Washington, where he was Southam's bureau chief, to tell *Time*'s editors what he thought such a section should contain. Within a week they had offered him the Canadian editor's chair, at a salary of $11,000 a year. Now, with the war over, Elson explained, *Time* was on a hiring campaign and combing key journalistic centres throughout North America for writers. The man in charge of the program, he said, was Eric Hodgins.

Hodgins was, at the time, riding a considerable personal boom as a result of having written a best-selling book called *Mr. Blandings Builds His Dream-House*, a saga of his own hilarious attempts to build a home in Connecticut. His story was reputed to have been sold to the movies for $500,000. At any rate, Mr. Hodgins was in a genial frame of mind when I was ushered into his office. A big, extroverted man, he pumped my hand, put his feet up on his desk and said: "Now Mr. Keate, tell me all about yourself from the beginning."

"Well," I said, "My parents were from Grand Rapids, Michigan, but they went to Vancouver in 1907 on a timber deal, fell in love with the place, and settled down as Canadians."

"Isn't that *interesting!*" cried Hodgins. "You know, my family did just the reverse. I was born in Canada but then we moved to Detroit and I grew up . . . "

Whereupon Hodgins launched into a vivid description of his boyhood, his life as a student, his entry into journalism, and his arrival at *Time*. For twenty minutes I sat transfixed as the story of his life unfolded. At the end of half an hour, he jumped up and said: "Well, I've heard a lot about you from Bob. This certainly has been interesting. Nice to talk to you. We'll be in touch."

I left his office bemused, though far from downhearted. But there followed two days of seemingly aimless wandering about the Time, Inc. building in which I was presented to numerous *Time* editors, offered the assurances of their most genial consideration, and silkily passed along to the next office.

I was only slightly baffled, in the midst of all this, when in the corridors of the Time-Life building I met Gordon Pushie, a Newfoundland journalist whom I had known during Navy duty in St. John's. I asked him what he was doing.

"Working, I guess," Pushie grinned.

"How did they hire you?"

"Well," he said, "I've got to admit it was a bit strange. At the end of the war I headed for New York. I tried Reuter's and Associated Press but they didn't have anything. One day I was passing this building so I said to myself: 'What the hell, why not go in?'

"The girl at the reception desk sent me to Personnel, who asked me where I came from. 'Newfoundland,' I said. They appeared thunderstruck. They had Yi-Ying-Sung from China, Urmila Kokatnur from India, and Mark Vishniak from Moscow — but *Newfoundland?* I was a prize specimen for the zoo. So they hired me. Simple as that."

"What are you doing?"

Pushie laughed. "Well, technically," he said, "I'm writing for Foreign Affairs. But frankly I've never encountered such a system in my life. My boss is a man named Whittaker Chambers. A very nice guy, but kind of mysterious. Every Thursday we have a story conference and I get certain assignments. I go back to my office and write my stories. Then I submit them to Chambers. He always thanks me politely, but then he places my copy beside the typewriter, writes 'Pushie' at the top of the copy-paper, and writes the story the way he thinks it ought to be written. It's always much better than mine. To be honest with you, I have trouble recognizing my own stories when they appear in the magazine. They're beautiful."

By the end of three days I was growing restive. The trade gossip, the long liquid lunches, the dining and the playgoing were seductive, but I didn't appear to be getting anywhere. I said so when I was presented to the managing editor, Roy Alexander.

"Sure," said Alexander. "Why don't we arrange an interview with the editor, Tom Matthews? He's the final authority."

Matthews was one of the most famous editors in America, the son of an Episcopalian bishop and probably the most handsome man I had ever met. He didn't waste much time.

"This seems to make sense," he said, riffling some papers on his desk. "How much money do you want?"

"Mr. Matthews," I replied, "they tell me it costs a lot to live in New York."

"That's true," he said crisply.

"How would $150 a week sound?" I fully expected him to toss me out of his window onto the Rockefeller ice-skating plaza.

"Fine," he said. "I'll give you a letter saying you're hired, you get a landed immigrant visa from the Consulate in Vancouver, and as soon as you get out of the Navy, get back here."

In high spirits, I repaired at once to a dingy bar across the street from *Time* to compare notes with another job-seeker named James Felton, who had been working for magazines in Los Angeles.

I found Felton at the bar. "How'd you make out?" he cried.

"Great," I said. "I'm in."

"How much they paying you?"

"A hundred and fifty a week."

"Sucker," said Felton. "I asked for $200 and they gave it to me."

There was only one catch to this, as I was to learn in subsequent months. It was true that *Time* would pay people what they asked, but they then demanded performance to match scale. At the end of nine months, Felton was called in and advised that he would be given three months to justify the $200 he had asked. He said that he couldn't work under that kind of pressure, quit, and went back to Los Angeles.

Back in Vancouver, it took about three weeks to get out of uniform, pick up my rehabilitation credits, visit the US consulate (for fingerprints and papers) and make fond farewells. A modest headline in the *Province* proclaimed: "Stu Keate To Big Time".

In a curious way, the headline rankled. I had returned from the wars fully expecting to spend my life in Canada; the fact that I had been hired by a famous American publishing concern seemed *ipso facto* to invest me with some kind of cachet unknown to Canadian journalism. All this confirmed to me only that (1) Canadians suffered a flaming inferiority complex vis-à-vis the United States; and that (2) a great many young Canadians were actually *driven out* of the country by employers who refused to pay them a respectable salary. (Years later I was told that the *Province* netted $500,000 a year all through the Depression, when the average editorial salary was about $25 a week. I also learned that my starting salary of $7,800 a year at *Time* was exactly $300 a year more than that of *Province* editor MacTavish, the man who had advised me to stay away from them in the first place.)

Nevertheless, the move to New York was an important turning-point in my life. *Time* was an exhilarating place to work, full of bright, intelligent young people who vied with each other for status on the magazine's famous masthead and would stare out the window for hours in search of *le mot juste*. A few of them seemed to me unquestionably geniuses. One, certainly, was the brilliant movie critic James Agee, who probably spent too much time being kind to aspiring reporters. Whittaker Chambers, a rumpled man with the face of a Pope, wrote like an angel but carried within him the daemons which emerged later in his celebrated confrontation with Alger Hiss.

Editor Matthews was at once perceptive, witty and remorseless in his assaults on foggy prose. When Bob Elson produced a prolix piece on the economic reconstruction of Germany, and titled it "Whale on the Beach", Matthews wrote at the bottom. "Fine. Now strip off 75 lines of blubber."

In my first story for *Time*, I wrote that the Canadian parliament in Ottawa had opened "with its usual pomp and circumstance". Matthews struck out the trite words and substituted "with pith and vinegar".

I redeemed myself with TSM, as he was known, when in describing a St. Andrew's debutante ball in Montreal I wrote that "some of the girls curtsied like short-stops going down after a hot grounder". Matthews liked the phrase so much that he (1) sent me a note; (2) invited me to lunch at his Park Avenue apartment; and (3) put my name up on the masthead three months ahead of schedule.

It was not long before I became (with John Brooks) a "swing man", available for any section of "the book", front or back. In sequence, I wrote about Canadian Affairs, Milestones, Miscellany, National Affairs, Foreign Affairs, People and Press.

Trained in the hurly-burly of daily deadlines, I was fascinated by the more leisurely approach of a newsmagazine whose work-week was from Thursday morning to Monday night, when final copy was transmitted from New York to the vast printing presses in Chicago.

Each Thursday at about 10 a.m. we would gather for a story conference in the office of the Senior Editor of our section: writers, researchers and art editors, usually totalling about a dozen. Story suggestions from correspondents scattered around the world were considered. Writers and researchers offered news-clips which might be developed into broader pieces. (We were expected, for example, to be reading all seven of New York's dailies regularly.) From time to time the Senior Editor would expound on a theme which he felt merited attention. Conver-sation was uninhibited, spontaneous, wide open; when debate was joined, sparks flew which illuminated both sides of the ques-tion and proved, to me at least, the benefits of "group journalism".

Stories were assigned to various writers according to their special interests and talents but they rarely knuckled down to writing them before Friday afternoon. In the meantime, research-ers (all of them women) had been digging into the files, sending out queries to correspondents for overnight filing, and plopping onto the writers' desks several thousand words of background. The trick then was to reduce these thousands of words to a few lines in the magazine. It provided an invaluable lesson in writing taut, spare copy which — after it had been refined in several editorial hoppers — emerged as the world-famous *Time* style.

I was quickly disabused of the notion that it was easier to write for a weekly than a daily. To be sure, Thursday was a three-martini day, but thereafter the pressure mounted relentlessly and reached its peak on Sunday night. First drafts of stories went to the Senior Editor. They were rarely approved. Back they would come for refinements, changes of phrase, additional nuances, complete recarpentering. A second treatment was almost inevitable, but sometimes, with particularly demanding editors, they went to a third, fourth or even fifth version. The ultimate degradation, which came rarely, was when a writer was all unknowingly taken off a story and the job handed to a colleague who would "write behind him". In the words of one practitioner, this process "ground your brains to powder". But it was extremely useful.

One Saturday night Senior Editor Ernest Havemann called Pushie and me into his office and ominously closed the door behind him. We were, at the time, both writing National (American) Affairs.

"Fellows," said Havemann, "We're in trouble. We've got two stories here that just don't come off. One concerns Clare Boothe Luce (whereat Pushie and I exchanged furtive glances) and another a radical labour boss.

"I don't care which one of you writes which, but it's got to be done, and done tonight. You can toss a coin if you want." We tossed. Pushie got Clare and I got the labour leader.

My heart sank for my old friend. I was able to get a satisfactory discharge on my story by 2 a.m. Pushie was still assaulting his typewriter with stolid Newfie fortitude when I left the building. He told me the next day he had finished his forty-five-line story at 6 a.m.

Mrs. Luce, while never seen in the Time-Life building, was nevertheless regarded by young editors as an *eminence grise* in the organization. Her husband, known to all staffers as "Harry" Luce, was a regular attendant at his office when in New York, but appeared to commune only with Senior Editors and executives.

With one exception. From time to time he would ask to be briefed in special areas by writers supposed to enjoy some expertise in their field. One day, a few months after arriving at *Time*, I was told that I had been tapped and to prepare myself for a "Luce luncheon". I received the summons with all the enthusiasm of a piece of ham facing the grinder. Luce was a brilliant, remote and arctic man, an intensely shy, private person who nevertheless enjoyed the cut and thrust of debate and could be dissuaded from a special stance if a challenger could down him with facts. He was known as a ferocious interlocutor, a man who could reduce writers to jelly with the curtness and acuity of his questions.

Only once to my knowledge had he been "topped" and that was by the irrepressible Travers Coleman, when public relations director of the Canadian Pacific in Vancouver. Luce was passing through the city en route to China by way of an Empress liner. Hearing this, Coleman delved into the Dominion Bureau of Statistics files and memorized every statistic he thought might capture the attention of the great publisher.

When they met, Luce wasted no time. "How much grain shipped through this port?" he demanded.

"Sir," said Coleman, "23,749,363 bushels last year."

Luce's jaw dropped a foot.

My "Luce luncheon" took place in a small, private dining-room in the Radio City building with about six *Time* people at the table. Luce, who had absolutely no interest in food, handed the menu to an aide and asked him to order something. Then from beneath his bushy eyebrows he surveyed his captive audience.

Fortunately for me, his eye lit on a young man named Emmett Hughes, one of *Time*'s top writers, later to become a special adviser to Eisenhower and a successful author.

"Hughes," Luce snapped. "Understand you're just back from Spain. What's going on?"

Hughes began to talk. And talk. And talk. When he reached twenty minutes, my numbness began to thaw. At half an hour, I actually began listening to what he was saying. At forty-five minutes, I knew I was home free. The meeting broke up without a single question about Canada.

Not long after, I met Luce standing at the intersection of 49th Street and Fifth Avenue, waiting for a light to change.

"Good morning, Mr. Luce," I said. He grunted.

Together, in lock-step, we started out into the traffic. It was quite obvious that he was thinking Deep Thoughts, but since we were headed for the same office, a block away, I did not think it prudent to break into a run, or feign a muscle spasm and collapse into the nearest gutter. Along 49th we walked, still not speaking, and into the Time-Life building. An empty elevator was available. Luce retired to a corner and stared glumly at the floor. At the 26th floor I got off. Luce rode on up to his office.

Luce's apparent lack of interest in Canada (at least until his son married a Nova Scotia girl) filtered down by some osmotic process to the many sections of the magazine. Otto Fuerbringer, a

Senior Editor, once asked me: "What do they call those divisions of territory up there — not *states*, . . ." When I replied "provinces" he slammed the desk with his fist and said, "Yeah, that's it — PROVINCES." The offical explanation was that "Canadians are not news-makers" — life in our country was so serene, so orderly, that it did not produce lively copy.

Nevertheless, at the end of the war Canada was accorded a full page in the magazine's US and international editions. In due course this was watered down to an occasional story in the magazine's "Hemisphere" section. Since Canada was the United States' best customer, and the two countries exchanged more trade than any other two countries in the world, *Time* indifference was difficult to understand.

But the establishment of a "Canadian" edition, with a maple leaf on the front cover and three pages of Canadian news inside — with Canadian advertising sold around it — was a dramatic success. Before long, this spin-off was netting close to $400,000 a year, causing the company president, Jim Linen, to say: "Give me the Canadian edition and you can have my job." This roaring success eventually led to the establishment of the O'Leary Commission, which held that *Time Canada* had an unfair advantage over its Canadian rivals because 90 per cent of editorial content could be dumped across the border at no cost to the Canadian edition. After some years of stalling on the sensitive issue, and vigorous lobbying from both sides, Ottawa ruled that Canadian businesses could no longer write off costs of advertising in *Time*. It was expected that this ruling would kill the Maple Leaf edition — which it did; but to the surprise of a great many, Canadians continued to pay higher rates to advertise in *Time*, and the business flourished.

In the main these were happy and rewarding days at *Time*. We were proud of our magazine. New York was an exciting city, not yet plunged into the lawlessness and disorder which converted it into the sink-hole of the Wagner and Lindsay eras. It was still safe to walk home from the theatre down dimly-lit side streets. There were restaurants to accommodate any wallet. It was possible to roam Central Park at night without fear, or take a subway to the ball game without being mugged.

But at the end of eighteen months in New York, disenchantment was setting in. The pressures of those late Saturday and Sunday nights were getting to me. My wife was finding New York a difficult place in which to raise a small boy. In Tudor City, where we lived, 8,000 people were jammed into a couple of square blocks of high-rise apartments. Social tensions were rampant. It was clear that dogs took precedence over children in New York.

I thought I would be happier, and do a better job, in one of *Time*'s bureaus, preferably in Canada, and tried to sell Bob Elson on the idea of opening a Vancouver office for the Canadian edition.

"Nothing doing," he stormed. "If anyone ever opens a Vancouver office, it will be me!"

"Would you believe Seattle?" I pursued.

"No," he said. "If you went to Seattle you'd be sneaking up to Vancouver every weekend."

A break came when word was filtered down that Time International was unhappy with its Montreal operation. A French-Canadian journalist had been chief of bureau for a year, but had published less than a dozen stories. His notion of covering Montreal was to place a case of Dewar's Scotch behind his desk in the Windsor Hotel, invite his friends to drop by and — over *un p'tit coup* — tell him what was going on.

*Time* decided to let him go. I applied for the job, and got it. In the dead of one of the coldest winters in history, 1947, my wife (who was seven months pregnant) and I entrained for Montreal.

# Chapter 6

"Four hostile newspapers are more to be
feared than a thousand bayonets."

— *Napoleon Bonaparte*

We arrived in a fierce snowstorm. The morning *Gazette* carried
a chilling story about a poor Samaritan who, in helping push a
car away from the curb, had caught his scarf in a snow-blower,
been sucked into the whirling blades of the machine and blown
out in bloody chunks onto the street. *Bienvenu à Montréal.*

*Time*, with its usual largesse, had arranged to put us up in the
comfortable and elegant old Windsor Hotel while we were house-
hunting. *Time*'s offices were directly across Dominion Square,
in the Sun Life Building. It couldn't have been more than a
hundred yards away but for a few minutes, that first morning, I
seriously doubted that I would make it. My rubber galoshes were
inadequate for the vast drifts of snow and my Navy great-coat,
stripped of brass buttons and braid for civilian use, almost too
heavy. I fetched up on the steps of the Sun Life gasping for breath,
my cheeks stinging, ears frozen and eyes running with tears.

From this glacial and inauspicious beginning emerged almost
four fascinating years that I counted, in retrospect, an invaluable
post-graduate course in the understanding of a nation. Like most
western Canadians, I was largely ignorant of *la belle province* and
thought of it (if I thought about it at all) in the conventional
clichés: the priest-ridden snowscape of aluminum church spires,
pea soup, pork pies and Piaf *chansons* . I left with a much different
impression.

It was, in fact, an exciting time to be in Quebec; a time of social unrest and a massive population shift from rural to urban civilization. Montreal was in the throes of one of its periodic vice probes, dramatically pursued by the young lawyers Jean Drapeau and Pacifique ("Pax") Plante, who went around wearing a shoulder-holster. Camillien Houde was out of concentration camp and working his considerable Gallic charm on the citizens from his secure post at the *Hôtel de Ville*.

Over in the capital of Quebec City, Premier Maurice Duplessis was declaiming: "L'Union Nationale, c'est moi!" and few would challenge his boast. Autocratic, a lover of puns as well as power, he had ruled his province (with one brief wartime exclusion) for more than twenty years.

One of my first duties was to make my number with *le chef*, who was regarded by my employers as the most interesting political personality on the Canadian stage. As I entered his large, tastefully-furnished office overlooking the St. Lawrence River, Duplessis leaped up from his desk, hand outstretched.

"My, you're a big bugger," he cried.

I took his hand; it was soft, almost feminine. He was wearing a suit of expensive checkered cloth, but he needed a better tailor: the suit was double-breasted, and tended to accentuate his formidable *embonpoint*. His linen was spotless, but his tie at half-mast. The most striking feature of his face was a pair of twinkling eyes which seemed to bore within you, from behind a generous Bourbon nose. It would not have been difficult to imagine him in ruffles and lace, taking pinches of snuff.

"Come in, come in," he cried. "Are you the Keith of Radio-Keith-Orpheum?"

I explained that my name was Keate and that I was an employee of Mr. Henry Luce, come to pay my respects.

"Excellent!" he shouted. "Together we will have the *Time* of our *Life* and make a *Fortune!*"

And thus, having delivered himself of three puns in a single sentence, the Prime Minister slapped his thigh in appreciation and doubled up in paroxysms of laughter at his own cornball joke. The rest of the meeting passed very amicably. Only as the months went by did our conversations take on a chillier air.

Few could match Duplessis on a fast ad-lib. When, during an

election campaign, a heckler shouted: "What about St. Laurent?" (then Prime Minister of Canada), Duplessis cried: "Never yet has the St. Laurent overflowed the St. Maurice," which was not only a pun on his own name, but indigenous to his riding at Trois Rivières.

When, on another occasion, he was being invested with an honorary degree by McGill University (which a number of alumni considered outrageous), and ascended the platform in scarlet robes, a French-Canadian reporter whispered from the press table: "Maurice, I never thought I'd see you wearing red" (the Liberal party colours). The Prime Minister grinned and quipped: "You'll notice I'm sitting on them." (It served McGill right. Duplessis never came through with the grants they hoped might flow from that honorary degree.)

In the years that ensued, it became painfully evident that the Prime Minister's gay, bantering exterior was a mask for one of the most ruthless, despotic personalities Canada has ever produced. Behind the jaunty platform postures and the cheap puns lay a tough, uncompromising will and a nineteenth-century mind in which the capacity for vindictiveness was vivid.

His grip on his party was so strong that many of his followers lived in downright fear of *le chef*. Once, during the 1948 provincial election, I asked a precinct organizer what I regarded as an innocent question: was it true that followers of the Union Nationale contributed 25 cents a month to the party coffers? The subordinate blanched perceptibly, and looked away in embarrassment. "You will have to ask the Chief," he replied.

Duplessis' election tactics were blunt and to the point. "Do you want a new hospital? Do you want a new bridge? Electric lights? A new school? Then vote Union Nationale. I would hate to force gifts on you that wouldn't be appreciated."

When Frank Roncarelli, the Montreal restauranteur, undertook to bail out about 800 Jehovah's Witnesses who had been arrested for distributing religious pamphlets, Duplessis hit him where he knew it would hurt: he revoked Roncarelli's licence. Within a year, his restaurant was broke. Roncarelli sued, and after years of delay and frustration, won a Supreme Court judgement.

Duplessis operated on a simple principle: Father Knows Best. His Padlock Law — declared *ultra vires* in 1957 — was introduced into the statutes in 1937 and permitted the Attorney-General (M. Duplessis) to close premises *suspected* of fomenting subversive ideas or propaganda. Those accused were compelled to prove themselves innocent, a remarkable switch on Commonwealth tradition.

Civil liberties accepted as commonplace in other Canadian provinces got short shrift at the hands of Quebec's Prime Minister. Censorship was tightened — on 16 mm. movies, "ham" radio operators and even bingo and two-piece bathing suits. These strictures made for some amusing stories. *Time* rejoiced when Duplessis' censors took aim at a Seven-Up billboard showing a family frolicking on the beach. In the foreground a two-year-old baby exposed her bare bottom. Censors promptly ordered some bathing trunks painted in.

As a recorder of these bizarre goings-on, *Time* was in a unique position. Published outside Canada, it could assume the role of dispassionate observer in a manner in which Quebec publications, both French and English (with the honourable exception of *Le Devoir*) could not, or would not. Both the Montreal *Star* and *Gazette* looked the other way. Their rationale was that, as spokesmen for a minority culture, they had "to get along" or be accused of fomenting racial strife. They might have argued, just as convincingly, that a lot of *Québécois*, raised in the authoritarian tradition, heartily approved of Duplessis' bully-boy tactics.

The fact that I mentioned this journalistic abdication in a couple of articles and speeches did not endear me to the Montreal *Star's* publisher, John McConnell Jr., who seized the occasion of a cocktail party in San Francisco to announce that he was going to "punch me in the goddamned nose." McConnell was, at the time, well into the paint and feeling bodacious. He was eased off to a corner.

Some years later, in Toronto, McConnell approached me at another newspaper party and apologized. "I'm sorry," he said. "That stuff of yours rankled. But it was true. My father was a friend of Duplessis. Our policy was to support the party in power as much as we could."

It was a sad fact, too, that a number of Quebec reporters, both French and English, were "on the take". Underpaid and overworked (this was before they were organized), they had come to accept as routine the brown paper envelope tucked under the dinner plate. The size of the bribe ranged upwards from $5 and was generally determined by the circulation of the reporter's paper.

More recent bribery charges by the late Réal Caouette, who claimed to have suborned a CBC correspondent, have given the impression that corruption of journalists has been common in Canada. This has not been my experience. In forty years of journalism, I was importuned only three times — once by a doctor who offered me $5 to put his name in a column; once by a promoter with an offer of some "insider" stock; and once by a Minister of Trade and Commerce in the Duplessis cabinet.

We had concluded an interview in his Windsor Hotel suite when this gentleman excused himself and returned with a brown paper envelope.

"What's this?" I asked.

"A little present for you."

I was embarrassed. "One reason *Time* pays us such good money," I explained, "is that we don't have to accept this kind of gift."

Now the Minister was embarrassed. "But you must realize," he said, "it is the accepted thing in Quebec."

"Thank you," I replied, "but I don't want it."

The Minister waved the envelope at me. "All right," he said, "*You* don't want it. So take it and by some flowers for your wife."

I left him with the envelope in his hand, shaking his head in disbelief.

Today, happily, there are higher standards. Quebec reporters are among the highest-paid in Canada. The Montreal dailies, both French and English, are hard-hitting and quick to expose shenanigans at all levels.

Directing one of these dailies today, ironically, is a man who had never written a line of journalism in 1947. As a fledgling author, Roger Lemelin had created something of a scandal with his first book, an anti-clerical story called *The Boy from the Town Below*. En route to becoming President and Publisher of *La Presse*, the second largest French-language daily in North America, he ventured into forest products, radio, TV ("The Plouffe Family"), advertising, insurance, and the distribution of blood puddings, and in the process became a millionaire. He once astonished me in a Montreal restaurant by producing a photostat copy of a cheque for $1.1 million, made out in his favour.

My close association with the talented and flamboyant M. Lemelin began when Ricky Daignault, a good reporter whom I had been employing as a part-time correspondent (or "stringer") in Quebec City left to take a permanent job with The Canadian Press. I asked him if he could nominate a successor. He suggested his friend, Lemelin. A meeting was arranged in Quebec City. I drove over with my wife and had an enjoyable meal with Lemelin —a big, good-looking, laughing fellow with an infectious *joie de vivre* and a booming belief in his own talents. He was, he confessed, not only the greatest writer in Quebec but a superb athlete, magnificent baritone singer, devastating lover and (just to balance his personality a bit) a ranking chess master.

When we got around to the brandy, it occurred to me that we had discussed everything but journalism. So, with characteristic Anglo-Saxon stuffiness, I steered the conversation around to the business at hand.

"Mr. Lemelin, have you ever written for newspapers?"

"No."

"Magazines?"

"No."

"You've never done journalism?"

"No."

"Never written in English?"

"No."

I was becoming a bit bewildered. "*Time*," I said, "is a pretty sophisticated publication. You say you have no experience, none at all. So what makes you think you could write for *Time?*"

At this point, Lemelin reared back haughtily and bellowed: "I have *intelligence*. Is that not enough?"

This answer so delighted me that I hired him on the spot. He was a great success; a natural-born story-teller whose mastery of English was just "quaint" enough to charm the editors in New York. When, shortly after he was appointed, the town of Rimouski was virtually destroyed by a fire, Lemelin wrote such a poignant and moving "mood piece" about the survivors that *Life* magazine grabbed his copy for a masthead display.

Lemelin was less successful with the New York brass, for whom he appeared to hold a thinly-veiled contempt. One year each bureau chief was asked to invite an outstanding "stringer" in his area to accompany him to a correspondents' seminar at the Park Lane Hotel in Manhattan. I asked Lemelin.

At the first day's session the main speaker was Roy Larsen, one of the founders and President of Time, Inc. In the middle of his speech I was horrified to see Lemelin with his head down on his chest, snoring audibly.

At our hotel that night, I said: "Look, Roger, these guys are paying all your expenses down here. The least you can do, when the President is speaking, is to stay awake."

Lemelin waved off the protest with an airy toss of his hand. "Stu," he said, "these are circulation data. They do not interest me."

"Well tomorrow," I replied, "the speaker is going to be God Himself, Harry Luce. I want you to promise me you won't go to sleep while he is talking."

"For you, Stu," he replied, winking irreverently, "I will do it. Now let us go to The Three Deuces and listen to some jazz."

The next day I was delighted to note that Lemelin was sitting forward in his chair, hanging on every word The Master was uttering. After the meeting, however, my attention was drawn to a knot of ten or twelve writers gathered in a corner across the room. In the centre, his back to the wall, stood Mr. Luce. Directly in front of him, and wagging a finger under his nose, was Roger Lemelin.

With sinking heart, I eased him away and said: "For God's sake, Roger, were you *lecturing* Luce?"

"Not at all," he replied, indignantly. "I was just telling him that his magazine was no damned good."

Luce appeared unperturbed.

This lusty irreverence and general go-to-hell attitude I found a most endearing trait. French-Canadians, while clearly subordinate to their English-speaking bosses in their day-to-day lives, just as clearly triumphed in the essential business of enjoying life.

I sensed this particularly when I was welcomed into the cluttered *ateliers* of Montreal's artists and sculptors. The art world at the time was full of yeast and ferment. Paul-Emile Borduas, regarded by many critics as Canada's finest painter, was fighting his expulsion from a teaching job by Duplessis. Two or three

French-speaking theatres were thriving, most notably that of Gratien Gélinas with his long-running play *Tit-Coq*. The painters Riopelle and Pellan were gaining international attention with their vivid canvasses. Louis Archambault and Robert Roussil were exploring new spatial concepts with their metal and wood sculptures.

As the representative of a powerful international magazine, I was equally welcome in the panelled boardrooms of the business community. The contrast was striking. But one institution which proved less easy of access was the Royal Victoria Hospital (where my daughter Kathryn had recently made her arrival on the scene). Dr. Wilder Penfield and his associates were working their black magic at the Neurological Institute and *Time* was desperate for a story on this man, reputed to be the world's finest brain surgeon. All efforts to obtain an interview were rebuffed until I negotiated a trade-off with principal Cyril James of McGill: an interview with Penfield in an exchange for a mention in *Time* of McGill's fundraising drive.

Once committed to this unlikely proposition, Dr. Penfield allowed me access to his laboratories and operating theatres for a full week. I attended day and night, in one of the most absorbing experiences in a life-time of journalism. But Penfield, a considerable writer, was sceptical of the approach of a popular magazine. Would I promise him that the *Time* story would contain no names? I could make no such promise. Could he see copy before it was filed? That was a journalistic no-no. Would I then permit him to write his own story of MNI's work, for forwarding to the editors in New York?

An unusual request, but I had no objection. In due course, my story was published and a wire came from managing editor Roy Alexander: "We are prepared to believe that Dr. Wilder Penfield is the greatest brain surgeon in the world. He is by no means the world's greatest journalist."

Access to St. James Street, where the power brokers worked their financial magic, was easier. When the Royal Bank announced that it was appointing a new President, James Muir, I asked for, and was granted, an interview. Mr. Muir and his public relations man, my former Toronto *Star* boss John Heron, entertained me at a stiff luncheon at the Mount Royal Club, during which the new

President recited with some relish his rise from boyhood in Peebles, Scotland, to the eminent state he had now achieved.

After lunch we returned to the head office of the bank. Heron and I were chatting amiably about the story when a loud buzzer sounded on the President's direct line. Heron jumped a foot. "Yessir, he's here. Yes sir. Yes sir." Heron began to make some notes. "Yes sir. I've got it."

He put down the telephone, put his head in both hands, and looked at me. "Stu," he said, "I hate to do this to you, but I've got to. The old man loves those funny captions they put under pictures in *Time*. He's written his own caption for the story you're doing and has instructed me to pass it to you. You're not going to believe this, but here it is:

FROM PEEBLES TO PRESIDENT . . . The Royal robes could be worn by no finer banker."

Needless to say, *Time* spurned this literary gem.

Far from being pleased with the story which appeared in *Time*, Muir was incensed (1) that it appeared only in the Canadian edition and (2) that his picture had not appeared on the cover " . . .as it has for all my friends". He instructed John Heron to telephone me, conveying his displeasure and announcing that an interview for a full-length profile in *Maclean's*, which I had agreed to do on a free-lance basis, was forthwith cancelled.

The French-Canadians took themselves less seriously. If there was any separatism around, it didn't show itself. At the Montreal Press Club, *les Canadiens* tended to hive themselves off, but the rest of us were always welcome at their table — and even when they predominated 5-1 they paid their English-language colleagues the ultimate courtesy of speaking in their tongue.

To be sure, there had been formed a society for the preservation of pure French (which objected to things like "Buvez Coke"), and there were some militant demonstrations by the Société Jean Baptiste on parade day, but separatism was not the flaming issue it was to become in the 1960s and 70s. What *was* evident was a growing demand for social justice: the French-Canadians were clearly second-class citizens in their own province, underpaid, barred from top jobs, casually dismissed as folk-singing *habitants* who would perform the drudge duties for their English overlords.

From the sidelines it appeared to me that the French had a perfectly understandable grievance. The turning-point, in my view, came with the strike at the town of Asbestos in 1949, an event I have always regarded as the most socially significant Canadian story of our times. From it flowed the "new Quebec" which has brought Canada to the brink of insurrection, dissolution and (for the lunatic fringe) possible civil war.

Hundreds of strikers were sleeping on the floors of St. Aimé, the parish church. We reporters had been tipped off that the provincial police were on their way to open up road blocks, "put down violence" and arrest as many strikers as possible. But by 4 a.m. we were pretty well convinced that plans had changed, that the police were not coming. I confess I was the first to give in. "C'mon, fellas," I said, "let's get back to the hotel and get some sleep."

With me was a combative and talented young photographer named Michael Rougier. Suddenly he leapt up and cried: "Here they come! Let's get cracking!"

Over on the horizon, on the main highway leading into the town, the headlights of a motorized caravan, twenty or thirty strong, advanced toward the beleaguered village. We followed. Out piled 150 policemen, in plain clothes, armed with tear-gas guns, sidearms and truncheons.

For an hour or so an uneasy peace descended on the square. Then a captain shouted *"en avant!"* and the raid was on. In front of St. Aimé — as in so many Quebec village churches — there was a statue of Christ with a circle of light at His head. A few flowers ringing the base were guarded by a single strand of wire. One of the charging police tripped over the wire, picked himself up, and joined his comrades. The heavy church doors yielded to the mass attack and the men stormed into the basement, shouting and swinging.

Rougier went in with them, snapping pictures on the run. He saw the truncheons flail and recorded the evidence. In a tiny kitchen, strikers were backed against a wall and beaten. His pictures showed them soaked in blood from head to foot — ghostly apparitions as they staggered out into the sunrise. Outside the

church, Louis Jaques of Montreal was taking more pictures —
until he sickened of the role and turned away.

This bloody confrontation rocked Quebec. For the first time,
the church appeared to be on the side of the workers. In Montreal
the gentle intellectual Archbishop Joseph Charbonneau ordered
a collection for the strikers. Not long after, he was relieved of his
post (for reasons of "ill health") and shipped off to Victoria to
become a humble Chaplain of St. Joseph's Hospital.

Asbestos was significant not only because it marked a turning-
point in the social history of Quebec, but because it threw into
prominence half a dozen personalities not widely known at the
time who became major figures in the political life of Canada.
Gérard Pelletier was there, as a correspondent. Representing *Le
Devoir* was Pierre Laporte, strangled twenty-one years later by
the FLQ. The eloquent and scrappy union leader was Jean Marc-
hand. Jean Drapeau was a young lawyer for the union.

But most of all, there was Pierre Elliott Trudeau, a rich man's
son and a lawyer in revolt against the established order, who
later found an outlet for his views in the critical paper *Cité-Libre*.
Years later, in a book of essays on the Asbestos strike, Trudeau
denounced "the bosses", the Liberal party and "the scabrous
politicking of the old parties". While he was, in fact, less calm in
his approach than his co-essayists, he was also by far the most
analytical and felicitous of style.

"It was the asbestos that caught fire," he wrote. And so, as we
have since learned, did all Quebec. The strike was finally settled,
after five months, by the much-respected Archbishop Maurice
Roy. The workers got a ten-cent raise.

That summer we rented a cottage at Brome Lake, in the Eastern
Townships — a pleasant interlude interrupted by a call from New
York. A federal election having been called, *Time* had decided
to do a cover story on Louis St. Laurent and required thousands
of words of research in a relatively short time. Would I high-tail
it over to Quebec City, talk to the Prime Minister, and provide the
necessary background for an in-depth look at "Uncle Louis" and
his electoral prospects?

I had been introduced to Mr. St. Laurent by Lester Pearson at
a 1946 New York reception for Canadian delegates to the UN. St.
Laurent was at the time Minister of Justice in the King government.

By any standards, he was an impressive gentlemen: striking, courtly, a complete charmer. He had entered public life at the behest of Mr. King, who was anxious to be succeeded by a strong French-Canadian, and had given up his lucrative corporate law practice only after he was persuaded that it was in the nature of a national duty to do so.

Once established at the Chateau Frontenac, I sought a personal interview with the leader. His functionaries advised me that Mr. St. Laurent was so caught up with his campaign preparations that he could not grant one-on-one appointments, but did promise that if I would draw up a list of questions, he would provide written answers.

Accordingly, I climbed on my Royal portable and drafted such a list. It was quite late in the evening when I set out from the Chateau to deliver the questions by hand to his home on the Grand Allée. It was my intention to drop the material in the St. Laurent letter-box. But, when I arrived at his home I found that it — like most of the old Quebec City mansions — had a vestibule. I tried the outer door. It was open. So I went in and tried the inner door. It was open, too. So I stepped quietly into the house, propped the envelope on the hall table, and departed. A simple thing, perhaps, but so damned *Canadian* that I had to ask myself: was there any other country in the world where such a process could be repeated? (I had a feeling that had I tried such a stunt in the US, a dozen FBI agents would have leapt from behind the rhododendron bushes and wrestled me to the ground as soon as I set foot inside the front gate.)

There remained another avenue to be explored. I knew that Mr. St. Laurent was a golfer. So, on the off chance that I might catch him on the fairways, I took a taxi out to his club on the weekend. The resident professional, one of the famed Huot brothers, confirmed that Mr. St. Laurent was on the golf course, but emphasized that this was a private club and he could not have so prominent a member as Mr. St. Laurent badgered by the attentions of an inquisitive reporter.

I could understand that. But perhaps M. Huot would tell me about Mr. St. Laurent's game. How did he play? The professional thought for a minute. Then he said: "Well, let me put it this way. He is neither to the left or the right, but always right down the middle."

Since this, in capsule form, was a precise definition of Mr. St. Laurent's political philosophy it elicited huzzahs from the waiting editor in New York and a perfect quote for *Time*'s cover story. The election, of course, was a rout. The prime minister scored the greatest triumph in Liberal history, taking 193 seats to George Drew's 41.

Not very long afterwards I received another telephone call from New York — this time from Bob Elson. After almost four years in Quebec, he said, the time had come for me to move on. Would I be interested in the Los Angeles bureau? Denver? Chicago?

None of these cities was well known to me; I shuddered at the thought of "going in cold" to make new contacts — a repeat, in effect, of what I had done in Montreal. Besides, as we shall see, an attractive invitation had developed in Canada. This brought me to a watershed: did I want to stay with *Time* and become an American, or did I want to remain in Canada as a Canadian citizen? Even though it meant less money, I opted for Canada. It was a decision I never regretted.

Elson, as usual, was both kind and understanding. "We'll send you off with a hell of a party," he promised. Thus, one balmy June day, about 250 friends gathered in the garden behind the Naval Officers' Club on McGregor Street for farewell drinks and speeches. In launching my successor, Jim Conant, we somehow contrived to consume $700 worth of Mr. Luce's booze. One report (which I could not confirm) reached us that a prominent Montreal matron was discovered the following morning, asleep under a rhododendron bush.

Some years later, in 1964, I drew on our four years' experience in Montreal to write an article for *Saturday Night* magazine entitled: "What The Hell Goes On In Quebec?" Although in those days one could walk outside *Saturday Night's* circulation in five minutes, no article of mine written before or since brought me such a flood of personal correspondence. In the piece (which took the form of an exchange of letters with my old friend Roger Lemelin) I deplored the possible loss to Canada of *la belle province* and attempted an analysis of the difference in life-style which made Quebec what it was. Perhaps rather naively, I rejoiced in the French-Canadians' capacity for song and laughter, the richness of their personalities, their innate courtesy and *joie de vivre*.

In his response in *Saturday Night* Lemelin argued, as gently as possible, that I was merely perpetuating the myth of the genial *habitant* in his touque and *ceinture flechée*, indifferent to his role in the marketplace, content to go along as a second-class citizen, singing "Auprès de ma Blonde" and sloshing back the *vin du pays*. Apropos of the early bombings the warm-hearted Lemelin amazed me by writing: "A certain amount of anarchy is part and parcel of a growing social maturity."

His reactions to my sentiments surprised me. So did those of Quebec correspondents who after the appearance of the piece, in dozens of letters, rejected out of hand my sincere admiration and love for their province.

Unhappily it would appear that Lemelin was right. Regardless of any referenda, provincial or national, the separatists will always be with us. (They have been, we sometimes forget, for more than 100 years.) Revolutions traditionally are rooted in bold dogma. Unless by the exercise of decent restraint and calm common-sense we can arrive at a *modus vivendi* with our Quebec brethren, I fear for the future of Canada.

# Chapter 7

"Great newspapers are made by great
editors."

— *Lord Francis Williams*

A few months earlier, in the spring of 1949, I was sitting in the
office of *Time* magazine in Montreal when my secretary, Made-
leine Roy, came in and said: "There's a Mr. Bell outside to see
you."

"I don't know any Mr. Bell in Montreal. What does he look
like?"

"Well," she replied, "he's kind of cute."

"Never mind that. What does he *look* like?"

"I don't know. He is wearing a sports shirt and no tie."

"You mean he's a bum?"

"No, I don't think so, because he is also wearing a camel-hair
coat which I think is very expensive."

"Okay," I said, "show the bum in."

.This was my introduction to Max Bell. It turned out to be one
of the luckiest encounters of my life. I had never met him before,
had heard of him only vaguely as a Calgary sportsman and fin-
ancier who had "hit it rich" in 1947 with the advent of the Leduc
oil strike.

In appearance, Bell was a locker-room guy — athletic, mus-
cular, snub-nosed, blue-eyed, with close-cropped curly grey hair
and pink cheeks. I judged him to be about my own age. In later
years, I sometimes reflected that his dress that first day personified

the man: the camel-hair coat reflecting his affluence, the casual
golf shirt his indifference to it.

At first Bell seemed shy, almost diffident. He apologized for
"breaking in without introduction". It was just that we had some
mutual friends out West and that he was looking into a newspaper
deal which he thought might interest me. What he had in mind
was purchase of the two newspapers in Victoria, the *Times* and
the *Colonist*. The *Times* deal was virtually complete; he would
pay the Spencer family $750,000 for the 18,000-circulation daily.
Bell thought he could buy the *Colonist* from H. T. ("Tim") Matson.
He was dickering for a minority position with the long-range
prospect of eventual take-over and a merger.

As he warmed to his topic — the whole monologue lasted
about forty-five minutes — Bell's voice rose in proportion to his
enthusiasm. To emphasize a point, he extended his right hand
like a claw, withdrew it to his chest, and indulged in what can
only be described as "a smiling grimace". I was fascinated with
the way he spoke. In many ways, he was a "voice double" for
Jimmy Carter. His style, while a trifle florid, indicated a fondness
for the English language. It was only when he soared into the
realms of high finance that he left me: his sentences were sprin-
kled with arcane business jargon such as "net quick", "liquidity",
"times-earnings", "roll-over" and "spin-off".

What Bell was arguing, with forceful conviction, was that Victoria was what horse-players call an "overlay". In short, it was a
potentially valuable, but overlooked, property. The *Times* and
*Colonist* were newspapers of good repute; indeed the *Colonist*,
founded by Amor de Cosmos in 1858, was the oldest daily of
continuous publication on the Pacific Coast. But the *Colonist's*
building was on the verge of collapse and the *Times* had anti-
quated equipment. The logical economic move was to put them
together in a spanking new building, let the *Times* use the presses
in the daytime and the *Colonist* at night. The market potential,
Bell suggested, was probably in the neighbourhood of $5 million
a year. With the economies inherent in joint equipment and a
combination advertising and circulation rate, such a venture "would
probably net about $700,000 a year."

I listened to this fanciful prospectus with mounting disbelief.

Serene, stodgy, stable old Victoria netting $700,000 a year? *Surely*, I thought, *this boy must be on the poppy*.

After an hour or so, Bell got up to leave. "Nice talking to you," he said. "I don't know you, but I have friends and they tell me you might be persuaded to return to the coast. I'm looking for a Victoria publisher. Would you be interested in the job?"

A remote warning bell sounded, something harking back to a family feud in Regina and Saskatoon in the late 1920s. At that time my father-in-law, Hugo Meilicke, and his brother Ted were partners with George Bell, Max's father, in the prairie newspapers. They did not approve of the way George Bell ran them, especially in respect of political patronage. With the support of a managing editor named Burford Hooke, who had been given voting stock in the company by Bell, they mustered enough votes to turf Bell out of office and take command. A long and bitter law-suit emerged, which Bell ultimately dropped. In addition, a Bell brother had married a Meilicke sister and family relations were strained, to put it charitably.

So I said to Bell: "Look, I'm flattered, but how could I work for you? My wife is Letha Meilicke."

"I know," he grinned, "but this has nothing to do with you. After all, you married into the family about ten years after that old fight. Forget it."*

So we parted on amicable terms, Bell promising to get back to me when his *Times* deal became firm. There followed a protracted silence. Then, more than six months later, Bell telephoned. "I apologize," he said, "I've been terribly dilatory about the Victoria thing. Do you think you could come out to Calgary and see me?"

It transpired that with the financial assistance of F. R. ("Ronnie") Graham and Edmonton lawyer H. Ray Milner, he had had not

---

* For years Max Bell believed that the Meilickes had conspired behind his father's back to sell the Regina and Saskatoon papers to the Siftons and defraud his father of a proper share. At a Canadian Press meeting in the 1950s Max checked the story with Clifford Sifton and was assured that the Meilickes had acted honorably throughout. It was characteristic of Max that he asked me to take him to the Meilicke home in Vancouver so that he could shake hands with my father-in-law and assure him that the family feud was ended.

too much difficulty in persuading the Spencers' department store people to off-load the *Times*. So in Calgary, we settled the deal. It was arranged that I would return to Montreal, resign from *Time*, and meet him in Victoria later to announce my appointment as publisher of the *Times*.

In some respects, it was a bit of a gamble. My starting salary, Bell said, would be $10,000 a year — $3,000 less than I was already earning at *Time*. But, he promised, if I succeeded in Victoria he would "cut me in for a piece of the action". Thus, in contravention of the classic dictum, I took a step backward with the hope that a little further down the road it would propel me two steps forward.

We arrived in Victoria on a beautifully sunny day, registered at the Empress Hotel, and walked the three blocks to the old *Times* building on Fort Street. The date was auspicious: July 1, 1950, smack in the middle of the twentieth century.

The five *Times* executives who met us in a third-storey office were clearly and understandably apprehensive. The youngest was 58, the oldest 72. And here confronting them was a new owner, 37, and an untried publisher, 36. Hard though it is to believe, their former editor, Benny Nicholas, had refused to accept for himself more than $60 a week, and largely because of this their salaries were pitifully low. They had no pensions. Thus my first job was to assure them that there would be no immediate house-cleanings and that retirement allowances, when they came, would be provided as the paper could afford them, out of general revenues. In this, I had the full and generous backing of Max Bell.

There was an ambience about the place that I found highly agreeable. The *Times* looked and smelled the way an old newspaper office should — slightly fusty, a bit run down, but pervaded by an attractive, easy-going camaraderie which is characteristic of small shops where every person has his job to do and there's little time for politicking. At the moment, understandably, staff morale was low. But, unknown to them, I had in my hip pocket news which would give them heart and demonstrate that we were serious about restoring the *Times* to its old vigour and effectiveness.

From his summer cottage at nearby Shawnigan Lake, Bruce Hutchison had scrawled me a hasty note. Hutchison was an alumnus of the *Times* who had started his career there as a cartoonist

and sports writer and gone on to become one of Canada's foremost authors and political journalists. Hutchison wrote:

Dear Stu,

You have been much on my mind lately — on everyone's mind
out here. I hope the premature announcement of your coming
to the *Times* is correct. . . . If you are coming, do come and
see me at my camp [Cliffside] 25 miles from Victoria, where I
can put you and your wife and kids up in comfort any time.
    I am most anxious (as the oldest inhabitant) to welcome
you and tell you some things you may not know about the
newspaper situation here. I turned down the *Times* offer long
ago. I am not an applicant for a job but I might be able to
help you, tho' you'll need no help. You can do this job with
your left hand, even if you're right-handed. . . .
    It would be wonderful to have a newspaperman out here to
talk to. I have no one now, and, as a result, have lost the
power of speech. But I can still remember. And I remember
when the *Times* was a great little paper and I sometimes wish
I were back in it.
    So much needs to be said — and no one west of the Rockies
is saying anything that I can hear. The town therefore awaits
your coming with palpitations. . . . Again thanks and very best
wishes for your success, which is assured.

This was like rooting around a log-pile and coming up with
the Varga diamond. Hutchison's prestige in Canada was enor-
mous. His book *The Unknown Country*, which I had read and
been moved by as a trainee at *HMCS Stadacona* in the early days
of the war, had enjoyed national success as the first popular
expression of the Canadian ethos. A lyrical work, it quickly made
its way into the school curricula as a classic.
    At the age of nineteen Hutchison had been assigned to cover
the legislature in Victoria. At twenty he had sold fiction to the
*Saturday Evening Post*. Possessor of a flaming prose style and
boundless energy, he had produced millions of words which
found ready acceptance in the newspaper, magazine and radio
markets of the world.

65

I remember vividly the first day I saw him. He was standing quietly at the entrance to the old *Province* newsroom, one day in 1935. He was wearing an old tweed jacket, a woollen pullover sweater, baggy flannels and scuffed-up shoes. With his shaggy forelock, steel-rimmed spectacles and hawk's nose, he looked not unlike a gentleman farmer who had wandered by mistake into this hotbed of communications activity. Silently, he was surveying the scene with what can only be described as "the look of eagles", his gaze particularly riveted on the southwest corner of the room where the late Roy Brown and news editor Bob Elson were deep in conference. "Aha," I imagine he would be saying, "a top-level conference. What are they up to? I know, the bastards. They're planning to move me from Victoria to Ottawa. Well, they'll never get away with it." Subsequent investigation, of course, revealed that what Brown and Elson were discussing with such gravity was where they would take lunch that day.

The second time I saw Bruce was four years later, during the 1939 visit of George VI and Elizabeth to Vancouver, when I found an empty seat beside him on the press bus. A very young reporter, I was intimidated by the magnitude of the assignment and said so to Bruce. He had been staring glumly at the floor of the bus, twirling a stub of yellow pencil between his fingers, and I realized that he was even then composing his opening paragraphs. But he turned to me, a neophyte, and said: "Stu, don't worry. Just write it like you would any other story and it will turn out fine."

That warm word of encouragement was just the first of many kindnesses Bruce was to show me in what became a lifetime partnership.

The next time I saw him was in 1943, when I was home on compassionate leave from the Navy to greet my new-born son, Richard. In the crowded parlour car of a CPR train, heading back for Ottawa, I was delighted to find Bruce and his friend, Jimmy Gray of Calgary. They were associates on the editorial pages of the *Free Press*.

This was my first exposure to Hutchison the economist. He had open on his lap the current issue of *Fortune* magazine and something in it had aroused his wrath. With mounting anger, he began to read aloud to Gray, jabbing a forefinger at the offending passages and working himself into a robust choler.

"For God's sakes, Jimmy," he cried, "listen to this boob. He's arguing that high taxes contribute to inflation; that you can fix prices without fixing wages; and that wartime spending will carry over into peacetime affluence. Hasn't he ever heard of Keynes? What a lot of goddam nonsense!"

One by one the other passengers in the parlour car laid down their newspapers. When, in a final burst of indignation, he flung the offending magazine on the floor, a mild ripple of applause spread through the car. He blushed when Gray and I suggested he should stand and take a modest bow.

Now, here in the summer of 1950, was the best newspaper editor in Canada *volunteering* his services to his old alma mater, the Victoria *Times*. I could scarcely believe my luck. With almost indecent haste, my wife and I repaired to Shawnigan Lake for a conference.

While Bruce's wonderful wife Dorothy and Letha sat beneath the arbutus trees on the patio, Bruce and I moved down to the water's edge. Bruce took a stick and traced patterns in the gravel while he talked about the great days of Benny Nicholas at the *Times*, of its slide towards a moribund state, of the need for a strong editorial voice in the provincial capital.

The upshot of all this was that Bruce agreed to write three columns a week for the incredible sum of $50. All we had to do to clinch the deal was to persuade his son Bobby, an Olympic sprinter, to act as a sort of native bearer between Shawnigan Lake and Victoria, carrying the Olympian editorial messages. To facilitate this arrangement, we took Bobby on as a junior reporter for the summer duty.

Within a year the incumbent editor, Harry P. Hudges, retired and Hutchison took over as editor of the paper. This was the beginning of an association between publisher and editor which lasted more than a quarter-century, on two newspapers, a relationship perhaps unique in Canada.

Despite the difference in our ages (thirteen years) and outlooks, the relationship flourished. We had in common a love of newspapers, books, theatre and the outdoors. There were important differences, too. While I immersed myself in community affairs, Bruce remained largely in the country to do the heavy reading and writing which would build weight and authority into the editorial columns of the paper. Politically, we were both small-l liberals and only rarely did we disagree on matters of editorial opinion. When differences did arise, I was always impressed with Bruce's sense of fairness and professionalism. "For God's sakes, Stu," he would say, "you're the boss. You're the one who has to take the ultimate responsibility. My copy's not sacred. Fix it any way you want." Yet young reporters today are prone to scream and chew the rug if so much as a syllable of their copy is questioned by an alert desk-man. Gradually Hutchison and I emerged as a good, harmonious working team.

Max Bell was delighted when I made my deal with Bruce Hutchison. With the passage of time, and a growing appreciation of Bruce's character and talents, Max began to regard us as his surrogates on the Coast, and in due course enabled us to buy some preference shares in the parent company which paid healthy dividends. But at the outset our starting salaries remained low. When we learned that our owner was due in Victoria for a visit, Bruce and I agreed that the time had come to Cat the Bell.

Max greeted us warmly at his suite in the Empress Hotel. He was en route home, he said, from a highly successful race meet at Santa Anita. How was the business? What was on our minds?

Our answer was simple: more money. While I was in the middle of my pitch, Max suddenly reached out to a suitcase by his side and produced an elastic exercise-rope.

"Excuse me, fellows," he said. "Just keep on talking," he said. "Don't mind me — I do this every day." And so saying, he began yarding the stretcher to its outermost reaches. In the face of this almost hypnotic procedure, I found it very difficult to continue. In the middle of my stammerings, Max tossed the exerciser to Bruce. "Here, have a try," he cried. "Nothing to it." Bruce caught the stretcher and regarded it with the utmost suspicion, like a snake charmer with a couple of recalcitrant cobras. His best efforts to separate the opposite ends of the gadget failed.

"Hell, I can't do this," he protested. "I'm not an athlete like you, Max."

"Well," Bell murmured, with a quiet grin, "I try to keep myself in shape. Used to be able to walk across the floor on my hands. Think I could still do it."

So saying, he got up on his hands and began a gymnastic march across the suite. As he did, bank-notes began to fall from his pants

68

onto the carpet. Hutchison and I gaped. They were American bills, of sizeable denomination. Slightly embarrassed, Bell began to pick up the crumpled bills. "Made a pretty good score at Anita," he confessed. "Just haven't had time to get to the bank."

Needless to say, this bid for monetary recognition ended in a complete shambles: we had met the Master, and been vanquished. But the following year, when the *Times'* profits were soaring, I went back to him. Bell responded handsomely, with raises of 50 per cent each.

His generosity was manifest on other occasions as well. Faced with some unexpected, and heavy, medical expenses, Bruce asked me if I might intercede with Max for a bonus payment. I cheerfully agreed; it seemed to me that Bruce was working for less than bargain-basement prices. The opportunity arose just before Christmas, when we were in Calgary for a meeting with Max. The meeting took place in his unique offices in the *Albertan* building. Max's main office featured an anvil which had belonged to his grandfather, a pioneer blacksmith. An adjoining passageway housed a refrigerator full of chocolate caramels, which Max adored. A spacious inner office was rich in leather, the walls adorned with bound copies of *The Racing Form*.

At an appropriate moment I took Max aside and told him of Hutchison's request, underlining the important contribution he was making to the success of our Victoria operation.

"Certainly," Max said. "Give him $5,000."

I went back to the Palliser Hotel to relay the good news to Bruce. He shook my hand warmly and said: "Thank you. I really appreciate that." Then he looked at me sharply and said: "For God's sakes, don't put it through until January. It will kill me, tax-wise."

In his autobiography *The Far Side of the Street* Bruce looked back on his re-birth as editor of the *Times* and wrote:

The best years of my life, and Dot's, had begun. We spent four months every year at our Shawnigan camp, with frequent winter travels, and I kept turning out books in my spare time. These cosy arrangments were possible only because Stu regarded me as a sort of historical relic, a museum piece, very frail in my old age, easily broken and needing tender care.

The truth is almost exactly the opposite. Far from regarding Bruce as "an historical relic", I looked on him as the most gifted editor in Canada, the conscience of the paper and its most valuable ornament. Our agreement, while unspoken and never reduced to chaste contractual language, was quite simple: I gave him freedom, and he gave our modest little paper a touch of class. He was a man of sound political judgements, nurtured in observation and coverage of twenty federal elections; of impeccable manners and morality. To these basic virtues he brought the added dimension of a singing prose style and an ability to infuse mundane events with high drama. It was always my feeling that Bruce could take an Air Canada timetable and convert it into a three-act melodrama.

At the same time there was growing conjecture — and a bit of sniffing by rival columnists — at the notion of a man simultaneously "editing" the Winnipeg *Free Press* and Victoria *Times* while buried deep in the rain forests of Vancouver Island. How could this be achieved? To the outside observer, Bruce's only links with the world were a beaten-up mantel radio and a telephone located in a gas station two miles down the road from his cottage. What his critics did not know was that the movers and shakers of North America were beating their way down a remote country trail to commune with the master in his native habitat — writers like Henry Brandon, Max Freedman, Blair Fraser and Peter Newman; American statesmen of the order of "Scoop" Jackson, Livingston Merchant, George Ball and William Bundy. The Chief Justice of British Columbia, J. O. ("Jack") Wilson, often stayed long enough to augment the Hutchisonian woodpile or assist with the digs of a new outhouse.

When Pierre Berton turned up on one of his periodic swings through his old West Coast haunts, Bruce sent me an amusing memo:

We had a queer weekend with Escott Reid, of the World Bank, the Arthur Irwins and the Bertons, locked up in a summer cabin by pelting rain but pursuing some good talk. Pierre is overwhelming. That's the only word — overwhelming. Amusing, infuriating, exhausting. He lives in the boy's dream of the candy shop and consumes the products furiously. We had no candy but nourished him on beef and whisky. He seemed to come through the ordeal quite well. But I returned to town wilting, mentally and physically. No doubt you had the same jolly experience in Vancouver.

As the years started to roll by with distressing speed, our admiration and affection for Bruce grew. To the young sprigs of the business, he was the consummate "old pro". Editorials and columns represented only a fraction of his output. Assaulting his old typewriter with jack-hammer ferocity and on a rigid, self-imposed schedule, he never ceased to amaze us with the volume of his copy, and with its quality.

Top mass-circulation magazines like *Life*, the *Atlantic*, *Maclean's* and *Readers' Digest* published Bruce's stories. Each week, as he had been doing for more than thirty years since 1919 and as he was to continue to do until 1975, he produced a piece on Canadian affairs for the *Christian Science Monitor*, becoming in the process its most senior correspondent. He went to Germany to talk with economic minister Erhardt about that country's amazing post-war recovery and visited Japan to write a series on its economy. In Washington, he conferred with Walter Lippman, Mike Mansfield and Ben Bradlee, as an old friend.

The books began to roll — *The Fraser, The Incredible Canadian, Canada: Tomorrow's Giant, The Struggle for the Border* and *Mr. Prime Minister*. Three Governor-General Awards. Two Bowater Awards. Two President's Medals. Three National Newspaper Awards. Honorary degrees from UBC, Yale and Calgary. And then, when the Royal Society of the Arts in London struck a silver medal, to be awarded to the best journalist in the Commonwealth outside the UK, the first winner and unanimous choice of the judges was Bruce Hutchison.

Our Washington correspondent complained: "That damned Hutchison can breeze in here and see more important news sources in three days than I can in a year." The reason, of course, is obvious. In Bruce they recognized a serious journalist, a man who did his homework. He could be trusted with a confidence.

Indeed, his concern for editorial security was legendary. It passed into folklore after a visit he made to Washington at the time of the Bay of Pigs fiasco. Somehow or other Bruce had got the ear of a person very close to President Kennedy and returned home with the inside details. It was a fascinating yarn but at the end Bruce wagged an admonishing finger at us and said: "Now look, fellows, this story must never go beyond these four walls. Don't even tell your wives. This is strictly classified." And then, pounding my desk to emphasize his point, he said: "Jesus Christ, just think what Nikita Khruschev would have given to have been in this office for the past thirty minutes!"

# Chapter 8

"Whosoever would influence the public must first learn to entertain it."

— *The Spectator, 1711*

My first task at the *Times*, it seemed to me, was to shore up its flagging morale. The paper was running a poor second to the *Colonist*, 18,000 to 28,000. It was losing money. Its facilities were archaic. The former owners had departed without even stopping by to shake hands with their employees. Salaries were miserable. Some of the staff rules were incongruous. Long-distance calls had to be approved by the managing editor. Reporters were not permitted to fly on assignments. A senior newsman told me that he had not set foot off Vancouver Island for eleven years.

At the same time, it was clear that the genial thirty-odd men and women in the editorial department were eager to change all this. Accordingly, in the first week I called them together in the newsroom for a pep talk. I told them I thought it was an "unnatural" situation for an evening paper, with the field all to itself, to trail a morning paper with the incredible name of *Colonist*. We were going to take dead aim on that paper. We wanted to produce a sheet from which the juice could be extracted by responsive readers. What's more, we wanted to have fun doing the job.

To move in that direction, we expanded the amount of space alloted to news; added six reporters and an editorial cartoonist (Sid Barron); overhauled the sports department; bought the complete stock market listings; had the paper re-designed by "Dea-

73

con" Farrar, the foremost authority in the field; and acquired new features, including the incredibly successful comic strip, "Peanuts".

On a trip to Montreal, I negotiated with my old sparring-partner, John McConnell Jr., to include his rotogravure section, *Weekend*, in the Saturday *Times* — a privilege for which he would cheerfully pay us money. This latter gambit disturbed Tim Matson, owner-publisher of the *Colonist*, who called me to try to intimidate me. His astonishing protest was that we were running a paper that was "too wide open" (translation: we were giving the public more news than he was).

Meanwhile, the re-designed and re-invigorated *Times* was beginning to attract both new readers and new advertisers. Towards the end of the first year I asked Bob Thomson, the venerable and courtly general manager, what he intended to do for the staff by way of Christmas bonus.

Bob permitted himself a wan grin. "I don't think we're that far along yet," he said. "Lineage has been good this fall but if we're lucky, we'll just about break even."

"Okay," I replied, "then let's give everyone a Christmas turkey."

"If you say so," said Bob. "I think we can manage that."

Never in the course of Canadian journalism has so little done so much for so many. On receipt of the news of this Yuletide largesse a waggish reporter named Humphry Davy repaired to the Court House and returned with a "warrant" for my "arrest", all duly signed and sealed by the proper authorities. The staff was assembled and the "warrant" read. It charged me with the heinous crime of "violating all tradition and history of the *Times* by doing something, voluntarily, for its staff. This precedent should not go unpunished."

I was seized by the arms and told to stand in a corner. Whereupon the women of the staff, led by the veteran editor Bessie Forbes, lined up and solemnly, one by one, marched by and kissed me. This was, for me, a plummy moment: a stamp of approval, so to speak, which united us in a determination to become #1 in the Victoria market.

Traditionally a sleepy, easy-going tourist and civil-service town, Victoria's delights had lately become apparent in the post-war boom. The city was on the threshold of a vigorous expansion. Its population was growing rapidly. From the newspaper point of view, it was an advertising manager's delight: all the major department stores (Eaton's, The Bay, Simpson's, Woodwards, etc.) were represented there, as were the food chains. More than a dozen investment and brokerage houses tended to the city's considerable "retired money". Advertising rates had been pegged artificially low because Spencers', who owned the *Times*, also owned an adjoining department store.

Yet there was an ambience, a milieu, which set Victoria apart. This was borne in on me very early in the game when I attended a luncheon meeting of the Chamber of Commerce in the Empress Hotel. A transportation executive named Conway Parrott took the floor and said: "Gentlemen, I have just learned of a plan to install a major pulp and paper mill on the Gorge, just a few miles from where we are meeting. . ."

(*"Great news,"* I thought. *"The old town is beginning to roll."*)

Parrott slammed his fist down on the table. "Gentlemen," he cried, "we've got to get together and *stop* it!"

Cries of "hear, hear," spread throughout the room. I could scarcely believe my ears. This was the *Chamber of Commerce*, protesting about the establishment of a multi-million dollar industry in its environs?

In the fullness of time, as I began to understand the Victorian mind a little bit better, I came around to Parrott's point of view. He was an environmentalist fifteen years ahead of his time. The long-range projection enunciated by succeeding municipal councils was for Victoria to develop, steadily and quietly, as a university and tourist town. The proponents of this philosophy were indubitably correct.

While addressing myself to my new duties with coltish enthusiasm, I was daily confronted with vast areas of newspaper operation of which I was almost totally ignorant. All my training, after all, had been on the reportorial side of the business. I did not know how to web up a press, cast a plate, set type, or calculate the cost per page of setting up classified ads.

I sought solace in a simple syllogism:

1.  The first job would be to produce an informative, lively and readable newspaper;
2.  Such a newspaper would attract readers;
3.  Readers constituted a market;

4.  A market had an intrinsic monetary value which would be reflected in advertising rates; and therefore surely in positive "bottom line" results.

Within limits, this was a workable formula. The catch, I soon learned, was to keep costs from going through the roof.

And there was another factor: promotion. It was an axiom of the business (not subscribed to by all) that it was not enough to produce a good feature, or a good newspaper; readers had constantly to be *told* that these things were good. This was particularly true at the *Times*, where spirits were low and in sore need of bolstering. If we could get people *talking* about the paper; if it could be developed as a positive force in the community, then staffers would hold their heads up, and go about their rounds with pride.

To that end, we not only set out to improve the quality of the paper, but embarked on a series of stunts which simultaneously aroused and bewildered the populace, and helped close the circulation gap between the *Times* and its morning rival.

Foremost among these was a campaign to erect in Beacon Hill Park "the world's tallest totem pole". The inspiration for this gambit came at a cocktail party, when I became engrossed in a conversation about the mighty cedars which abounded in the area. It was a happy coincidence that this conceit arose at a time when the famous Indian carver, Mungo Martin, was in town to do some work for the provincial government. Why not put the two together? Why not find the tallest, straightest cedar, and put Mungo to work carving it?

In a few days Mungo, his son David and nephew Henry Hunt were in my office, signing a contract prepared by the Victoria Press lawyer, Edwin E. Pearlman. How to pay for it? Circulation director Stewart Kidd came up with a brilliant notion. We would sell "shares" in the project for 50 cents apiece. For this sum, "stock-holders" would have the right to (a) observe the carving in progress, in Thunderbird Park; (b) get a chip from the pole autographed by Mungo Martin; (c) attend the pole-raising ceremonies. Eventually, 12,000 persons subscribed, including Bing Crosby, Gracie Fields and Winston Churchill.

The beauty of this simple charade was its ongoing attraction as a news-feature. First there was the contest to find precisely the

76

right tree — in which we had the full co-operation of the local forest-products companies. The technical job of felling the tree without damaging it made for an interesting photo-feature. Then there was the business of hauling it out to tide-water and towing it to Victoria's inner harbour. On the Saturday morning that the mighty log fetched up in front of the Empress Hotel, all hell broke loose. The crane employed to lift the tree across the esplanade moved slowly, took up the entire roadway, and backed up traffic for blocks. This unforeseen development delighted us as much as it annoyed the motorists.

To ensure that the pole would be securely anchored, Harold Husband of the local machinery works had fashioned a "candlestick" cement and steel base. To the cheers of the assembled thousands, Bill Heaney's crane lowered the totem into its base and there it stands today — 127 feet, seven inches of it. For about fifteen years it remained the world's champion until some envious Indians in the Alert Bay area went berserk and fashioned a pole 187 feet high.

The totem pole caper, acclaimed by the trade paper *Editor and Publisher* as "the best newspaper promotion in North America", lasted about three months and ended up in a splendid ceremony, enlivened by speeches in Kwakiutl, Indian tribal dances, and the throb of tom-toms. But its impact on the city paled in comparison to the frenzy engendered by the Straits of Juan de Fuca swims.

These treacherous waters curve around the south end of Vancouver Island, separating it from the State of Washington, eighteen miles away. Walking in Beacon Hill Park one day, I looked across to the smoke rising from the Washington State mill-town of Port Angeles and asked myself: "Would it be possible to swim that distance — from the United States to Canada?" It had never been done before.

On the map, it appeared to be a test equal to that of the English Channel, where the American Florence Chadwick was churning up records. Would it not be possible to bring Miss Chadwick to Victoria as the world's pre-eminent distance swimmer, to make a first attempt? Of course, we had no money in the budget for such shenanigans and I had a hunch it might take money to interest Miss Chadwick. But I had a friend, Fred Manning, who was an executive of a highly successful and civic-minded paint company. I went to him and offered him co-sponsorship of the project for $10,000. Fred consulted his father-in-law, a former mayor of Victoria named Carl Pendray, who readily concurred.

We brought Miss Chadwick from her home in San Diego and took her out for a look at the Straits. On the advice of some tug captains, who towed logs through the waters, we warned her that the tides were quixotic and that the temperatures would be less than 50 degrees. We also put her in the care of Archie McKinnon, a Canadian Olympic swimming coach and a favourite son of Victoria. After a test plunge Flo accepted the challenge, on simple terms: $7,500 if she tried and failed; $10,000 if she were successful.

Unhappily, in the last week of her training Flo decided to import her own navigator from San Diego. A good man, who had worked with the champion in her Catalina swims, he had no knowledge of the swirling Juan de Fuca currents and refused the advice of the old tug captains. Thus, in a sense, Flo was doomed before she entered the waters off Cadboro Bay. She swam about five miles and gave up when she found she was losing headway against the tricky waters. A plucky champion, she was in tears of dismay when she was taken out. She was also as blue as an Arctic iceberg.

In her dressing-room, she threw her arms around her venerable sponsor, Carl Pendray, and sobbed on his shoulder.

"There, there, my dear," said the gallant Carl. "You made a great try. I'm going to give you the $10,000, anyway." Which precipitated further sobs from the distraught Miss C.

As Mr. Pendray shrewdly surmised, it didn't much matter — win, lose or draw, Flo had put Victoria and the Straits on the map. There ensued a summer which could only be described as "The Juan de Fuca Follies of 1954". The town went crazy about the Straits challenge. Before it was over, some fifty-three swimmers from all parts of the world — some authentic athletes and some certified kooks — plunged into the frigid waters in quest of a $1,000 prize, which they fully anticipated would be augmented by endorsements, commercial contracts, film rights, and a lifetime supply of thermal underwear.

The first person to succeed was an ex-Marine and Tacoma logger named Bert Thomas, who plunged in on the American side, at Port Townsend, and fetched up in Esquimalt some eleven hours later. A story was promptly circulated that the burly Mr.

T., swimming through the night, had cleverly hitch-hiked part of the way at the end of a tow-rope. This canard was investigated and proved to be untrue, or at least unprovable. At a jetty in front of the Empress Hotel, Mr. Thomas demanded his $1,000. Somehow, this little detail had been overlooked. I made out a personal cheque and ran to the bank to ensure that it was covered.

The mid-summer madness achieved new plateaus of frenzy two years later when it was announced that the Straits would be tested by Marilyn Bell of Toronto. Miss Bell, whose recent conquest of Lake Ontario had earned her the sobriquet "Canada's Sweetheart", came to Victoria with her famous coach, Gus Ryder, and with Cliff Lumsdon, a long-distance swimmer from Toronto who had also successfully swum the lake.

Miss Bell, like Florence Chadwick, quickly captivated the natives with her bubbling personality and gracious manner. There was something very close to gloom — and a certain snarkiness on the part of the Toronto press — when she gave up on her first try and Ryder was reluctant to take her from the water. The Toronto scribes insisted that she was on the point of being embalmed in ice. A scorching few minutes in a canvas bath quickly thawed her out.

Gamely, Miss Bell scheduled a second attempt from Port Angeles — and this time she made it.

The scene as she neared the beach below Beacon Hill Park was incredible. Ten thousand Victorians looked down from the cliffs. The beach itself was jammed. Tug-boats whistled their acclaim. Dozens of little boats clogged the tiny bay. A leading chartered accountant of the city, G. Fitzpatrick Dunn, stood in the water, in hip-waders, cheering the Toronto girl home.

The heading in the *Times* that night — in what newspapermen call their "Come To Jesus" type, said simply: "MARILYN WINS — BREAKS ALL RECORDS"

One week earlier her team-mate Cliff Lumsdon had succeeded in swimming the other way, from Canada to the US.

Perhaps the challenge was the thing with other contestants; perhaps the publicity. At any rate, I was hardly prepared for the telephone call I received from a Vancouver matron a few nights later.

"You've got to help me," she cried. "A young German friend of mine, John Giese, just telephoned and told me he's going to swim the straits. He's going out tonight, with only a friend in a rowboat. In fact, I don't even know if he can swim. You've got to stop him!"

She gave me a Victoria telephone number and I called the boy. The story was absolutely true. I pointed out to him the folly of attempting such a feat with no training, no knowledge of the tides, no back-up support except the rowboat. I promised that, if he would call off the swim for this night, I would arrange for him to meet the next day with Harold Elworthy, who owned a fleet of tow-boats and had been most generous in providing both boats and skilled navigators. Reluctantly, Giese agreed to the deferment.

The following morning Elworthy pronounced his verdict: "Son," he said, "you are a goddamned fool."

Giese eventually took the plunge. They picked him out of the waters after three miles.

But, when the lunatic summers of 1954 and 1956 had ended, we had proved two things: (1) it *was* possible to swim across an international border, from the United States to Canada (2) the waters, at an average of 46 degrees, were a bit on the chilly side for the average swimmer. This latter intelligence did not endear us to the Tourist Bureau.

We had also proved that the traditional "summer doldrums" which plagued newspaper circulation managers could be thwarted by lively, off-beat copy; and that the public would always respond positively to stories of physical courage in the face of stern obstacles.

This was certainly the case when we engaged Edmund Hillary and his Everest Team to speak and show slides of their epic ascent, at Victoria Arena. An arrangement was made with his Chicago agent, Ford Hicks, to guarantee a fee of $3,500. The tickets were placed on sale at Eaton's.

Old mountain climbers emerged from every thicket, moraine and enclave on Vancouver Island. As we had suspected, Sir Edmund's name was box-office magic to the thousands of Brits, Anzacs, Aussies, and Scots who had retired in the area.

Imagine our chagrin, then, when Hicks called a few days before the lecture to advise that the Hillary team was over-booked with engagements in San Francisco, Pasadena and Vancouver and that the Victoria lecture would have to be cancelled.

80

The resolution of this impasse has clung to me as one of the strangest interventions of my life. Was it a psychic phenomenon? Or just a happy coincidence?

I flew to Chicago to confront Hicks. He turned out to be an affable, silver-haired giant of a man, perhaps seventy-five years old. For several minutes we chatted, exploring the possibility of a revision of schedule, but invariably we came back to a dead end. Mr. Hicks said he would try again, but was not too hopeful. "When are you leaving Chicago?" he asked me.

"Tonight at 10 o'clock," I replied.

"Well," he said, "give me your card so that I can get in touch with you."

When I handed him my card he looked at it with interest and remarked: "That's an unusual spelling. I've only seen it once before. I had a good friend once named Bill Keate. In fact, he got me my first job, on a small newspaper in Kalamazoo."

"That was my father," I said.

"But you're a Canadian," Hicks replied. "How could that be?"

"My father was born in Grand Rapids, Michigan. He moved to British Columbia in 1907."

Hicks studied my face. "It was in 1905 that I got that job," he said, "and I never saw Bill again." Still staring at me, he smiled and said: "You *are* Bill Keate's son. You look like him." Then he arose. "We'd better get going on this deal," he said.

Two hours before my plane left Chicago he telephoned. "I've been on to London, New York and Halifax," he said. "We've made an extra date. Victoria gets the last booking for Sir Edmund."

There were 200 million persons in the United States. What miracle brought me to this one man my father had helped fifty years ago?

Sir Edmund flew in with his Everest Team (which included James Morris of *The Times* of London, later to achieve further renown, after a sex-change operation, as Jan Morris) and proved to be a modest giant. The first thing he demanded was that we stop addressing him as "Sir Edmund" — he insisted on just Ed. He also showed himself to be a man of some fibre. Discussing arrangements for his lecture, I mentioned that we had, with some difficulty, found the New Zealand national anthem and persuaded the band of *HMCS Naden* to play it, in opening ceremonies.

"No," said Hillary, "that won't do. This is not a New Zealand show. A lot of other nations were involved, and the sherpas were absolutely invaluable." So we settled for "God Save The Queen".

The lecture went on as scheduled and was a smash hit. To accommodate the more than 5,000 spectators, a floor had been built over the ice, which created a genuinely glacial atmosphere for the chilling feats of derring-do Sir Edmund was describing on the platform.

And we managed to overcome the Commonwealth language barrier. Late in the afternoon, surveying arrangements for his projector at the Arena, Sir Edmund had turned to me and asked: "Will it be icey or dicey?"

"Oh, I wouldn't worry about it," I replied. "The floor covering works pretty well. People will probably have to wear coats but I don't think they'll be uncomfortable." This reply seemed to bewilder Sir Edmund.

"No, no," he said. And then, pointing to his magic lantern, he repeated: "Will it be icey or dicey?"

Finally the light dawned. What he wanted to determine was whether the Arena was AC or DC!

Entertaining the public was, of course, only a minor diversion. Throughout our years in Victoria Bruce Hutchison and I fought battles both bloody and hilarious.

Most of them were political. By coincidence, we had arrived on the Victoria scene at almost the same moment as William Andrew Cecil ("Wacky") Bennett, the Kelowna hardware merchant who was to dominate the province for two decades. To be sure, Bennett had been there before, as a Conservative backbencher and Coalitionist, but he had been beaten in a bid for the Tory leadership and, when he sensed that the Coalition was breaking up, had shrewdly moved to take command of the fledgling Social Credit party.

Thus began a "twenty-year war" between Bennett and journalists. Because his Liberal and Tory opposition was fragmented and dispirited, newspapers moved into the vacuum, *Time* magazine referring to the Victoria *Times* as "Mr. Bennett's most effective political opponent".

I first met Bennett in the main lounge of the Union Club in Victoria. When I was introduced as publisher of the *Times*, Bennett beamed broadly and said: "I'll have to watch your editorials."

Whereupon he whipped out a cheque-book and signed for a year's subscription to the paper, the first one I had "sold" since my carrier days.

Within a year Bennett tried both to hire me (as his information officer in an abortive "On To Ottawa" campaign) and fire me (describing Bruce Hutchison and myself to our owner Max Bell as "menaces to good government"). It is amusing, in retrospect, to reflect that we had a hand in his accession to power. The 1952 election was so close — Social Credit and the CCF separated by a single seat — that the defeated premier, "Boss" Johnson, could not make up his mind on whom to recommend to the lieutenant-governor. We called on "Boss" and found him hesitant and uncertain. When he asked our advice, we told him he would have little choice but to recommend the free-enterprise partisan, Bennett. This was done.

In spite of Bennett's hostility to the press, it was possible to sympathize with him in those early days. The public was leery of the "funny money" theories of pure-Major-Douglas Social Credit. Few of Bennett's cabinet colleagues had any experience. Some of his followers were certifiable crazies. To reconcile the quirks and quiddities of this motley assemblage called for considerable diplomacy, and Bennett managed it.

In the process, he made some astonishing alliances. His intimates seemed as far removed from him in personality and character as one could imagine. Bennett was proud of the fact that he did not smoke, drink or swear. He was a strong family man and a regular church-goer. Yet one of his closest aides was a flamboyant publicist who was suspended by his golf club for heaving a vase of flowers into a grand piano, and another was a gambler and alley-fighter who drank the lights out at every party. The test with Bennett appeared to be loyalty. Those who had supported him in the tough, early days were assured of reciprocal backing.

This was manifest in his support of Robert Sommers, whom he described as "as a brilliant minister of the Crown", and who became the first Cabinet minister in the Commonwealth to be sent to jail for accepting bribes in the matter of forest management licences. The evidence against Sommers had been gathered by a young lawyer named David Sturdy and was reported in the *Times* by Tom Gould, then a Victoria political reporter and now an executive of Global TV in Toronto. Sturdy placed his evidence before attorney-general Robert Bonner, who tended to dismiss it as baseless and unworthy of his attention. But under the relentless pressure of the press and the opposition, Bonner was compelled to act. Exactly 707 days after he had first received the information, charges against Sommers were laid. The trial, which fascinated British Columbians and gave forest companies the fidgets, lasted six months. In the end, Chief Justice J. O. Wilson packed Sommers off to jail for five years, branding him a rascal and betrayer of the public trust.

Perhaps Bennett's strangest initiative occurred when, at a gaudy press conference, he welcomed to British Columbia the Swedish industrialist, Axel Wenner-Gren. Mr. Wenner-Gren had made a fortune in vacuum cleaners, a fact which doubtless impressed the former hardware merchant of Kelowna. Less impressive was the fact that Wenner-Gren had known ties with the Nazis and had once assured President Roosevelt that German U-boats had nothing to do with the sinking of the *Athenia* in the early days of the war.

With that as background, it was astonishing to learn that Bennett had granted Wenner-Gren developmental rights to one-fifth of central British Columbia, an area the size of Nova Scotia. The Swedish tycoon responded with a grandiose plan which included a monorail, to run at 110 miles an hour through the Rocky Mountain trench and thus open up the hinterland.

In spite of the wild nature of his pledges, Wenner-Gren was wined and dined and hailed as a new saviour of the province. To objective viewers, it appeared that the establishment had taken leave of its senses. The last straw was an announcement that Mr. Wenner-Gren would be transported to Victoria in the lieutenant-governor's yacht and feted at a State dinner. This fawning reception was too much for me. I sat down and wrote a front-page editorial documenting Wenner-Gren's dubious record and concluding: "We intend to watch you."

Developers tut-tutted but the broad mass of *Times* readers commended the paper for its vigorous opposition. The most interesting reaction of all emanated from the premier.

"Keep it up," Bennett told me. "The more you protest, the better deal I can make with these people. Now I can go to them and say: 'See, the people of BC really don't want you.' "

Before long even the politicians saw through the Wenner-Gren pipe dream; it dissolved and he departed. But in the meantime Bennett was busy on a dozen different fronts, completing the north and south ends of the "railway to nowhere", the Pacific Great Eastern; building roads, ferries, schools, hospitals and court-houses. Against strong press opposition, he established a Bank of British Columbia which, under the wise guidance of Albert Hall, was a success from the outset.

In Gordon Shrum, the retired UBC physicist, Bennett found an amazing expediter. At the age of 65, Shrum was asked to bring the Peace River on stream as a major source of hydro power; perhaps mischievously, Bennett named Hugh Keenleyside, a long-time adversary of Shrum, to do a similar job on the Columbia. The two veteran academics showered sparks in their scramble to deliver the juice.

In 1963 when Shrum was 67, and the massive Peace dam was in place, Bennett asked him to create an "instant university", Simon Fraser. Shrum worked with architect Arthur Erickson and, incredibly, was still working with Erickson in 1979 at age 83 in the development of the stunning Law Courts building in down-town Vancouver — for Bennett's *son*, Bill.

In all, it was a remarkable record, with Bennett a clear victor over a hostile press. But after sixteen years in office the premier had achieved a degree of sophistication which was reflected in a letter he wrote to me, copy to Max Bell:

Dear Stu,

I know you and I have had genuine differences of opinion in the past on the conduct of public affairs in British Columbia and may have in the future! In view of the serious responsibility we both owe to the people of the Province it would in fact be surprising if we took the conduct of public business so lightly as to always agree on how these responsibilities should be carried out.

For this reason and because I know you had grave doubts regarding the wisdom of the Government's policy on power development, I am doubly grateful for your generous editorial comment in Tuesday's paper concerning the completion of the Peace River project.

Thanks again, and kindest personal regards.

# Chapter 9

"Two papers are better than one."

— *Harry S. Southam*

Close students of Max Bell's business techniques quickly discerned a couple of constants: his capacity for investigative detail, and his patience. In building his newspaper empire from the unlikely base of the Calgary *Albertan*, which had never been a financial success, he studied the papers around him, put together an offer, and waited for the other publishers to succumb.

A pattern emerged in Bell's successful bids for the Lethbridge *Herald* and the Victoria *Colonist*. (He would later use it again in his purchase of the Vancouver *Sun*.) In each instance, the second-generation owners lacked the will or the spark to carry on the endeavours their pioneer fathers had so laboriously fashioned. Apparently convinced that they could not compete with the developing chains, they were content to "take the money and run".

In Lethbridge "Billy" Buchanan had begun as an itinerant printer and had built the *Herald* into the authentic voice of southern Alberta, rising in the process to the Senate of Canada. On his death, his newspaper passed into the hands of two sons — Donald, who elected to work in the fine arts and made a notable contribution to cultural magazines in Canada; and Hugh ("Bucky") Buchanan, who came out of the RCNVR to impose his considerable journalistic talents on the *Herald*.

Bucky's problem was that he was a playboy. At first he was content to sell off a minority interest in his paper to his friend Max, who constantly warned him about his dwindling patrimony.

But, as his demands for money continued insatiable — including a bill one year for a $75,000 villa in the south of France — he decided to sell out, ending his days as a writer of whimsical editorials for the Hamilton *Spectator*.

In Victoria, as we have seen, Bell's long-term goal was to buy both dailies and put them together in a new plant. But the *Colonist* proved a much tougher nut to crack than the *Times*, for here Bell found himself face to face with the quixotic H. T. ("Tim") Matson, a journalistic pecan of the first chop.

At first, Matson had no difficulty in selling off 49 per cent of his holding in the *Colonist*. And yet he was troubled. Earlier, he had actually sold his paper to Roy Thomson but had had misgivings and ordered his loyal general manager, Jack Melville, to fly to Toronto and beg out of the deal. With considerable (and unexpected) gallantry, Thomson had said: "Well, a deal's a deal: but if he's not happy, I guess we'd better call it off."

So now Matson was faced with the prospect of selling his heritage to another of the financial whiz-kids from across the Rockies. It made him nervous.

A scrawny bantamweight of somewhat simian countenance, Matson had once described himself, sadly, as "the runt of the litter". His father, Sam Matson, was a domineering entrepreneur in transportation, politics and real estate and a big man in the life of Victoria. His solution to the problems of his younger son was to pack him off to a succession of British public schools, which he cordially detested.

Sam's clear preference was for his older son, Jack, who was a good enough golfer to play in an exhibition with Walter Hagen. If Jack couldn't match Hagen on the golf course, he could at the nineteenth hole, where his capacity for gin fizzes was legendary. Jack, in fact, was everything that Tim was not: carefree, confident, a popular local figure and the inevitable heir to the *Colonist*. But his untimely death resulted in this obligation being dumped on the shoulders of Tiny Tim.

One of Tim's first reactions to the new responsibility was that he should become a war correspondent. While the Canadian Army in western Europe was staunchly ready to join battle with Hitler it was ill-prepared for its encounter with Matson. A petulant fellow, whose chief literary talent lay in composing doggerel, Tim set about correcting the errant ways of Army brass. This, coupled with his fondness for the malt, quickly landed him in the stockade. His infrequent dispatches, highlighted by his wild verse, caused his superiors to wonder if he wasn't conveying dark secrets to the residents of southern Vancouver Island. Among those attempting to decipher that arcane Matsonian intelligence was Col. Dick Malone, chief of public relations for Canadian forces in the area.

In due course Matson returned to Victoria. In his absence, the *Colonist* had been run by a brilliant young businessman named Harold Husband, who had been associated with Sam Matson in Vancouver Island Coach Lines. Husband had done such a good job, and found the newspaper game so interesting, that he made intercession with Ada Matson, Tim's mother, to buy the property. Tim, in a fit of pique, handed Husband a terse note in which he announced that his general manager's services were no longer required. Husband went on to national renown as a ship-builder and president of Victoria Machinery Depot.

Matson contented himself with some golf at Royal Colwood, dropping in to read his mail at the *Colonist*, and embarking on a new career as a columnist. In this he exploited his talents as a writer of doggerel and in one famous bout of poesy managed to describe a Lyons' Tea House in London as a "bug-trap". Distance did not lend enchantment to the Lyons people. They sued for a hefty sum, resulting in an apology and suitable monetary recompense.

The amiable life of a successful Victoria publisher also allowed Tim to indulge his predilection for fine cars. A local salesman boasted that he, personally, had sold Matson $65,000 worth of automobiles in one year. One day Matson called me to ask whether I would like to inspect his new Bentley, of which he was inordinately proud. I told him I would be delighted and together we set off from the Victoria Press building on foot, down Douglas Street and east on Yates to "automobile row". This was a good twenty-minute hike and I was a bit puzzled; particularly so when we fetched up at the side of a sleek little roadster.

"Surely, Tim," I said, "this is not a Bentley?"

"No, this is a Skoda," he replied, with some asperity. "This is the car I use to *take* you to the Bentley."

Off we wheeled, in the frisky little European car, in the general direction of Esquimalt. Matson unlocked the garage door at his suburban estate and there, in all its glory, stood the splendid Bentley. Around the walls of the garage were ranged several rows of electric heaters; their purpose, Tim explained, was to keep the Bentley *warm*. Unfortunately, there was only one thing wrong. The Bentley wouldn't start. Soon the air was alive with screams, oaths and imprecations.

A few months later, coming out of the Banff Springs Hotel, Tim found a knot of curious and admiring car-lovers gathered around his luxurious vehicle. By some strange reasoning Tim regarded this as an invasion of privacy and could hardly wait to get back to Victoria to sell the car, which he did at a knock-down price.

Nor did Tim react positively to the challenges being posed to the *Colonist* by the upstart *Times*. Within a year of being moved to the joint premises on upper Douglas Street he decided to sell control of his paper to Max Bell.

To advise and assist him in negotiations, Matson took along with him a man named Tom Bailey, a soft-spoken and highly regarded chartered accountant who had looked after Matson family affairs for decades. Flying across the Rockies to Calgary, Bailey asked Tim how much he intended to ask for the newspaper.

"I was thinking of $750,000," said Matson.

Bailey pondered the matter for a moment and then said: "That's not quite enough, Tim. I think you ought to ask for $1 million."

Matson snorted. "Oh, he'll never pay *that* much," he replied.

Before long they were in Bell's office. As usual, Max came directly to the point.

"I'm ready to deal, gentlemen," he said. "You name a price. If I think it's fair, I'll sign right now. If not, I'll let you know. In that case, you'll still have your paper and I'll still have my money."

Matson, screwing his courage to the sticking-point, murmured: "One million dollars."

Max put his hand out. "Gentlemen," he said, "you've made a deal."

Thus did control of Victoria's newspapers pass from the capital to another province, and set the stage for formation of Federated Papers (FP) Publications Ltd. Max Bell was now the owner of four dailies whose total circulation was roughly the equal of the Winnipeg *Free Press*, his eventual partner in the new group.

Some years later Tom Bailey added a delightful footnote: "I guess my suggestion on that 'plane ride added $250,000 to Tim's

89

profit. But in the spring of next year he sent me a bill for $66. He claimed I made a mistake in that amount when I made up his income tax."

The *Times* and *Colonist*, like most joint newspaper operations insisted that their staffs should not fraternize on the job, the theory being that an arm's-length policy would intensify the competitive spirit. But, some years after Tim had left journalism, I found myself involved with the Matson family in an unusual project — unusual for a newspaperman, that is, because it also involved religion.

Ada Matson, the matriarch of the brood, had willed a spectacular piece of property overlooking Esquimalt Harbour to the Salvation Army as a site for a senior citizens' home. I was invited to head up a citizens' campaign committee whose target would be $240,000, the rest of the money coming from various levels of government.

To their intense surprise, about a dozen members of my staff found themselves out on the street, rattling the tambourine for the dear old Sally Ann. For about six weeks we worked our butts off and on the final night of the campaign were able to hand over a cheque for $265,000.

The home was built — all cedar and glass, with attractive suites for the oldsters and a patio with a telescope where they could scan the busy marine traffic on the waters below. There were, to be sure, more dramatic events in a lifetime of journalism, but few more satisfying.

# Chapter 10

"Money doesn't consume me. But it's a kind of yard-stick."

— *Max Bell*

In the summer of 1958, with his newspaper enterprise humming, Max Bell handed me a unique assignment: to organize a "Think Tank" at his Twin Isles resort, north of Powell River. The idea was to bring together about twenty-four eminent gentlemen from disparate fields, to commune with nature (and each other) on the problems of the day. Max had not long before acquired a stunning yacht, *MV Campana* and two islands with log-cabin accomodation worthy of Jasper Lodge. Why not bring the two assets together and generate some useful talk?

Why not, indeed? After two months of negotiation, during which I neglected the Victoria *Times* shamefully, I had lassooed a reasonably formidable cast of characters — financiers, union leaders, politicians, publishers, editors and one university president.

They were headed by Lester B. Pearson, then leader of the Opposition in Ottawa and a recent winner of the Nobel Peace Prize, and included Premier Ernest C. Manning of Alberta, Democratic Congressman Frank Coffin of Maine, journalists Blair Fraser of Ottawa and "Stuffy" Walters of Chicago, Elmer Brown of the International Typographical Union, and Max's partners in FP Publications Ltd., Col. Victor Sifton and Dick Malone. A mixed bag, to be sure, but interesting. Such forays were not entirely new. Already Cyrus Eaton had become famous for his "Thinkers' Conference" at his home town of Pugwash, Nova Scotia, where world issues were discussed and debated by global intellects of top degree.

When word of the impending hegira filtered out to the Vancouver press, considerable interest was evinced, if only because it was the first such undertaking on the West Coast. Was Max Bell attempting to upstage Cyrus Eaton? Was this an early step on his way to a press baronetcy? To all such questions, Bell replied goodnaturedly that he "just had these facilities and wanted to put them to work". "Who knows?" he kidded with one reporter. "Some good may come out of it."

The fact that he wasn't in it for publicity was evident in his dictum that the talks should be off the record and that the press would have to content itself with a prepared statement at the end of the meetings.

The party left Vancouver on September 28 in *Campana* and the *MV Jorholm*, requisitioned by Bell from his friend "Red" Dutton, the former hockey star and NHL executive. In laying in the provender Bell had, as usual, gone first-class. To call the first night's meal "hamburger" was an outrage; what Bell's chef provided, in hamburger form, was prime beef, hung especially for the occasion.

From the outset, Bell had only one injunction concerning hospitality on the *Campana*: it had to be the best. Thus, while he did not drink or smoke himself, and watched his diet carefully, he insisted on serving the choicest viands, finest imported wines and Cuban cigars. He was also extraordinarily generous in his loans of the yacht. When he learned, for instance, that my mother was celebrating her 80th birthday in Vancouver, he cheerfully offered use of the vessel for a harbour cruise and buffet supper for some twenty-four relatives. The yacht, when chartered, brought $800 a day. But for friends like Bing Crosby, Bob Hope, Phil Harris, Bill Morrow and Johnny Mercer, who liked to fish and play golf in British Columbia, *Campana* was offered free.*

The Twin Isles conference was somewhat more formal. After

---

* Mercer repaid the moral debt by writing and dedicating a song to Max called "Clams, Clams, Clams," which Crosby sang and recorded. The concluding refrain went like this: "Max Bell has his horses/While we eat six courses/Of clams, clams, clams..."

it was over, Mike Pearson wrote to me: "The conference really was a great success. My only criticism — and this is a tribute to those of you who arranged it — is that everything was so pleasant and we were so well looked after that it was difficult to be sufficiently argumentative or controversial. There is a serenity and a beauty about Twin Isles which is more conducive to quiet enjoyment than to argument."

But it was a memorable conference for me in another sense. While cruising north from Vancouver, Bell approached me and said: "Victor Sifton is down in my cabin. He'd like to talk to you. Why don't you drop down and say hello?"

I had never met the legendary Winnipeg publisher, despite the fact that Max had made me a director of the parent FP chain a year before, and assumed that Sifton wanted to make some pleasant small talk, shake my hand, and wish me well as his junior out-rider from the bleary mists of the Pacific.

I was quickly disabused. When I entered the cabin, Sifton was holding a blue financial folder, which looked suspiciously like the ones we used in Victoria, and which he was tapping with some pince-nez depending from a ribbon around his neck. Without any greeting, or formality, he said: "Keate — what's wrong with Victoria? Why aren't you making more money?"

I was completely taken aback. I had no financial statements with me, nor had I expected to be called on the mat in these salubrious surroundings. But some inner voice whispered to me: *Don't argue with this guy. Don't get into debate. There's no way you can win.* So, after a moment's hesitation, I stammered: "Well, Mr. Sifton, I thought we were doing pretty well there. Our return on equity is something like 30 per cent. I think that compares pretty favourably with other returns I have seen, both here and in the US."

"Not at all," he replied. "The situations are not comparable. You have the whole ball of wax. You ought to be doing better." And he proceeded to go over the expenditures, item by item, while I sat like an errant school child, being ticked off by his principal.

In retrospect, two conclusions seem valid. First, Max was not above steering me into a little greening by his tough, autocratic new partner. Second, the old soldier knew the value of establishing his command by jabbing his young lieutenants off balance at the first opportunity.

It was not a happy experience, nor an isolated one. Some months later, at a meeting in the editorial offices of the Ottawa *Journal,* attended by all FP publishers, Sifton took off on Cleo Mowers, the amiable and easy-going chief of the Lethbridge *Herald*. In looking down the road to future FP development, Mowers revealed that he planned to beef up *Herald* coverage by appointing a man to an Ottawa bureau. Sifton lit into him unmercifully, dressing Mowers down in language which seemed altogether excessive for the occasion. As his indignation waxed, his voice rose to a pitch which bordered on the irrational. The atmosphere was electric until the "get-acquainted" meeting broke up. With heavy hearts, a few of us walked back to the Chateau Laurier. When he saw Sifton in the lobby, Max Bell walked over, put his hand on Sifton's shoulder, and said: "Victor, you were pretty rough on my boy." Sifton looked at him sharply but made no comment.

Bell and Sifton were an unlikely pair of partners. In an interview at the time of the merger between Bell's four western dailies and Sifton's *Free Press* which created the FP chain, mention was made in the press of Sifton's stables, which dated back to 1905; there was a deathless quote to the effect that horses were meant for jumping and not gambling. In fact, Sifton intimated, a man who would bet on horses was no gentleman. Max, of course, was known as one of the best-informed punters in Canada, a man who kept a separate bank account for his wagers and was reputed to be one of the very few who could "beat the system". (On a certain visit to Calgary, I was told by Bell that he was running $33,000 ahead on the year's wagers. On another visit, I heard him confirm on the telephone an arrangement to fly one of his horses on the Pacific Coast by private charter to a $100,000 stake race in Chicago, at a fee of $7,500. Bell's system was to look for the right odds, study the blood-lines, and keep a sharp eye out for "over-lays", horses which had been off for a while and were overdue for a win.)

There were other differences. Sifton vicariously dabbled in spiritualism. Bell was a regular church-goer, a strong contributor to his Presbyterian faith and a student of the Bible. But Bell was also a jock at heart, an easy-going man who laughed a lot, enjoyed the company of track roustabouts and beautiful women, told hairy stories and gambled like a burglar. Sifton was an austere elitist, proud and haughty, who had fought a superb war in 1914-18, and was never thereafter quite able to separate the military from the civilian.

Both men were regarded as modest, but the truth is that each managed to conceal that streak of vanity which runs in most men of achievement. Bell, for example, rejoiced when his horse Meadow Court won the Irish Sweeps in 1965. He appeared for the occasion in a Moss Bros. outfit of cutaway and grey topper, and was delighted to introduce as a one-third partner Bing Crosby — an arrangement which was effected without the knowledge of the other partner, Frank McMahon, and caused that normally-genial man to mutter some sour imprecations.

A gamble on the success of the Leduc oil fields in 1947 when he was in his mid-30s had provided the base for Max Bell's fortune. He could easily have adopted the role of playboy or international jet-setter, but was more interested in a meritocracy. By the time he was forty Bell had laid the foundation of a newspaper empire which, through mergers and acquisitions, became the largest in Canada, with a circulation in excess of 1,000,000 — a figure surpassed in more recent years in a flurry of acquisitions by Southam and Thomson.

When he made his deal with Victor Sifton in 1958 to form FP Bell was able to contribute his four western dailies — the original *Albertan*, the Victoria *Times* and *Colonist* and the Lethbridge *Herald*.

In May of 1959, Bell and Sifton established a voice in the nation's capital by buying control of the Ottawa *Journal*. This was to be followed in 1963 by purchase of the Vancouver *Sun* and in 1965 by a deal to bring into partnership Howard Webster and the *Globe and Mail* of Toronto. In 1972 an amalgamation was worked out with the Montreal *Star* and *Weekend*. Thus FP came to dominate the major markets of Montreal, Winnipeg and Vancouver, and held the most prestigious newspaper in Canada in Toronto's *Globe and Mail*.

Along the way, Bell expanded his commercial interests and

became "the boy wonder" of Canadian finance by achieving the position of top single shareholder in both the CPR and the Hudson's Bay Company.

I remember one day in 1959 driving with him down Douglas Street in Victoria, past the Hudson's Bay Company department store.

"Is that a good operation, Stu?" he asked.

I told him it had a good name in the community; that it had originally been built a bit far north of the city centre but was rapidly being overtaken by the Victoria boomlet of the post-war period.

"Good," he said. "I'm thinking of buying the company." This brash statement astonished me. I looked at him with a surely-you-jest expression.

Bell then launched into one of his virtuoso performances and by the time he was finished, half an hour later, I was prepared to believe him. There were a lot of things wrong with The Bay, he argued. While it was the first big Canadian merchandiser, its headquarters were still in London. Its chief operating officers did not understand the ethos of Canada. It had not exploited to the full the advantages it held in the marketing of whisky, blankets and furs. In short, it had a tremendous potential which could only be fulfilled by the application of aggressive North American techniques.

In due course, Bell set about buying Hudson's Bay stock until he became the largest single shareholder in Canada. To friends, he insisted that he was serious in his intent to take over control of the company. He never quite made it — although subsequent events, such as the transfer of headquarters to Canada, indicate that he shook up the old guard when the annual meeting was held in London. A story, perhaps apocryphal, is that Governor Keswick in London listened respectfully to Bell's pitch and when it was over murmured: "Well, Mr. Bell, there are two points of view on that — yours, and the other."

Max would, however, listen to the other point of view. On one occasion I invited him to speak to the Vancouver Institute, an academic forum at UBC which had been offering intellectual discussions each Saturday night for more than half a century. I was a bit surprised when he accepted.

He chose to speak on the Canadian economy and, since he

was a major shareholder in the CPR and Hudson's Bay as well as a multi-millionaire newspaper tycoon, he could speak with authority. But one of the audience started to heckle him, accusing him of being "a lousy capitalist" and advocate of a system which "ground down the workers". The audience, losing patience with the interloper, began to boo and entreated him to "shut up and sit down".

During the altercation Bell leaned on the lectern, an amused smile on his lips, but when the crowd turned on his tormentor, Bell said: "No, no. Let the fellow say his piece."

Which was in keeping with his attitude to his newspapers. Each was left to determine its own editorial policy. In the twenty-two years I was associated with him, I can recall only one occasion on which he asked me to publish an item of interest to him. He had been impressed by an encyclical of Pope John XXIII. Would we take a look at it and see if it was worthy of comment? It was, and we did.

At times, indeed, we found it necessary to write editorials which we knew were in direct conflict with Bell's interests, but he never complained. On one occasion, the CPR directorate decided to meet on the Pacific Coast, on the very day that the *Times* unleashed a furious editorial blast at the company.

"Look, fellows," Bell said, a mite wanly, "I don't mind the editorial — but couldn't you have arranged to publish it some other day?"

On the other hand, Bell was never subservient in the presence of authority. With a Board of Trade group, he visited Moscow in 1964 and found himself in a teeming crowd of thousands in Red Square, observing the May Day parade. Unhappily, they were hived off behind rope-guards, attended by Red Army soldiers with sub-machine guns. Sizing up the endless parade, Bell reckoned it would take him hours to fight his way through the mob and get back to his hotel. To the delight of his friends, the arch-capitalist ducked under the restraining ropes, ran to the procession, and marched off the square with the Russian soldiers, some of whom broke out into metallic grins at the impetuous caper.

Disquieting news about Bell's health began to filter through the FP group in 1967. For all his concern about conditioning, and despite his ruddy outer glow of health, he was reported to be suffering from severe headaches and a loss of balance so bad that he was compelled, at times, to crawl across the floor on his hands and knees.

For a time, Bell pursued a hyperactive life — wheeling and dealing in oil, natural gas, newspapers, potash, cablevision and real estate; he followed his horses at home and abroad; played in the Bing Crosby pro-amateur golf at Pebble Beach; and in the process became the best single customer of Alberta's long-distance telephone system and Canadian Pacific Airlines.

Eventually, of course, he was ordered into hospital for thorough tests and a harsh fact emerged: he was suffering from a brain tumour behind his left ear. An operation was scheduled at the Montreal Neurological Institute, where the famed surgeons Wilder Penfield, Theodore Rasmussen and William Feindel took a personal interest in the case. Preliminary reports were encouraging. The tumour was benign. But in the delicate brain area doctors could remove only so much of the tumour. There was always the possibility that it would grow back again. Which is what happened. Over the next five years Bell endured four major operations, one of them requiring eighteen hours on the table.

Bell met this ordeal with classic courage. Between operations, he carried on as active a life as was possible. While admitting, for example, that he wasn't "feeling too good", he made a point of attending a testimonial dinner marking the fifty-second anniversary of the entry into journalism of Bruce Hutchison, by that time editorial director of the Vancouver *Sun*. He kept active in the Calgary Stampede and imported Bobby Kennedy, with his huge family, to serve as parade marshal.

After each operation, Bell sought restorative measures in the sunny climes of Palm Desert. He jogged (and remained inordinately proud of the fact that he could run a mile in just over five minutes). He golfed, and he swam in his private pool. But by the time of his fifth operation, he needed the services of a male nurse to help him around. He had been compelled to give up on a heroic stratagem to continue swinging a golf club: he ordered his man to tie him to a tree so that he would not fall down when he swung.

One day he called me on the telephone and asked me to fly down to the desert, with Letha, for a good talk. I found my old friend lying on a bed in the room off his swimming pool, wearing pink polyester shorts and a matching shirt. He greeted me with a cheery wave of the hand and asked me to sit beside him. Thereafter, he embarked on an analysis of all his newspapers which was nothing short of amazing. Circulation figures, advertising lineage, labour negotiations, "net quick" and "liquidity" statistics flowed from him in perfect sequence, and his facts were bang-on. For an hour I listened, fascinated. And when he finished, I thought to myself: *the doctors have got it all wrong. There's obviously nothing wrong with Max's brain. He's going to make it.*

Alas, this proved to be wishful thinking. Back in his little room at the Montreal Neurological, overlooking the playing-field where he had starred as a McGill football player, Max's life slowly ebbed away. Father David Bauer, the hockey coach and old friend, held his hand and spoke to him quietly. Max's gallant wife, Agnes, and newspaper publisher Frank McCool took turns sponging his forehead on hot summer days.

On July 20, 1972 Max died. He was three months short of sixty.

Tributes began to pour in to Calgary from around the world. The one from Hal Straight, publisher of a North Vancouver weekly, said:

Everyone who worked for Max became his best friend. . . . He once told me he had three main ambitions — to win some of the world's most famous horse races; to work with boys and possibly endow a boys' camp; and to own the CPR. He achieved his goals with the boys and the horses and darned near made it with the CPR. His influence on that company is well known to top financial people throughout Canada.

Another lifelong friend was Jim Coleman, the Southam sports columnist who had introduced Max to the intricacies of race handicapping en route to McGill by producing a copy of *The Racing Form*. Max had never seen the publication before but was immediately entranced with the mathematical problems posed in picking winners.

In a column published the day after Max's death, Coleman praised his friend's skills in hockey and football:

On a misty October late afternoon, many years ago, I sat in an upper row in the concrete stands [of Molson Stadium] and watched Max Bell kicking for McGill Juniors. Gawd — how he could kick that ball!

He was magnificently disciplined in athletics, as in every other phase of his life. He hád a funny little habit. In each kicking situation, just before he called for the ball to be snapped to him, he'd make a complete turn of 360 degrees on the spot from which he had decided to punt. He'd make this funny little complete pivot and he'd clap his hands, to call for the ball. He never wore a helmet. He stood there, bareheaded and serious.

As he let the ball slide from his hands, his right leg swung in a perfect arc; his spiral punts rocketed 60 to 70 yards, every time. Sitting high in the stands, you could see Max's foot strike the ball and then, slightly delayed, you would hear the echoing sound — PUNG — while the ball was soaring in the autumn twilight.

On July 24 Max was buried in a pleasant little country cemetery at Okotoks, fifteen miles southwest of Calgary, where he and Frank McMahon had maintained a fine thoroughbred stud farm. The sixty-car cortège was guided to the city limits by local police, after which a special detachment of RCMP took over.

As the procession approached the little cemetery along a narrow, winding country road, a wonderful thing happened. More than a dozen thoroughbreds, cavorting in the fields of Golden West farms, turned and ran to the fence, as if to get a closer look at the cortège. Soon they were in a row, perfectly still.

Msgr. Athol Murray, the renowned director of the Notre Dame "Boys' Town" at Wilcox, Saskatchewan, wrote to me:

"I was moved to see that, as the funeral cortège approached and was passing the Okotoks ranch, the horses in the paddock moved over to the fence, with bowed heads, and even moved over to a spot close to the interment. They seemed to know.

"I loved Max — deeply."

# Chapter 11

"Now is the winter of our discontent
Made glorious summer by the sun . . . "

— *William Shakespeare*

There is some evidence abroad in North American newspapers today that morning papers are showing greater growth than their evening rivals. Light rapid transit, with its invitation to easy-to-handle tabloids, is believed to have had some impact on the field. Another theory is that early-evening television has cut into the reading time of newspaper subscribers: the admonition to carrier boys has been: "Get that paper on the doorstep by four in the afternoon!"

Curiously, Vancouver has never followed this trend. On the contrary, it has always been known as a "tough morning-paper town". Both the *News-Advertiser* of 1887 and the *Star* of 1929 had foundered as morning sheets. The *News-Herald*, where I had made my first tentative overtures in the craft, changed hands three times between 1932 and 1957, when its final owner, Roy Thomson, decided he'd had enough.

So when I grew up in Vancouver, the strength lay with the two embattled evening newspapers, the *Sun* and the *Province*.

Of these, the *Sun* was the working-man's paper — at once raucous, rambunctious and dedicated to the proposition that the simple business of a newspaper was to raise hell. At that time it also espoused with the utmost vigour the curious enthusiasms of its publisher, Robert J. ("Bob") Cromie. An uneducated man who nonetheless had a canny sense of what interested newspaper readers, Cromie at various times championed Dr. Couě ("Day by day, in every way, I'm feeling better and better"); Angelo Patri, the child-care specialist; Arthur Brisbane, the Hearst columnist; Technocracy; and almost every diet known to man.

Jack Patterson, the late *Sun* sports editor, used to tell of the time Cromie telephoned and asked him to have lunch with him. Greatly flattered, Patterson met the boss at the front door of the old Sun Tower on Beatty Street, and they started walking south, Cromie talking eight-to-the-bar. Patterson was baffled as they approached Cambie Street bridge. Were there any good restaurants in this industrialized area of the city? None that he knew of. His apprehensions accelerated when Cromie strode off, south across the bridge, still gesticulating and inhaling deep breaths of the pleasant summer air.

Suddenly it dawned on Patterson: my god, we're going to Cromie's *home* for lunch, out on the south Shaughnessy slopes, a good seven miles away. When they reached the Cromie mansion, the starving sports editor was served a luncheon of carrot strips, celery sticks and water-cress.

Some of Cromie's friends contended that his diet fads hastened his demise. He died at 49. The *Sun*, for all its pizzaz, had never been able to catch up to its stately rival. The *Province* moved inexorably toward the magic figure of 100,000 subscribers, helped by a strong classified advertising section; the *Sun* trailed at 75,000 and at times had difficulty meeting the pay-roll. But the rivalry between the two papers was intense. The *Sun* needled the eastern-owned *Province* by proclaiming on the front page each day: "The only daily newspaper owned, controlled and operated by Vancouver men." The *Province*, in the face of this provocation, maintained a lordly silence.

The entire Vancouver newspaper scene was convulsed in 1946, however, when the *Province* decided to take a strike by the International Typographical Union, and the *Sun* kept on publishing. In a tumultuous six weeks the traditional Vancouver pattern was turned upside down; the *Province* suffered grievous blows from which it has never really recovered.

A shrewd advertising manager of the *Sun* named George Cran took advantage of the *Province* hold-out to hire a battery of telephone solicitors and instruct them to take every classified ad. they could find, even if it meant throwing out retail and national lineage. This was in keeping with the old newspaper maxim that "the paper that gets the classified gets the readers."

By now control of the struggling *News-Herald* lay with Clayton B. ("Slim") Delbridge, a stock-broker and financial whiz who knew very little about the editorial side of the business but was wise enough to leave that aspect to those who did. He had taken over the paper on the departure of the *News-Herald*'s founder and editor Pat Kelly for a job in Toronto as publicity director of the Canadian Red Cross.

Delbridge was an old friend of *Sun* publisher Don Cromie, R. J.'s son. Over lunch one day Cromie remonstrated with Delbridge for accepting some newsprint from the strike-bound *Province*, adding that he (Cromie) was so hard up for paper that he was considering entering the black market in New York, at an exorbitant price.

The *News-Herald* quota, while not large, was significant when valued at the price Cromie intended to pay for paper in New York. Before the luncheon was ended, Delbridge had agreed to sell the *News-Herald* to the *Sun*, contingent upon the Powell River company being able to transfer the newsprint quota. A few days later Powell River's president Harold Foley agreed to the transfer in the event of a sale. The deal was made. Cromie got the morning newspaper and its quota for no more than he would have been compelled to pay for newsprint in New York.

Not unnaturally, the *Sun* (which by now was romping away from the *Province*) began to curtail the amount of newsprint available to the *News-Herald*. When circulation dropped below 30,000 daily, and the size of the paper was pegged at only ten pages, Delbridge warned Cromie that any further cuts would result in closure. Cromie insisted that he needed the newsprint.

The *News-Herald* was a Liberal newspaper and its publisher was a good friend of the then-premier, Byron L. ("Boss") Johnson. Delbridge took his story to his friend in Victoria, who persuaded Crown-Zellerbach to allot the morning paper an extra 1,000 tons, at regular prices.

But Cromie, riding the crest of his boom with the *Sun*, didn't really need the daily he had bought for the sake of some newsprint. When Roy Thomson arrived on the scene in 1955, surveyed the Vancouver economy and decided to make a bid, Cromie sold him the *News-Herald*. It was one of those rare occasions in which

Thomson had ventured into a competitive metropolitan market. In spite of the fact that he moved the *News-Herald* to new premises on stylish Georgia Street, installed new presses, hired a respected editor in G. M. ("Gerry") Brown and changed its name to the Vancouver *Herald*, he could not hack it. In future British Columbia acquisitions Thomson stuck solely to one-paper, monopoly towns.

The 1946 strike at the *Province* was comparatively short, but violent. When the paper attempted to publish with the aid of some non-union printers flown in from Winnipeg, delivery trucks were over-turned, papers set afire and staffers beaten. In spite of a good Southam record in labour relations the *Province* was branded "anti-union", a title which was to haunt them for many years to come.

Once the strike was settled, the *Province* set out on a vigorous campaign to regain its position as leader in the Vancouver evening field. There began a decade of frantic competition which did little credit to either paper. Instead of returning to its original role as a low-keyed, responsible journal, the *Province* sought to match the *Sun* with sensational headlines and a "scoop" for each edition. All this was accompanied by a promotion assault in which each newspaper spent $500,000 a year to seduce the populace with a bewildering array of give-aways — sets of steak knives, Panda dolls, TV lamps and cheap insurance policies. It soon became evident that the evening Vancouver market could not maintain two successful dailies.

This harsh fact set the stage in the late fifties for the creation of Pacific Press, which was to divide the Vancouver market into morning and evening papers, each produced from a common building. The *Province* had already purchased property at the north end of Burrard bridge with the aim of building a new plant; the *Sun's* landmark Tower was old and so full of circular stairways that (in Eric Nicol's view) it gave reporters a giddiness that was reflected in the news columns. Southam's suggested putting the two together in one spanking new plant.

The idea was simple enough and already in practice in a number of US communities. But its execution was complex, with batteries of lawyers employed by both participants. A Combines commission from Ottawa held extensive hearings and eventually approved the merger, with some strictures about maintaining a balance. The new company, Pacific Press Limited, would acquire the assets of both the *Sun* and the *Province*. Under a formal "Sun-Southam Agreement", the *Province* would enter the morning field (vacant since the previous year, 1957) and the *Sun* would continue to operate in the evening. The papers would compete, albeit from the same building and using the same equipment.

Because the *Sun* was clearly winning in the Vancouver market and the *Province* was losing, a substantial "equalization payment" was required to bring the partnership into balance. Clair Balfour, for Southam's, was offering $3.5 million but Don Cromie was holding out for $4 million. Cromie likes to recall that, when negotiations appeared to be at an impasse, he had an astonishing long-distance call from Philip Fisher, the urbane and patrician president of Southam's. "Don," he said, "I understand you're a gambler. Why don't we flip a coin — if we win, we'll pay $3.5 million and if you win, we'll pay $4 million. If you want, you can toss the coin on your desk right now." Cromie, who *was* a gambler, blanched at the thought of a coin-toss for $500,000 and said he would have to refer it to his directors. Clair Balfour ultimately concluded the deal for Southam's at $3,750,000. It was one of the shrewdest deals in Canadian newspaper history.

For Max Bell, the *Sun* continued to loom as a glittering prize. It was the largest daily west of Toronto; it was functioning in a booming city; and if the economies of Pacific Press production worked out as indicated, it could be a substantial money-maker. So Bell began his quiet Chinese water-torture treatment on Don Cromie, calling on him whenever he was in Vancouver and letting him know that he was ready to deal at any time. One day in 1963 he caught Cromie in a receptive mood and offered him $10 a share over the current market value of $20.

Cromie was running a profitable newspaper. But he wondered if he, as an independent, could withstand the long-term challenge of the Southam group. He had also been shattered by the 1957 death by drowning of his younger brother Sam, who had been mechanical vice-president of the *Sun* and the most popular executive in the plant. As in the case of the Siftons, there was a history of early deaths in the Cromie family and there were times when Don didn't feel he would make it to age 60. (He did.) As majority holder of the family's 55 per cent of *Sun* stock, he felt a responsibility for the financial security of numerous children and in-laws.

He sold control to Max Bell — and years later conceded it was "a great mistake", a virtual forfeit of his patrimony and millions of dollars. Street talk in the trade was that Cromie had actually made an offer to buy back the paper but it was academic on at least two grounds: Cromie by this time did not have the money to buy, and Max Bell was not inclined to sell.

Pacific Press was now owned 50-50 by Southam and FP, who would divide the bottom-line profits. Each group appointed its respective publisher, who was responsible for policy and appointment of staff.

By the spring of 1964, the Vancouver *Sun* was in a restive and demoralized state. The Big Apple of western Canadian journalism, it was shiny on the outside (circulation, 240,000; pre-tax February profit of $480,000) but bitter at the core. For three months it had been without a publisher. Major decisions were being left in limbo. The new building was being built at a cost of $14 million and there were serious problems of over-runs and delays in its construction.

On sale of the paper Cromie had been offered, and had accepted, an invitation to continue as publisher "indefinitely" at a salary of $45,000 a year. He stayed six months.

Like his father, Don was a brilliant but quixotic fellow who had thought, among other things, that it was a stroke of journalistic genius to have football writer Annis Stukus go to the Far East to interview Chiang-Kai-Shek. An inveterate traveller himself, Cromie, like Lord Beaverbrook, had been fond of roaming the world and blistering his editors by long-distance telephone from various corners of the world.

In the mid-1950s he had become concerned about the length of *Sun* editorials and news-stories and imported a New York word-count specialist to do a study. ("Our aim," former managing editor Himie Koshevoy recalls, "was to reduce the fog index in the paper.") The visiting semanticist recommended that no editorial should exceed 300 words, and no sentence nineteen words. This remarkable decree posed severe problems for many writers.

After the sale of the paper, for some reason, Cromie laboured under the delusion that he could sell his newspaper and continue to run it in his own way. Max Bell felt differently. So did Richard Malone, who, as FP's general manager, was now working for John

Sifton, Victor Sifton having died in 1961. While conceding that the paper was bright and aggressive, Malone also regarded it as "irresponsible, a bit junky and bigoted on some issues". Bell believed that "there was some fat on it", that salaries were distorted (Cromie had been paying himself about $85,000 a year) and that the new owners could improve its performance by the simple imposition of some sensible management principles.

When these took the form of memos from Winnipeg, Cromie blew up and quit, with a stentorian blast at his erstwhile partners. With a few million in his pocket, as his share of the sale, he could afford to be belligerent. To a friend, he confided about Malone's chivvying him for absentee publishing: what the new owners wanted, Malone said, was a publisher who was on the job every day and could wield "total authority".

But three months had passed since Cromie's blow-up and nobody was in command. The old Sun Tower, a landmark on the fringe of Vancouver's Chinatown, was buzzing with rumours. Although Malone had suggested in casual conversation that there would be no appointment of a publisher "for about a year", newsroom gossip was that the job would go to Bell's old friend Hal Straight, a former *Sun* managing editor. Another report was to the effect that first in line was Clayton B. Delbridge. A third rumour was that the logical choice for the office was Larry Dampier, who had come out to the Coast from Montreal to be assistant publisher of the *Sun* after the death of Sam Cromie. (An interesting rebuttal to this latter theory was that Dampier, a former executive of Lever Brothers, was basically a soap man; since Fred Auger, the publisher of the *Province*, had come up via Procter and Gamble, it was argued that Pacific Press could not stand two Rinso white personalities in the top publishing jobs.)

At any rate Ed Benson, general manager of Pacific Press, telephoned me from Seattle to provide background on what he described as "a tense situation". According to Benson, senior *Sun* executives were "scared to death" and "full of apprehensions". I was puzzled by his call. Why should a man in charge of production of 350,000 daily newspapers bother to brief a publisher with one-tenth that circulation, in another (and much smaller) city? Was Benson, a master of intrigue, making a few tentative chess moves?

In the British Columbia legislature the ham-handed Victoria

member Waldo Skillings had flatly told the House: "Stu Keate is going to succeed Don Cromie as publisher of the *Sun*. Queried on this by The Canadian Press, I replied that I knew nothing about it, which was the truth.

Not that I was averse to the idea. After fourteen years as publisher of the *Times*, I was beginning to feel the need of a new challenge. The paper was in good shape and making a pile of money. There was plenty of time for golf and fishing. Life in Victoria was amiable and comfortable — perhaps too comfortable. It occurred to me that I could sit there, quite happily, for the rest of my life; no worries, no sweat, no involvement in the mainstream of Canadian journalism. Vancouver was different. It was exploding. It was tough. And it was my home town.

As a director of the parent FP company, I was appalled that a powerful paper like the *Sun* should be allowed to drift for another year. Accordingly, I wrote to Max Bell in February, making the following points:

1. The staff of the *Sun* was in turmoil, jittery and uncertain about its future.

2. As an interim "policy", Dick Malone had decreed that Dampier would handle business matters, but consult with him on "crucial decisions"; when in doubt about editorial policy, *Sun* people should telephone Victoria and take direction from Bruce Hutchison. In other words, the third largest daily in Canada — which had built its reputation as "Vancouver's only home-owned newspaper" — was instructed to look to Toronto and Victoria for major decisions.

3. Earlier in February, Jack Webster, the hot-liner, had blasted the *Sun* for "absentee ownership" with much emphasis on the fact that Don Cromie represented the last firm link with Vancouver.

4. All this drift was occurring at a time when Val Warren, a Vancouver advertising salesman, was announcing to a TV audience that he would shortly start printing the daily Vancouver *Times*, giving the city "a new voice" which would employ 300 local people and undercut the *Sun* both on advertising rates and home-delivered circulation.

In short, a dog's breakfast, virtually incomprehensible in the light of the business acumen of the paper's new owners.

Within a few days, Bell called me from Calgary and talked for thirty-five minutes, during which time he did everything but make me a firm offer for the job as publisher of the *Sun*. He was calling, he said, on a personal basis and that it would be up to me to read his mind as best I could. The appointment, he said, would not be "long in the wings". There was a Board meeting in a month and it should be settled by then. The job, he felt, was worth a starting salary of $36,000 a year, far less than Cromie paid himself, or even his assistant ($45,000). There would have to be "a degree of tolerance" in assessment of others' roles in the new structure. With his customary percipience, Bell pointed out that senior employees might have yielded to Cromie's wishes, against their better judgement, in order to protect the generous salaries he had instituted. What Bell was saying, in effect, was that these men might well turn out to be better operators than the new owners suspected.

Toward the end of the conversation Bell said, "I haven't said that this is your job," but then added: "There is no one I can think of . . . there's a great job to be done."

I told him that my relationships with Dick Malone were, at best, prickly, to which Bell replied: "Dick is just playing it cool."

Within a month, I was offered the job. Malone wrote from Winnipeg asking me to come to Vancouver with Bruce Hutchison, for a meeting with Bell and himself in the Hotel Vancouver. But what should have been a festive occasion quickly degenerated into a confrontation with all the élan and *joie de vivre* of the Nuremberg Trials.

Late in the afternoon, Malone summoned me to his room in the hotel and proceeded to read to me a solemn ukase which might easily have been titled: "How To Be Publisher Of The Vancouver *Sun* And Find Misery." This incredible document, unfortunately, is four typewritten pages long and too prolix for these pages. So let me cite, verbatim, just a few of the highlights:

1.  We [Malone read] cannot have the "big shot", bon vivant type of publisher — a Bassett or an easy-going Auger. We must not rock the boat too sharply or start any panic and gloom.
2.  The new publisher should conduct himself on a strict routine to set the example (i.e., on the job from 9 a.m. to 5

p.m. each day without afternoons off for golf, boating, etc., which will have to be confined to Saturday afternoons and Sundays, or after 5 p.m. on weekdays.)

3. The publisher should also make a point of being in the office for a while on Saturday morning as often as possible and occasionally dropping in at night to learn what happens in terms of night staff, customer service, complaints, want ads and so forth.

4. The new publisher should strictly confine his vacations to three weeks each year without extra long weekends and so forth, to set an example. [The Guild contract at that time called for five weeks' vacation for people with fifteen years seniority.]

5. Except where absolutely essential (the publisher) should avoid business trips out of town and becoming involved in association committee work which will take him away from his office.

6. For the first two years the new publisher should strongly avoid the social swing and cocktail circuit of Vancouver, the Press Club, drinking or partying with other employees, etc. He should proceed as quietly and seriously as possible. Above all, he should avoid criticizing, gossiping or in any way encouraging scuttlebutt as to any internal problems or staff relationships with Pacific Press, both inside and outside the office.

7. There will be, of course, considerable pressure for the new publisher to join dozens of Vancouver organizations, from Symphony and Opera societies, to business and sports organizations, but it is recommended that the new publisher should avoid all such outside diversions and demands on his time and confine himself strictly to his knitting for a considerable period. As far as possible, he should divest himself of outside offices and appointments for a considerable period.

8. It is quite impossible to be one of the boys on the town one night and hold the serious respect of the staff on the following day.

9. Above all, the publisher must demonstrate that he knows his business and show that he can apply himself directly to each problem rather than simply leaving it up to his

subordinates. The advertising and circulation departments must be given drive and enthusiasm.

10. I would strongly urge that the new publisher should refrain from public personal statements, speeches, declarations and so forth. It is more important to build the paper than any single individual.

11. Unquestionably, there are a number of problems to be resolved but the new publisher should not discuss this with people about town, his friends or visiting firemen . . . he should keep his thoughts to himself.

I sat in the hotel room, listening to Malone reading this sombre catalogue of Thou-Shalt-Nots — actually *reading* it, with an occasional furtive glance to ensure that I was Getting The Message — with mounting dismay. I felt a bit like a juvenile delinquent being lectured by a stern and disapproving father.

I was at the time fifty. I had been in the newspaper business thirty years, for almost half that time as publisher of one of Malone's papers in Victoria. I had led that paper, with the help of a great staff, from the position of a box-office loser to a very handsome winner. When we left, 500 of the staff were to turn out at a party in honour of my family; I was presented, among other things, with a scroll saying: "Sorry to see you go," and signed by every single member of that staff, both union and management.

The more I thought about Malone's austere injunctions, the more I came to realize: *this guy doesn't really want me to take this job.* For the person he had described, and the procedures indicated, were the precise antithesis of my own style, personality, and philosophies of leadership.

Quickly, I tried to break down as much as I could remember: No golf? I loved playing golf, and sometimes managed as much as one game a week. Stay away from Symphony and Opera? I loved the theatre in all its forms and held season's tickets for just about everything. No travel? If nothing else, I was coming up for presidency of the Canadian Press, which required six or eight trips a year; I was a director of the Inter-American Press Association, and of the International Press Institute.

No speeches? It had always seemed to me essential to establish a paper's identity and views on public policy. I believed wholeheartedly that a newspaper should immerse itself in community activities, if only because it had a fundamental duty to know what was going on. As a result, in my first couple of years in Victoria I had accepted speaking invitations from organizations as disparate as the First Baptist Men's Club and the Associated Chambers of Commerce of Vancouver Island (where a drunken chairman delighted me by checking his introductory notes and whispering in my ear: "You're in janitors' supplies in Nanaimo, aren't you?"). Since there are never enough speakers to go around the service-club circuit, I had found the invitations piling up. In one year there were 150, of which I accepted about eight.

"Don't leave problems to subordinates?" My philosophy tended to the opposite. The job of publisher, it seemed to me, was to get the right people in the right places and then let them loose, with a minimum of neck-breathing. Trust them. A publisher's fundamental task was to create an atmosphere of freedom, a climate in which intelligent people could work comfortably, and without fear.

Malone tossed his Sermon on the Mount on a coffee-table. "Read that carefully," he said, "and think about it. I'll see you at dinner."

As I always did when deeply troubled, I went to Max Bell.

"Max," I said, handing him the document, "this is impossible. I don't see how I could live with it. It's insulting."

Bell grinned. "C'mon," he said. "Those are not rules — they're just guidelines. You know the situations at the *Sun*. There's got to be some revision of scales imposed in the first year or so. You can stick-handle your way through that. Don't let it get you down." Then he looked at me directly and, in a quiet voice, delivered the clincher:

"Malone isn't the final authority in all this."

Nevertheless, I asked him to speak to Malone; to tell him that I couldn't change my personality after all these years, and that I couldn't run the *Sun* without autonomy.

An hour or so later we gathered at the Panorama Roof for a somewhat edgy dinner. Bell meanwhile had relayed my misgivings to Malone and I gathered that Round One had ended in something approaching a Mexican stand-off. But before we broke up, Bell put his hand on my shoulder and said:

"Stu, I want you to know that you were my first and only choice for this job."*

So I accepted. It was decided to keep the appointment quiet until the directors of the company had been notified. Further, a propitious moment would have to be chosen at which Larry Dampier would be advised and offered alternative employment — possibly my old post at the Victoria *Times*.

But the annual Canadian Press meetings were on in Toronto, industry gossip was being exchanged in smoke-filled bedrooms, and the secret could not be kept. The story broke when John Bassett, then publisher of the Toronto *Telegram*, approached Malone, said he knew that I was going to be appointed, and that he proposed to announce it in the *Tely* the next day. Malone scurried around, found Dampier, and on the mezzanine lobby of the Royal York Hotel advised him that he would not be getting the top job at the *Sun*. As assistant publisher and trouble-shooter for Cromie, Dampier had a legitimate claim to the office. Although disappointed, he took the news with good grace and promised his loyal support. He stayed four years as assistant publisher and left in 1968 to assume the presidency of a food chain, while continuing as a director of the *Sun*.

All this happened on the day of the Canadian Press annual dinner, at which I was to be installed as president of the wire service. I suppose, as anyone looks back over his career, there is one day which stands out as a summit and major turning-point. For me, this was it.

At dinner-time, I took over as president of CP — which I felt was a great honour, since the post is elective of all members, and I was the first from British Columbia to be chosen. At midnight, after I had just climbed into my pajamas, a knock at the door of our suite brought a reporter and photographer from the *Telegram*, and a man from *Time*, to do stories on my appointment. (The *Tely's* interview the next day appeared under the Horatio Alger headline: "From Paper-Boy to Publisher.")

The first person to know about the appointment, outside the press, was, of all people, US Attorney-General Robert Kennedy, who had come to Toronto to address the CP annual dinner.

---

* Years later I learned that this was not true. Both Malone and Bruce Hutchison testified that Bell had initially pushed for the appointment of Hal Straight.

While we were chatting before his speech, Kennedy asked me: "What is your home paper?"

"As of midnight tonight," I replied, "I'm moving from the Victoria *Times* to the Vancouver *Sun*."

Kennedy's face lit up in his familiar Bugs-Bunny grin and he held out his hand. "Congratulations," he said. I was impressed by the fact that he regarded this as a promotion. It was, after all, a long way from Washington, DC.

When I got back to Vancouver, Don Cromie was cleaning out his desk at the *Sun*. He paused to hand me a package in a familiar Birks' blue box. I opened it, and found a beautiful walnut gavel with a silver band on which were engraved the words: "Stuart Keate — Total Authority."

And then we both had a good laugh. Although he turned out in later years to be a relentless critic of the paper he had sold, we remained friends.

# Chapter 12

"The First Law of Journalism (is) that a
newspaper inevitably reflects the character
of its community."

— *Tom Wicker*

In a far-ranging survey of the media in Canada in 1970 which
was often critical of newspapers and of their editorial performance, the Davey Commission nevertheless stated that, "...the
daily and weekly newspapers of this country are, in general, doing
a praiseworthy job. Let us remember the obvious: newspaper
people produce a wholly new product *every day*. Each edition
is the result of hundreds of human decisions, each calling for
swift judgement, instant clarity, and the fine balancing of other
people's perceptions. Journalism, however humble, is a sort of
art; there can be very few occupations that are so demanding in
terms of speed and judgement. The wonder is that newspapers
are as good as they are. They really are a daily miracle."

It's worth looking at what is involved in the "daily miracle" for
a metropolitan evening newspaper such as the one I was about
to join. How in a span of three or four hours are 200 columns
of news, opinions, features and art-work fitted together into a
paper which will vary from 60 to 120 pages — a process which
involves the distillation of 300,000 words of wire copy and the
production of the equivalent of two novels a day?

At the Vancouver *Sun*, "dummies" of the advertising content
are handed to the newsroom at 1 p.m. daily as a framework for
the next day's edition. While the ratio of advertising to news will
average approximately 70 per cent to 30 per cent, a "news-hole"

of 200 columns is guaranteed and editorial maintains the right-of-way in any crunch situation. Flexibility is essential: in a Kennedy assassination, or comparable calamity, the entire front section of the paper will be ripped apart and the existing work jettisoned.

The first man on the scene each day is the art editor, who starts his working shift at 4 a.m. He reviews all the projected art, clears the wire-photo machines, examines the photos submitted over-night by a twelve-man staff and assesses their merit for later consultation with the assistant managing editor. The night editor has gone home at 3:30 a.m.; there is only one hour in each day that the newsroom is vacant but, as a precaution, the wire room is manned so that the paper is protected against "things that go bump in the night". At 4:30 a.m. an editor and two desk men arrive to start processing copy for a first-edition press start at 10:00 a.m. As a general rule the paper is filled from back to front, calling for shrewd judgements about copy which will "stand up" for the rest of the day. Pages 1, 2 and 3 are left open for spot news and stories which breathe vigour and freshness into the day's edition.

While most of the city is still sleeping, the National Editor and wire-copy chief start their day at 5:30 a.m. Most of the news-desk staff begin their 7½-hour day at 6 a.m. (For this responsibility, they are paid an average of about $24,000 a year.) The assistant managing editor arrives at 6 a.m. and presides over a first-edition news conference at 7:15 a.m. With the art editor, he checks over available pictures and selects art which may or may not survive the rest of the day, including the all-important page 1 illustration. News editors submit their story lists, which are evaluated and assigned space, with the full knowledge that late-breaking copy may squeeze them out. (A critic of newspapers once remarked that the job of these people was "to separate the wheat from the chaff — and then print the chaff.")

The managing editor arrives at 7:30 a.m. His role is crucial. He hires and fires and directs a newsroom staff of 175, including Sports, Business, Features, Entertainment and Leisure. He re-solves debates arising out of earlier conferences and keeps a wary eye cocked for questions of taste and libel. One of his prime functions is to see that the publisher is never surprised. The editorial and background pages are beyond his jurisdiction, but he keeps in touch with the editorial pages editor, who administers a staff of thirteen, and makes his people available for background briefings.

Deadline for the home edition, which most readers receive, is noon. (In Vancouver the first edition traditionally goes to the hinterland and Vancouver Island.) The home edition, in turn, may be "chased" by late-breaking news. The final edition, or "buff" (so-called in Vancouver because it was originally printed on peach-coloured paper) closes at 2:15 and runs off the press at 3:30 p.m. in time to catch downtown news-stands and a complex schedule of bus and ferry connections.

All this is achieved in an atmosphere of mounting pressure.

When I arrived at the *Sun* in 1964, the impelling challenge, it seemed to me, was nothing less than a complete change in its character and personality. From its inception it had been an erratic and unpredictable newspaper — vibrant, yeasty and aggressive, but nonetheless erratic, sensational and strongly partisan.

Indeed, its original charter committed it to support the policies of Sir Wilfrid Laurier and the Liberal party. Many years later, in the 1950s, this fact was discovered by Premier W. A. C. Bennett, who seized on the intelligence with great glee and trumpeted it in an election speech. The *Sun* board quickly met and struck the offensive passage, proclaiming its independence with a mast-head line from Macaulay saying: "Men are never so likely to settle a question rightly as when they discuss it freely."

It had appeared to me as an interested bystander in Victoria, that the *Sun* had not kept pace with its community. Vancouver, in the post-war boom, had surged forward to become a first-class city, deserving of a first-class newspaper. But the *Sun* seemed content to needle the *Province*, preoccupy itself with local issues and thus give off an aura of parochialism.

My aim was to reduce the strident tones of its columns; to take the paper out beyond the bounds of British Columbia to concern itself with national and international affairs; and in the process to make it as independent and responsible as humanly possible. I reckoned this change, introduced quietly and subtly, would take about five years. In the end, it took ten.

What was needed, obviously, was a change in newsroom

direction. Newspapers, after all, were the work of human hands. The trick was to find the talent and use it wisely. With Bruce Hutchison as an ally (Hutchison had been appointed nine months before I became publisher) there was no problem with the editorial pages; his writing brought both intelligence and consistency to those columns. In Cliff MacKay he had found the perfect editorial partner and in Len Norris a comedic genius whose cartoons were renowned across the land.

But the newsroom situation was not as happy. In charge was Erwin Swangard, who had immigrated from Germany in the depression years and risen through the ranks to become first sports editor and then managing editor. Swangard had many positive attributes. He was hard-working, a "bulldozer" who got things done. But he was not above using the news columns for his own pet causes, and he seemed to me to belong to the "Front Page" school of another era. It soon became apparent that we could never produce the kind of paper we wanted with Swangard in charge of the news columns. In due course, I advised him that he would be retired at age sixty. Swangard balked. There ensued some acrimonious negotiations, at the end of which there were threats of legal action for wrongful dismissal. Before it reached that point, we "settled out of court" with a graduated series of payments totalling some $85,000.

Characteristically, Swangard bounced back. Our agreement stipulated that he would not work for a rival medium during the run of our "pay-out". But when he called one day to ask permission to accept a position as news editor of a radio station I told him to go ahead. Swangard took the job, imposed on it his considerable knowledge of news-gathering techniques, and developed it into a winner. This in turn led to a position as president of the Pacific National Exhibition.

To his credit, Swangard had brought along behind him as assistant managing editor a superb newsman in W. T. ("Bill") Galt. A native of Vancouver, Galt had served as a bomber pilot in World War II, had attended Columbia Journalism School in New York and later found a job as news editor of the Victoria *Colonist*. From there he had been summoned by the *Sun* and established, in due course, as its Washington correspondent, where he made his name with riveting coverage of the Little Rock de-segregation riots.

K.'s mother, Ethel Anderson Keate

K. and "Louie" at Sproat Lake, 1927

*HMCS Uganda* in the Pacific, 1945 (S.K. is the one with the five o'clock shadow)

Thousands watch as Marilyn Bell nears the shore at Beacon Hill Park in Victoria—the first woman to swim successfully across the Straits of Juan de Fuca

Prime Minister Pearson and S.K. at *Sun* Salmon Derby, 1965 (photo: Brian Kent)

Bruce Hutchison at work on his famo Shawnigan Lake log-pile (photo: Vanc *Sun*)

This "family group" set a Vancouver precedent (photo: Vancouver *Sun*)

Gillis Purcell on a press visit to Mosc

American couple wed on Garibaldi Mountain—too much white space?
(photo: Vancouver *Sun*)

...med Indian carver Mungo Martin
...eaks at the raising of the World's
...llest Totem Pole in Beacon Hill
...rk, Victoria (photo: Bill Halkett)

Max Bell (photo: Vancouver *Sun*)

R.S. Malone—president and general manager of FP Publications

Lord Thomson visits the Vancouver S[...] 1974 (photo: Ralph Bower)

CLOUDY

MUtual 4-7141   46 PAGES   VANCOUVER, BRITISH COLUMBIA, MONDAY, JAN. 25, 1965   ★★★★   PRICE 10 CENTS

Index: Letters 4; TV, 7
Sport 15; Finance
18; Names in News, 21
Women, 24; Comics, 26; Bridge
31; Gardens, 36; Crossword
31; Theatres, 26;

# 'orld Mourns Gallant Winnie

# BLOOD, TOIL, SWEAT-- AND NOW OUR TEARS

## Royal Rites Ordered

LONDON (CP) — Amid a tumultuous outpour
of sorrow, Sir Winston Churchill, the great human
soul of courage and freedom, will be borne through
streets of London in a state funeral unrivalled in sol
grandeur in Britain's long and colorful history.

Saddened by "inexpressible grief" as the 90-y
old warrior-statesman slipped into death Sunday m
ing, the Queen knelt at the tiny Sandringham Pa
Church.

She immediately requested Parliament set a
next Saturday for a state funeral to high-domed, ba
quered St. Paul's Cathedral where she will attend.

### End Came Peacefully

Parliament today quickly approved the Queen's
quest. State funerals are seldom granted common
Royalty seldom attends funerals of anybody other t
other royalty.

Death came quietly and peacefully to the bril
statesman Prime Minister Harold Wilson describe
"the greatest man any of us have ever known."

Gradually weakened by a stroke announced Jas
but which may have occurred some days previous,
wartime leader slipped into unconsciousness and

*Churchill in Words, Pictures*
*And Memory, Pages 1A to 1F*

shortly after 8 a.m. (midnight Vancouver time)
his family by his side.

For the 79-year-old Lady Churchill, Sir Winst
wife for 56 years, the long and exhausting vigil
over.

Death came to her world-famous husband 54 d
after his 90th birthday, on the 70th anniversary o
father's death.

### Many-Sided Genius

Tributes to what the Queen called "his many-s
genius" poured out from all corners of the world.

Flags were dropped to half staff.

The powers of this orator, writer, prime mini
painter, parliamentarian and bricklayer were rec
in scores of television programs.

They brought sharply to mind his jutting jaw
celebrated cigar and his famous V-for-victory sign
brought cheer in Britain's darkest hours.

From the unpretentious home at 28 Hyde P
Gate where he has spent his declining years, Sir V
ston will be borne to the huge, cavernous Westmi
Hall to lie in state for three days starting Wednes

Then, like the Duke of Wellington, the great
queror, Sir Winston will be carried through the st
of London on a gun carriage preceded by massed
talions signifying the magnificence and strengt
Britain. A 90-gun salute will be fired.

Many of the world's leaders will be in the cor
along with Churchill's widow and the three surviv
children, Randolph, Mary and Sarah.

### Traces Nelson's Path

At St. Paul's, which holds the remains of
Wellington and Admiral Lord Nelson, royal her
will carry Churchill's banner, shield, crest and spur

Following the service, the body will be borne
Tower Pier to be placed on a barge—as Nelson's b
once was carried—for a journey up the Thames
Festival Hall Pier for its final journey to Bladon s
70 miles northwest of London.

In the little churchyard of Bladon, with
Churchill's family in attendance, the body will be
ered into a family plot close to Churchill's mother
father.

e Vancouver *Sun* won the world award of the London Press Club
the best front page on the death of Sir Winston Churchill (photo:
ncouver *Sun*)

Stuart and Letha Keate at Inter-American Press Association meetings
in San Diego

Stuart Keate

It was impossible not to like Galt. Quiet-spoken, but with a dry wit and hilarious talent for mimicry, he enjoyed the respect of the newsroom because reporters knew he could do any job they undertook, only better. A rumpled, corpulent man with straight black hair combed back over some painful psoriasis on his neck, he was fondly known as "Injun Joe". His hawk nose and jet-black hair gave him a native countenance, whereas in fact he was a descendent of one of the Fathers of Confederation.

Galt's office was always open to young reporters, most of whom were graduates of UBC and partisans of the campus revolts then plaguing North America. What they were seeking was nothing less than control of their copy, consultation on hirings and formation of a committee which would advise management on day-to-day operations.

One reporter Galt had hired, an American, decided to challenge British Columbia's health minister on a rubella immunization program (or lack of it) by daubing spots on his face, hanging the minister in effigy, and unleashing a vicious harangue before the TV cameras. This, of course, was in direct contradiction of the newspaper's policy of non-involvement of staff in political issues, and of objective reporting. But there was no way the offender could be fired. The only grounds possible, under the Guild contract, were for "gross misconduct" and these were unlikely of success.

Galt's solution was to move the renegades (at least two of whom were Maoists) to less sensitive beats, and to stage a few downtown "beer sessions" to which the dissidents were invited, to air their squawks against the paper. There Galt made it abundantly clear that management did not intend to abdicate its control of the newsroom. Eventually the clamour subsided.

In spite of this ferment — or perhaps because of it — the paper continued to flourish. By the end of 1969 circulation had risen to 261,000, making it the second largest daily in Canada (a whisker ahead of the *Globe and Mail*). Profits, too, had been steadily climbing, with a dramatic increase in classified advertising which clearly established the *Sun* as the leader in this field throughout Canada.

At quarterly board meetings of Pacific Press a high-class problem presented itself: exactly how much profit should the operation produce? The question was never answered, definitively, although Max Bell once murmured that he thought "about $2.5 million" annually would be right.

The *Sun* by this time was showing a before-tax profit of approximately $12 million. But it was an illusory figure. Under Pacific Press accounting, this amount had first to be reduced by the $1 million loss on operations of the morning paper. The $11 million remaining was sliced in half by corporation taxes and other charges. This left a net of $5.5 million to be divided, under the Sun-Southam agreement, equally between the two shareholders — a bizarre arrangement which thus left the *Sun* with a bottom line of $2.25 million on its gross profit of $12 million and the *Province* with exactly the same reward on a *loss* of $1 million.

This performance infuriated Dick Malone, who came to each Pacific Press board meeting in Vancouver loaded with tough questions. Why, he demanded to know, did the *Province* need almost as many circulation personnel when it had roughly half the numbers of the *Sun*? Why didn't the *Province* cut back its circulation to 85,000 (from 125,000) rather than squander money on flying newspapers into non-profitable areas in the hinterland? Why was it that the Victoria *Colonist*, with less revenue, could make money in the morning field and the *Province* was rolling up ever-increasing deficits? In frustration, Malone declared that he would refuse to approve annual financial statements and budgets, and "wanted his dissent recorded".

In this, he had the solid backing of Howard Webster, a major shareholder in FP and chairman of the *Globe and Mail*. Webster contended that a partnership was just that; that there was no law suggesting that a winner could go on indefinitely subsidizing a loser. At one point he brought along a New York lawyer who argued that the Vancouver omelette could, indeed, be unscrambled.

While muttering dark threats from time to time, Malone did not press the point. The contract, under Canadian law, was perfectly valid and had, as a matter of fact, realized the objective of the Ottawa investigation in 1958, namely the continuance of two dailies of disparate views in Vancouver. In that sense, the Pacific Press structure had worked. It is certain that no private entrepreneur (Roy Thomson, for instance) would have sustained the ever-increasing losses of the morning paper, which were soon rolling along toward $1.8 million annually. As long as the *Sun*'s money tree continued to blossom, the *Province* would continue to publish and rake up $2 or $3 million "profit" to its own account.

Now, however, after a decade of operation, relationships between the principals were becoming increasingly chilly. To Clair Balfour's credit, he never lost his cool. The brunt of Malone's verbal assaults inevitably fell on the shoulders of Paddy Sherman, publisher of the *Province*, and he responded ingeniously.

In boxing parlance, Paddy "dazzled 'em with footwork". He purported to show, from a maze of statistics, that the *Province* could produce a column of type cheaper than the *Sun*. The reason the *Province* needed almost as many circulators as the *Sun* was that they had to cover the same districts, albeit with fewer subscribers. A crippling burden, he argued, was the *Province* share of Pacific Press buildings and production costs. It was not their fault that they were sharing elaborate premises with the *Sun*; operating solo, in a building more suited to their size, their costs could be substantially reduced.

Wound up, and in full voice, Sherman managed to convey the impression that the *Province* was somehow carrying the *Sun* on its back. At the very least, its cost-conscious operation was subsidizing the *Sun* and making it possible for the evening paper to roll up handsome profits. *Sun* directors often left the meetings chastened and resolved to do better.

To be sure, costs were mounting, the result not only of tough union settlements but inflation. In less than a decade the *Sun*'s news-gathering budget doubled, from $2.5 million to $5 million. But this in turn enabled the paper to improve qualitatively: to strengthen its bureaus, acquire new wire services like the Washington *Post* — Los Angeles *Times* and Chicago *Daily News,* undergo some typographical face-lifts, and hire new staff.

All this was done in the full knowledge that readers, whatever their protestations to the contrary, did not much like reading foreign news. Circulation directors could prove that a hot local story would always out-sell an international report. The *Sun* could point to a classic Vancouver feature about a sailor and his girl friend who got stuck into the wall by an erratic Murphy bed. With a slight shift in emphasis, however, the *Sun* eventually arrived at a workable balance: one-third international news, one-third national (mostly Ottawa) and one-third provincial or local.

The Davey Commission, in its 1970 survey of the press, found that the wealthiest dailies in Canada, not unnaturally, tended to be the best. Of the 109 dailies in the country it contended that only nine did a hard-hitting, conscientious job: the first one it listed was the Vancouver *Sun*.

In a memo to me, columnist Allan Fotheringham wrote: "You would be surprised at the stature of some people across the country who would like to come here and work now." This observation, if true, applied also to journalists in Britain, the United States, and Australia. Rarely a week went by without a wandering journalist fetching up on our door-step. One of them, Jack Wallace, sat himself down firmly in the managing editor's office and said he would not leave until he had some assurance of a job. He had made up his mind to leave San Francisco, settle in Vancouver and that was that.

Wallace came with gaudy credentials. One of his first jobs had been as secretary to Walter Winchell in New York. Thereafter, he had risen in the Hearst organization to become managing editor of one paper and a "newspaper doctor" to several others. With a passion for typography, he had set up a print shop in his home and experimented endlessly with new fonts and typefaces de-signed to make papers easier to read and more physically at-tractive.

In spite of some "Yankee-go-home" grumbling from junior staff, we hired Wallace and in due course turned his hyperthyroid talents loose on a re-design of the newspaper. We were rewarded not long after when the *Sun* won the nation-wide MacLaren Awards for "best front page" and "best sports page".

From London we picked up Eric Downton, a Canadian who had spent fifteen post-war years as a foreign correspondent for the *Daily Telegraph*. Paul St. Pierre returned from one term as an MP in Ottawa to resume his sparkling column. Doug Collins came over from CBC to do investigative reporting, was given a column of his own and within six months had rocked the entire community with his strong right-wing views. Trevor Lautens and Christopher Dafoe contributed graceful columns, one critic liken-ing them to the work of E.B. White. Denny Boyd, a writer of considerable talent who had defected to radio, was lured back into the newspaper fold and charmed his audience with columns on night-life, politics, and the creation of superior recipes for corned-beef hash. Jim Taylor, originally from the Victoria *Colonist,* developed such a popular sports column that the Toronto *Star* offered him $33,000 a year to move East. Cartoonist Roy Peterson resisted the same blandishments and went on to win first prize in an international competition.

Sheer serendipity brought Lisa Hobbs to the *Sun* from the San Francisco *Chronicle.* Author of four books, including the best-selling *I Saw Red China,* Ms. Hobbs had joined her husband Jack in flight from the big city rat-race to the misty forest delights of Kildonan, on Vancouver Island. A deal with Bill Galt was made which enabled her to research features for four days in Vancouver which she then wrote on weekends at her island retreat.

A feisty, no-nonsense journalist, she was later assigned by Galt to take over an ailing TV column and very soon found herself embroiled in a libel action with the CBC and its regional director, Bob McGall. A jam-packed courthouse listened with fascination for eleven days as Hobbs documented her charges of CBC ineptness — although the corporation had 432 employees in British Columbia, it could spare only one man to cover the BC Legislature. Hobbs lost her case and was ordered to pay damages of $1; a "contemptuous award" if ever there was one. For the next opening of the House the CBC dispatched thirty-two staffers!

Not long after, Hobbs was appointed associate editor, the first woman named to the *Sun* board. She stayed two years before succumbing to a handsome offer to join the National Parole Board in Ottawa.*

Another who disappeared into Ottawa, but for different reasons, was Dave Ablett. A political science graduate of UBC Ablett performed brilliantly as a *Sun* correspondent in Washington and Ottawa, specializing in energy problems, before being tapped to return to Vancouver as editor of the editorial pages. At thirty-six, Ablett had everything going for him. I saw in him a potential successor to the publisher's chair. But somewhere along the line, for reasons I could never understand, Ablett turned sour and began to churn out interminable (and, to some extent, incom-

---

* When her former *Sun* colleague, Simma Holt, was elected an MP and named to the prison reform committee, Allan Fotheringham quipped: "Some deal! Simma puts 'em in — Lisa lets 'em out."

prehensible) memos, one of which argued that Pacific Press had "destroyed the confidentiality of his news sources" by refusing to issue him a company credit-card. A protracted wrangle over a requested sabbatical, which would have taken Ablett out of the office for seven months, could not be resolved and by mutual consent we parted company. Ablett found employment in the Privy Council Office in Ottawa.

Another brouhaha involved the liverish but brilliant Allan Fotheringham, whose column had become the talk of the town. Off parade, Fotheringham was a charming companion: witty, urbane, full of gossip and a sartorial dandy. In front of a typewriter, a strange transformation took place. What emerged from his typewriter keys was frequently sheer bile.

The reasons for this were difficult to determine. Born in the whistle-stop town of Hearne, Saskatchewan, "Foth" had gone to school in Chilliwack and thence to UBC, where he attracted the attention of Don Cromie with a savage satire of the *Sun*. So incensed was Erwin Swangard that he entreated Cromie to fire Fotheringham as a campus stringer and take him to court. Cromie's wise response was to hire him.

As an editor of *The Ubyssey*, Fotheringham had met — and later, in 1963, married — a talented young writer named Sallye Delbridge. It was mere coincidence that she was the daughter of Clayton B. Delbridge, chairman of the board of the *Sun*. Thus, if not directly in the money, "Foth" found himself with rich resources behind him.

In an attempt to keep pace with Fotheringham's upward mobility, and to recognize his considerable abilities as a judge of news (and talent) I appointed him as Senior Editor, along with Dave Ablett. It was a title that I had seen working well at Time, Inc. It did not work at the *Sun*.

The problem was that "Foth" saw himself as an administrator and was hell-bent to run the shop. Before long, he was being described on national TV as "editor" of the *Sun,* personal policy adviser to the publisher, and the man to see if you wanted to be hired by the *Sun*. Serious schisms developed between Fotheringham and Bruce Larsen, who had succeeded to the managing editor's chair following the death of Bill Galt. Within a few months I realized that I had made a mistake. Accordingly, I re-cast the masthead to identify Ablett as editor of the editorial pages and Fotheringham as contributing editor. The result was several weeks of bitterness and misunderstanding. Eastern newspapers and magazines leaped in with extravagant bids for the services of the provocative columnist.

I reasoned with "Foth", as best I could, that he was not cut out to be an administrator; that his great gifts as a writer would be wasted and that he should develop along the lines of a commentator, not only in newspaper but in television and magazines — all of which came to pass when a local television station, CKVU, hired Fotheringham as an interviewer and political pundit and *Maclean's* magazine engaged him to write a weekly, back-page column. This extended "Foth's" clout and established him as a communications superstar, proving along the way that it was possible to write a successful national column from a base in Vancouver. It also placed him in the $100,000-plus income range.

In the end Fotheringham accepted this role and our personal relationship ended as it had begun, happily. Nearing my last day in office "Foth" treated me to what he called a "slap-up" lunch at Toulouse-Lautrec and presented me with a biography of Max Perkins inscribed: "For the Boss from the Foth, with affection after fourteen good years — The Stump Club, December 29, 1978."

Surveying this line-up, Bruce Hutchison remarked: "Stu, you're sitting on a powerhouse of talent." True. But in pursuing a no-holds-barred policy, in respect of both opinion and fact, I took considerable heat and was often reminded of the maxim that "a newspaper publisher can't have any close friends".

When reporter Moira Farrow uncovered a "bugging" of automobile sales rooms, and wrote a devastating series exposing the racket, car dealers reacted violently and instituted a boycott on advertising, worth $25,000 a month. The *Sun* stood by its story and in due course the dealers drifted back. Support for this position came from an unexpected source. Max Bell's son Chester was taking training as a business writer at the *Sun* and reacted strongly. In a memo, he wrote:

> I think that if we lost some advertising business as a result of the bugging, we should make mention of it in the news. We are always being chided for having too much advertising

as opposed to news; let's show them we aren't afraid to sacrifice the profit 'for the sake of the public'. This will serve as a warning to other advertisers that we don't necessarily knuckle under to their demands just because they have 'x' number of lines in advertising with us each year. This sounds crazy coming from a person with vested interests in the *Sun* but I feel it's an essential and honest report of the whole story.

At the same time, I deplored the *Sun's* proclivity for boasting about its triumphs. Thus, when the "bugging" story resulted in paroxysms of backpatting, I was moved to send Erwin Swangard a memo, saying: "While we did a fine job on this, I think we were a bit immodest in patting ourselves on the back six times in one story (per attached)... Excessive self-praise is usually a sign of some insecurity and I don't think we need to feel insecure about an honest job, honestly done. The facts will speak for themselves."

For more than twenty-five years, the *Sun* had been a leader in the publication of consumer reports, mainly expressed in the bitchy columns of Penny Wise, who hated spongy bread and supermarket fiddling. As newspapers became more financially independent, their freedom increased. The growth of investigative reporting brought with it well-researched attacks on strip mining, telephone rate increases and "moonlighting" by university professors. None of this added to the *Sun's* popularity. But its reputation for integrity was enhanced. Readers began to realize that the *Sun* could not be bought and was quite prepared to take on the giants as well as the petty crooks.

As one result, the *Sun* was described by Ron Haggart, then a tough columnist for the Toronto *Telegram,* as the "most sued" newspaper in Canada. Many *Sun* editorial people believed that it was better to settle out of court than undertake long and costly litigation. My own view was exactly the opposite — if there was a fighting chance of winning, pursue it hip, boot and thigh. Legal costs in some years exceeded $50,000. But the *Sun's* stand seemed vindicated by the actual disposition of cases. If a dozen suits were joined in a year, only one or two reached court. Many actions were instantly dismissed as trivial, or mischievous, designed to shut up the newspaper on the grounds that discussion was *sub judice.*

126

The most serious defeat it sustained was a judgement for $16,000 in favour of the Bennett brothers — Bill and "R. J." — which resulted from a garbled rewriting of a dispatch from the Victoria legislature. Bill Bennett, ultimately to become Premier of British Columbia, rubbed salt in the *Sun*'s wounds when, asked what he intended to do with the damage money, he replied coolly: "Buy a Ferrari."

Chief target of readers was Allan Fotheringham, who indeed set some kind of record by receiving three writs in a single week. In one year, it cost the *Sun* $32,000 in legal fees to defend Fotheringham, but beyond the occasional out-of-court settlement, for a few hundred dollars, the paper suffered no significant losses and its reputation for fearless reporting was enhanced.

Concurrently, and to demonstrate that not all its activities were polemical, the *Sun* entered vigorously on a round of good citizen projects. It originated the "March of Dimes" campaign in Vancouver and assisted in the founding of the Community Chest. In co-operation with the Variety Club, it instituted a series of Christmas campaigns on behalf of the mentally retarded and for a Children's Hospital rehabilitation unit in memory of its popular night-life columnist Jack Wasserman.

It raised money for Dr. Lotta Hitschmanova and her Unitarian Service Committee campaign to feed the hungry in India and the Far East. With the Vancouver Symphony, it created a Christmas series called "The *Sun* Family Pops" which quickly became a local institution. In co-operation with the Vancouver Institute, it brought to UBC as *Sun* lecturers such well-known journalists as Alistair Cooke, Harrison Salisbury and Mary Hemingway.

Allan Fotheringham was put to work on a special campaign to return Jericho Beach to the public from the Department of National Defence, which had conscripted that gorgeous, 120-acre piece of property at the beginning of the war as a seaplane base. "Foth" produced a stinging piece which showed that the priceless stretch of park and surf had been pre-empted by a handful of Army officers and a few minions. Eleven days after Fotheringham's blistering article hit the news-stands Ottawa capitulated and offered to sell the land back to the city.

On civic affairs the *Sun* launched a drive to establish a planning department at City Hall, to abolish the ward system and the poll tax; insisted on measures to relieve home-owners of much of the burden of education; and was instrumental in setting up the commissioner plan of administration at City Hall as an answer to its own call for the appointment of a city manager.

On civil liberties the *Sun* urged passage of Bills of Rights, appointment of ombudsmen, provision of legal aid for the poor, bail reform, jail reform and abolition of the fiat system. In the outcry against the columns of "Redneck" Doug Collins, these fundamental policies were overlooked by the "small-l" liberals.

In national politics in the 1960s. the *Sun* supported "Mike" Pearson and Pierre Trudeau. But it broke with Trudeau on the issue of wage and price controls and in 1972 backed Robert Stanfield, who supported the measures the *Sun* was advocating. It was the first time in history that the *Sun* had ever urged its readers to vote for a Conservative leader. Interestingly enough, the most prolific writers of letters-to-the-editor refused to believe that the *Sun's* conversion was serious, or lasting. Pierre Trudeau, who is known to have a low opinion of journalists, nonetheless wrote me a personal letter saying that he could not quarrel with editors who wrote out of honest conviction and that, while he was sorry to lose *Sun* support, our friendship would remain unimpaired.

When the national women's magazine *Chatelaine* undertook in 1978 an in-depth study of Vancouver, it concluded: "For many years now, the Vancouver *Sun* has been the best newspaper in Canada."

I would never make such a claim. Among the first three, perhaps; a paper to be ranked with the Toronto *Star* and *Globe and Mail.* It had won just about every possible newspaper honour: the MacLaren Awards for typography and make-up, the Michener Award for public service and all-round excellence; dozens of National Newspaper Awards. But I had by this time been around long enough to know that a newspaper was only as good as its last edition.

Finally there was the question of influence — or lack of it. While Max Bell had expressed a desire in putting together his papers to create "a strong voice in the West", this laudable objective was confounded by the stubborn facts of geography. Canada's postal service being what it is, it often took ten days or two weeks for the *Sun* to arrive at the Parliamentary Library in Ottawa, much too late to be of influence in any debate.

In an attempt to improve this situation we evolved a system of clipping four pages a day — editorial, op-editorial, background and "break page", which carried the trenchant Fotheringham column — and air-mailing them to BC members in Ottawa. This service was warmly received by the Parliamentarians, although one or two wrote to say that the clips were still taking four days to reach the capital. It was clear that the communications problem that had beset British Columbia since 1871 would not go away.

# Chapter 13

"A news story originates in a collision of
fact with an interested mind."

— *Tom Griffith*

Few new stories agitated the local media as quickly as the arrival
in Vancouver of Howard Hughes. Curious stories had contributed
to his growing legend as America's foremost mystery man. It was
said that the multi-millionaire-genius-eccentric had developed a
dirt phobia; that he was subsisting on a diet of Campbell's soup
and ice cream; that he had allowed his finger-nails to grow eleven
inches long; that he was bearded, emaciated, and plagued with
sores on his body.

All this was hard to square with the testimony of responsible
people who had had a rare glimpse of the mystic, or had heard
him speak. Thus, after he had "come out" briefly to denounce
the fraudulent Clifford Irving biography, and spoken by long-
distance telephone to seven newspaper correspondents whom
he knew, he proceeded to Nicaragua where US Ambassador
Turner Shelton saw him at Managua airport and described him
as "looking very well . . . very alert . . . very personable".

Whatever the truth, Hughes went into seclusion at the Bayshore
Hotel when he flew into Vancouver on March 14, 1972. With no
less than fifteen aides, he took the entire nineteenth and twentieth
floors at the top of the Bayshore towers, and imposed a tight veil
of security. Special closed-circuit TV screens guarded the fire-
escapes. When a Vancouver *Sun* team tried to take an elevator
to the top floor of the tower, it was discovered that the elevator

would not go beyond the eighteenth floor. The hotel manager, Warren Anderson (who confessed that he had not laid eyes on Hughes), explained that Hughes and his party had requested keys with which to lock the elevator controls to their floors. A new lock had also been placed on the inside of the fire door.

All this was extremely frustrating for the dozen-odd lurking *Sun* reporters and photographers, and back at the office managing editor Bill Galt and city editor Patrick Nagle were bemoaning their fate. "We're getting nowhere," Galt grumbled. "What can we do to keep this story alive?"

It was at this juncture that I mentioned to them my having met Hughes in 1946.

In the classic newspaper injunction, Galt bellowed: "For God's sake, don't *tell* it — *write* it!" So I sat down at a typewriter and recounted the following incident which dated from my earlier years at *Time*.

One day *Time's* managing editor Roy Alexander had called me into his office and asked me to write Medicine until the regular editor returned from a sabbatical.

"I don't know anything about medicine," I'd said.

"Nothing to it," said Alexander, grinning. "You'll have a trained biochemist as a researcher, and a doctor comes in every Monday night to check copy for accuracy." Warming to his pitch, he threw his arms up and cried: "Stu, think of the excitement of it all! The romance of medicine! Through the vagina with gun and camera!"

So for six weeks I had written Medicine. One assignment took me to San Francisco for the annual meeting of the American Medical Association and led to a stop-over in Los Angeles. It was there, on the morning of July 7, 1946 that Sid James, then the Los Angeles bureau chief, had called me and said: "How would you like to meet Howard Hughes?"

I told him I would be delighted.

"He's out at Burbank testing a new plane," James said. "Let's run out and have a chat with him."

En route James explained that Hughes was not much given to talking to reporters. After long Hollywood experience with press agents, and some unfavourable publicity, he was quietly edging over into anonymity. But James had written honestly about Hughes, had won his confidence; hence the invitation.

An astonishing sight met us when we arrived at Burbank. A

ladder was propped up against the imposing tail of the XF-11, a new, twin-engined plane designed for army photographic reconnaissance. Atop the ladder was a tall, wiry man who seemed to be plastering the rudder with long strips of masking tape. It was Hughes.

After a few minutes' tinkering, he clambered down the ladder and came over to shake hands. He was wearing what was apparently the Hughes "uniform" — a straw hat, white shirt open at the neck, rumpled grey slacks and running shoes. I guessed his height to be six-foot two or three.

He greeted us cordially. "Got a problem there today," he said. "Don't imagine I'll take her off until I get that tail fixed — probably just run her up and down the field for a while."

He and James fell into easy conversation, mostly about the aircraft. It was described as "experimental", was reputed to be the fastest, newest twin-engine plane ever built and had cost $8 million. I could determine nothing odd or eccentric about Hughes' behaviour. His record as a young pilot, and his extraordinary success in enhancing his father's tool business spoke for itself.

After half an hour or so, Hughes went to the plane, climbed into the cockpit, and started up the engines. We lingered a little longer, watching him run the aircraft up and down the field without attempting to take off. Then we left.

I was standing at a bar later in the afternoon when the telephone rang. The bartender answered it, then came back and said: "There's been an awful plane crash, right into the residential section of Beverly Hills."

"I'll bet it's Howard Hughes," I said.

Later that day the news-boys came out into the traffic, waving late editions with banner headlines: Hughes' plane had indeed crashed and he was critically injured. Less than ten minutes after take-off, the plane had developed motor trouble and Hughes had realized he was going to crash. He tried to reach a nearby golf course but couldn't make it and plowed into three homes — one of them owned by the chief army interpreter at the Nuremberg trials. There was a parachute aboard, but Hughes did not attempt to use it. Friends later said he disregarded personal danger in an attempt to save his new aircraft from becoming a total wreck.

His injuries were immense: his chest and left lung crushed, collar-bone fractured, twelve ribs broken, possible skull fracture, badly-burned left hand, broken nose and contusions. A young US Marine sergeant named William Lloyd Durkin was generally credited with saving Hughes' life. He had plunged into the burning wreckage and pulled the pilot out. It was reported later that Hughes set the young sergeant up with a life-time annuity.

At the Good Samaritan hospital Hughes asked the doctor: "Am I going to live?"

"I don't know," the doctor replied.

Then Hughes did an astonishing thing. "I want to give this message to the army," he said, and proceeded to dictate a detailed account of procedures leading to the crash, adding: "I don't want this to happen to somebody else."

An equally remarkable demonstration of Hughes' sinew was revealed a month later. Unhappy with his hospital bed, he called in some plant engineers and designed a "tailor-made" bed, complete with hot and cold running water. It was built in six sections and had thirty electric motors. One of his associates remarked: "I thought the damned thing was going to fly," but the push-button features Hughes installed were credited with easing his pain during the thirty-seven days he spent in hospital.

Hughes was once quoted as saying: "What I am tremendously interested in is science."

I wrote this story for the *Sun* in 1972, reporting that back in 1946 I had found Hughes "a courteous, civilized and highly intelligent 'technical man' ", and concluding with the words: "I hope he can find some happiness, however brief, here in Vancouver."

Two days later I received a telephone call from Dick Hannah, Hughes' public relations man. Hannah said that Hughes had liked my article and would like to talk to me.

At a time when every medium was starving for news of the mystery man, this was a stunning invitation.

I said to Hannah: "I don't think for a minute that Hughes will remember me — but he will certainly remember Sid James."

Hannah replied: "As a matter of fact, he does think he remembers you. He would like to meet you and chat about the accident. Does 3:30 or 4 p.m. this afternoon (a Sunday) seem workable?"

I decided to play it cool. I told Hannah that I had a commitment to take my family to a hockey game but would be home by 4:30. Would he call me then?

At 5:30 Hannah called and asked if the meeting could be postponed. "The boss apologized," said Hannah, "but a few things came up and he asked me to call to see if Monday morning was all right. The boss wants to block out the time 10 to 12 as he does not want to rush it when you do meet."

I told Hannah I would look forward to it. Privately, I concluded that I had blown a great exclusive for the *Sun*; what I was getting was the familiar run-around.

But at 11:15 a.m. on Monday Hannah came to my office, asked if I had a private line, and placed a call to Howard Hughes. This was the first indication that our "meeting" would be by telephone.

Hughes greeted me cordially. He spoke with a strong voice, perhaps a bit louder than usual, as is common with people with a hearing deficiency. (Hannah had told me that Hughes normally employed an amplifier in his telephone.) When I began with a remark about Vancouver's coolish weather Hughes said that, after the heat of the Bahamas and Nicaragua, it was "wonderful" in Vancouver, which he thought was a great city. He liked the cool air and was delighted with the prospect of the mountains on this sunny day.

The conversation lasted more than forty-five minutes and was preponderantly about aircraft. In fact, Hughes said that the purpose of his visit was to study the possibilities of getting Hughes Air West into Vancouver; he knew that various airlines were compelled to stop in Seattle, and thought that this was silly.

What convinced me that that the man at the other end of the line was Howard Hughes was his detailed recollection of our conversation on July 7, 1946, twenty-six years earlier.

"Oh yes," he recalled, "Sid James was a good friend of mine. He was doing a cover story on me for *Time* and wanted to check a couple of points." I knew that to be true, but had forgotten it.

I said to Hughes: "I seem to recall your mentioning, after the crash, something about a steering difficulty with the plane."

Hughes launched into a long, technical description of his troubles. It was not the steering that was at fault; a warning button told him the landing gear was malfunctioning. While his dials indicated full power, the engines weren't responding sufficiently to give him the lift indicated. There was "a terrible yaw" and it was like "pulling against a forty-foot board fence". Hughes' intricate and vivid description of the accident left no doubt in my mind that he was the person involved.

"Did it leave any scars?"

Hughes laughed and replied: "Not externally, at any rate — maybe internally, who knows?"

Hughes went on to talk about a wide variety of planes — his second version of the XF-11 "which might be classed as a failure, since it never went into full-scale production"; the Spruce Goose, which flew about a mile at a height of seventy feet, and was later stored for years in a warehouse; the Lockheed 101-1, the jet he had flown to Vancouver from Nicaragua; the Vickers Viscount, which he had first flown out of Montreal; the SST (on which he thought the government had made the right decision, even if it did cripple Boeing); and the DC-8 which (astonishingly) he said he had never flown.

In the course of this, he took off on some technical language which only another aeronautical engineer could understand. He talked about the twenty-eight cylinders on the XF-11 ("made it look like a corn-cob"); about fat propeller blades, about torque and thrust and other arcane principles of aviation.

He also recalled that he had visited Vancouver for a month in August of 1942, in the plane he had flown around the world in approximately three days. While here he met Yvonne de Carlo, the Vancouver actress, and (laughingly) "spent one of the finest months of my life." He had played golf, he said, at a course near the mountains, with a "Tudor-style clubhouse with some white stone" — easily identified as Capilano.

Hughes said that he felt "a bit penned in" at the Bayshore and wished he could be out flying. He had been watching small float planes land in the harbour and "some of them were pretty bumpy".

I asked Hughes when he proposed to end his isolation and meet the press.

He said: "I'll probably do it in three stages. First, I'll get a new picture taken, to prove to people I'm all right and not incapacitated, as some people have said. Second, I feel an obligation to those seven newsmen who were on the telephone line with me about the Clifford Irving book fraud. I would like to see them first as they have been very good and helpful; maybe I could get them up here. Then, when that's out of the way, I'd like to see

135

you and talk to you." In the meantime, he said, there was quite a lot of heat on him to meet the press. "But I'm not the kind of fellow who would just walk into the press room and say 'Here I am, fellows' — I'd be scared of that."

"It's been nice talking to you," I said, "and I'd certainly like to meet you before you leave Vancouver, Mr. Hughes."

"Hey, let's forget that 'Mr. Hughes' stuff. Surely we know each other well enough to use first names even on the telephone. I'm Howard. Okay, Stuart?"

Hughes indicated that he would be in Vancouver for several days yet. He had "no idea this country was breaking out as fast as it was". Just before noon the conversation ended.

Dick Hannah had stayed in my office and heard the entire talk. I said to him: "Do you think Hughes would mind if I wrote a simple story, saying we had chatted, leaving out any confidential material (his quest for new air routes), and merely recording some of his observations about Vancouver?"

Hannah said no, it should be treated as off the record. Otherwise, they would be inundated with requests for exclusive interviews.

Later, over lunch, I asked Hannah why so much secrecy surrounded the moves of his client.

"Because," he said, "of all the litigation involved with TWA; investigations by the Nevada Gaming Commission; personal lawsuits; and dangers of being misquoted, which could be damaging to Hughes' 50,000 employees."

What was the Hughes domestic situation? "None. His first wife was Ella Rice, of the Houston family. No children. Howard was twenty-three when they were divorced. Then Jean Peters. He was sorry to lose her."

As everyone knows, Hughes died in a private jet, en route from Acapulco to his home town of Houston in April 1976. Thus, after four frustrating years, I felt free to write the story of our Vancouver conversation. Not that it was all that important. But I felt, in fairness, that the public was entitled to know that four years before his death Hughes was in full command of his faculties and spoke with the vibrant good humour of a well man.

One former Hughes associate, a fugitive in Vancouver from tax evasion charges in Nevada, insisted publicly that Hughes had died in 1970. That, of course, would have made my interview a complete fantasy. I was grateful when some documents were discovered, logging Hughes' activities while at the Bayshore, and confirming the fact that we had talked on March 20, 1972.

# Chapter 14

"A man had better make his son a tinker than a printer. The laws of tin he can understand but the law of libel is uncertain, unwritten and undefinable. It is one thing today and another thing tomorrow. No man can tell what it is."

— *John Almon*

When I eventually retired from the Vancouver *Sun* I received a nice note from a senior reporter named Martha Robinson, wishing me well but adding: "I was never quite sure exactly what a publisher does."

She wasn't the only one. In the industry itself, the title seemed to vary from one country to another. In Britain, it indicated a concern with distribution and circulation. In the United States, more often than not, it meant "owner". When I asked an American friend to define his responsibility as publisher, he grinned mischievously and replied: "When I say 'go' they go, and when I say 'come' they come."

In Canada, it reflected a mix. Most independent newspapers were operated by family proprietors — the Dennises in Halifax, McConnells in Montreal, the Atkinson-Honderichs in Toronto, Siftons in Winnipeg, Graybiels in Windsor, Whiteheads in Brandon, Currans in the Sault, Matsons in Victoria.

But the advent of the chains changed all this. As their reach and influence grew and the family interest declined, owners began to appoint "hired executives", a new breed who managed the business but had no fundamental financial clout. Their rewards came in superior salaries and, in certain rare instances, stock participation which guaranteed them a comfortable retirement.

138

Max Bell preferred to call his FP appointees "publishers" on the shrewd theory that a portentous title provided a bit of ego-stroking which cost no dollars. When he acquired the Lethbridge *Herald* he promptly promoted its editor, Cleo Mowers, to the position of publisher. Bell's FP partner Victor Sifton — who had inherited the title from Sir Clifford and was thus an owner-publisher in the pure sense of the word — objected on the grounds that this sacred designation should not be bandied about indiscriminately. But Bell persisted and his faith was handsomely fulfilled when Mowers built the *Herald* into an influential (and profitable) voice of southern Alberta.

If a "journalist" was described in the craft as "a reporter with his coat on", then a publisher could be described as "a journalist with a Homburg hat". Not that all publishers were journalists. As competition for the advertising dollar with TV, radio and magazines grew, more and more newspaper heads were recruited from the ranks of advertising executives and business-management consultants.

In Vancouver, the duties of the publisher were clearly defined. The Sun-Southam agreement decreed that the publisher was directly responsible for the successful operation of four departments: editorial (the news-gathering function), advertising, circulation and promotion. He set salaries for his executives and other non-union people, within guidelines (an increase for anyone earning more than $30,000 a year had to be approved by a salary committee of Pacific Press). He could hire, and he could fire, though only for "gross misconduct".

What was, perhaps, even more significant was the area in which he did *not* directly participate — a sort of demilitarized zone embracing labour relations, the purchase of newsprint, and mechanical production of the newspaper. This, inevitably, led to frustrations and a lack of communication which exacerbated prickly labour disputes.

To the public, the publisher was the spokesman for the paper. He was also (as I learned to my sorrow) legally responsible for every line of copy printed. Not infrequently he found himself served with an action over some story published while he was out of the country and of which he was totally ignorant. The bailiff and I became good friends. A bit apologetically, he would shuffle into the office with a blue paper (the writ), drop it on the publisher's desk, make a few genial observations about the weather, and depart. The publisher in turn would simply bung the document off to the company lawyer and await developments.

As a guard against libel, a lawyer in the building was retained to check sensitive stories and warn of impending disasters. But the ultimate decision — to print or not to print — remains with the publisher. As a general rule, newspaper lawyers tend to be conservative, and are regarded with amused condescension by journalists, who much prefer Hugh Cudlipp's famous injunction: "Publish and be damned!"

For the reader who is sure he has been slandered, there is always the advice of Edward Everett: "Do nothing! Half the people who bought the paper never saw the article. Half of those who saw it did not read it. Half of those who read it did not understand it. Half those who understood it did not believe it. Half of those who believed it are of no account anyway."

I was at first bemused, in moving from Victoria to Vancouver, by the startling increase in sheer bumph that fetched up on my desk. No matter how assiduously I addressed myself to the opening wave, I could not leave my office for ten minutes without returning to find a fresh pile on my desk. In a veritable torrent they descended: government communiqués, copies of speeches, appeals for money, trade papers, new books, magazines, invitations, press releases both bizarre and bewildering. Somehow or other, for example, I got onto the mailing list of a Los Angeles firm named Solters and Roskin: they were publicists for a rock band and dutifully informed me of contracts negotiated for each new gig.

From time to time — particularly during an election, when partisan juices flowed freely — the mail took on a sinister tone and death threats were not uncommon. Most of them were the work of cranks but a few seemed to warrant further investigation. When, for instance, the *Sun* ran a series of articles exposing a wayward cabinet minister, I received a single-page, typewritten message which said, simply: "We're going to get you. If not today, tomorrow, or next year." This stark warning disturbed me enough to notify the police, who responded promptly by sending to my office a detective named (I am *not* making this up) Dick Tracy. Mr. Tracy took the letter but could find no fingerprints and advised me to forget it.

On another occasion my wife and I returned from the theatre to find our house smeared with doggy-do — windows, door-knobs and knockers. A statue Letha had created for our front garden had been wrenched from its base but abandoned because it was simply too heavy to cart away.

A different statue, this time a public one, also came in for rough treatment. When the two Pacific Press papers moved to their elegant new premises in December of 1964, they effected the shift from downtown over a weekend, without missing an edition. But the shot-gun marriage had scarcely been consummated before the principals became involved in a quarrel which set the whole town laughing.

It had been agreed that a sum not to exceed $50,000 would be set aside to grace the new building with art-work. Sculptor Jack Harmon was commissioned and in due course submitted a mock-up which he called "Family Group". It showed a father and mother and two children, the mother holding a little girl in her arms and the father standing stoically behind his son. With some of the prudery common to medical art-work, Harmon had presented the two males without reproductive equipment. Fair enough. The mock-up was approved by the *Province* publisher at the time, Fred Auger, and by myself, and Harmon proceeded to create a larger-than-life sculpture of considerable power.

But with a difference. When the finished work was hoisted into place, in a garden in front of Pacific Press, it was discovered that the young boy had suddenly sprouted a penis. The father had not. This was, at the very least, a biological contradiction which puzzled many viewers and enraged Fred Auger, who argued that Harmon had breached his contract with the ad-lib appendage.

Very soon, "Family Group" became the target of collegiate high-jinks and morality groups. An elderly woman telephoned me in near-hysteria to cry: "I have to avert my eyes when the bus stops in front of your building. How *dare* you show that little boy's privates in public!" After a series of clandestine raids, the offending organ became a sort of hitching-post for a variety of ornaments: a glazed doughnut, a garland of buttercups, even a condom.

But worse was yet to come: some students, believed to be UBC engineers, painted the boy's penis bright red, to appreciative guffaws from passers-by. I called Pacific Press's manager Ed Benson and asked him if one of his maintenance men could remove the paint. The emissary assigned to this task (who said it was embarrassing to perform such an act on busy Granville Street) unfortunately decided to do the job with Brillo. The result was twofold: the red gave way to a gleaming bronze, and the statue was immediately christened by staff members as *"Le coq d'or."*

Not long after I received a telephone call from Richard Simmins, curator of the Vancouver Art Gallery. "When can we come up and get the statue?" he asked.

"I don't know what you're talking about," I replied.

"Fred Auger says we can have it for the Gallery."

"The hell you can," I said.

Nor did we yield.

At the end of a year, "Family Group" was accepted as a part of the Vancouver landscape. It was a first — the first-ever nude statue in the city. Some people even professed to like it.

Because of the *Sun's* circulation and clout in the community, invitations flowed in at the rate of a dozen a week — from art galleries (of which there were twenty-eight in Vancouver), new restaurants, theatre openings, consular dinners, symphony and opera concerts, sports benefits, touring cabinet ministers and financial houses celebrating the arrival of a president or appointment of a new bank manager.

The latter occasions quickly assumed a pattern. Perhaps 150 to 200 of the city's financial gurus would assemble at 5 o'clock in a social suite of the Hotel Vancouver, the Four Seasons, the Bayshore or the Hyatt. Rich *hors d'oeuvres* simmered over copper braziers in the centre of the room. In a corner, a cocktail pianist tinkled some discreet background roundelays. The company officials, each adorned with a red or white carnation, received the guests, who for two hours would gather in knots, chatting with exactly the same people they had left at the office an hour earlier. The conversation was entirely predictable: the crippling burdens of taxation, the intransigence of the unions, the gaucheries of the press, the vagaries of the market, the stupidity of politicians.

Inevitably, it became necessary to develop a technique for early escape. First, a brisk charge through the receiving line. Then a furtive drift over to the food tables and the most remote of the three bars, a wink at the pianist, a gliding exit through the far door.

Obviously, some ground-rules were called for. Very early in the game, my wife and I decided to give up on cocktail parties, except where close personal friends or family were involved. Post-theatre receptions, which meant very late hours, were abandoned. Government House garden parties, where as many as 2,000 guests trampled the flowers, were avoided.

No doubt each publisher in Canada evolved a style of his own. It was said of Beland ("Bee") Honderich of the Toronto *Star* that he showed up at his office at 6 a.m., supervised the lay-out and make-up of each edition, presided over an editorial conference, took lunch at his desk, attended to the multifarious duties of his burgeoning empire in the afternoon and carried work away with him when he left, usually after 6 p.m. A crushing schedule, and certainly beyond my capacity, but one which met the ultimate test: for Honderich and the *Star,* it worked, and worked well.

My own day began at 7 a.m. with a little light exercise, five minutes on the stationary bicycle, fifteen minutes in the swimming pool, a hefty breakfast, and a drive of five minutes to the office. (On especially health-conscious days, I would walk to work. That took about fifteen minutes.)

The general rule we followed was that the morning belonged to that day's newspaper, the afternoon was for visitors, meetings, forward planning and (after 5) reading, when the office was quiet.

Thus when I arrived at my desk around 9 a.m. the first job was to cast a quick eye over proofs of the opinion pages, editorials and columns which had been made up the night before. Only rarely were changes called for; a phrase here, a potentially-libellous word there. I refused to let Doug Collins describe the Prime Minister as "a creep" and accepted his alternative: "a disaster". The most libel-prone member of our staff, Allan Fotheringham, screamed when his trenchant prose was touched but it remained a fact that, over a period of ten years, I killed exactly one of his columns in its entirety.

The mail, carefully winnowed down to a manageable pile by my diligent secretary, Hilda Weston, provided an endless bag of despair and delight. Policy was to attempt a personal reply to each letter, although I confess to a certain puzzlement over the proper protocol in dealing with a correspondent who began *his* letter: "Listen, you Commie sonofabitch . . ." To a woman who addressed me as "a spaniel", I replied with a two-word letter

("Arf! Arf!") and in a surprising number of instances I was able to assuage anguished breasts with H. L. Mencken's famous injunction: "You may be right."

Sometime during the morning the managing editor would come in with a catalogue of *his* problems: he had lost a deskman and wanted to hire a new boy. Jim Kearney wanted to go to the hockey matches in Czechoslovakia; it would cost $2,500. And, hey (the managing editor always began his pitches with the word 'hey'), here's a new comic strip from the *Star* syndicate which will be bigger than *Peanuts*.

This last request would be referred, automatically, to the strangest committee in all Canadian journalism. Called "the comics committee", it consisted of the managing editor, the women's editor (Ann Barling), the rock critic (Vaughn Palmer), a city-hall reporter (Randy Glover) and myself. Ex-officio was a labour reporter named Rod Mickleborough, appointed on the curious grounds that he was the only journalist in Canada who thought the comic strip *Nancy* was great.

Ann was there because she was believed to be a woman of impeccable taste. I was included because my brother, Jeff, was a cartoonist and I therefore enjoyed a symbiotic relationship with the craft. My credentials were jeopardized, however, when I made so bold as to cancel the strip called *Rex Morgan, M.D.* The subsequent uproar was so vivid, and so vitriolic, that the CBC morning show called me at home, and I volunteered an abject, on-air apology. Dr. Morgan, needless to say, resumed his practice in the *Sun*. My credibility was slightly restored when the morning *Province* made a fundamental mistake and I pounced on it. Defying a maxim of the craft — "never cancel a dog strip" — the *Province* let Fred Bassett off his leash. The *Sun* promptly picked him up and he became a blue-ribbon winner in every readership survey.

At 11 o'clock the first edition rolled off the press, calling for a quick check with the managing editor on his plans for a remake of inside pages or play of home-edition headlines. Thence off to lunch, occasionally in the staff cafeteria but more frequently in the genial ambience of Toulouse-Lautrec, a splendid French restaurant just five minutes from the office. Once a week I lunched with the Round Table, where twenty-five or thirty of Vancouver's elder statesmen gathered to discuss affairs of the day. At least twice a week I ate with a *Sun* editor or columnist, often joined

144

by "the Oatmeal Savage", Jack Webster, or other blithe spirits who were *au courant* with town gossip. A basic tenet of the craft, we believed, was that a newspaper should know what was going on in its town, even if it could not be printed.

In the afternoon, the delegations descended. Most of them were pleasant people, willing to discuss their problems in a rational and equable manner. Others were blatantly hostile. A picture of an Arab mother holding a dead baby in her arms, victim of an Israeli bombing attack, provoked a violent reaction from the Jewish community. Identification of a machete murderer as an East Indian invoked charges of racism. The right-wing column of Doug Collins brought insistent demands that he be shot, or otherwise disposed of, as an agent of fascism. (The fact that Collins had fought fascism for five years and escaped from nine prisoner-of-war camps during World War II was conveniently ignored.)

A frequent late-afternoon caller was Jack Wasserman, the columnist. Wasserman was a remarkable journalist. He knew just about everything that was going on in Vancouver but would not publish until he had checked and re-checked his facts. A Supreme Court judge told me that he considered Wasserman the best reporter in Vancouver. Certainly every survey showed him at or near the top in *Sun* readership. But for all his confident bearing and streets-smart demeanour, "Wass" remained a very insecure person. Any criticism of his column, however mild, gave him a severe case of the galloping fantods. At contract time, when negotiations became tense, he ran between labour and management officials, desperately offering home-grown solutions and trying to ascertain which way to jump.

On one notable occasion he decided to jump to radio, as a talk-show host on CJOR. In actual fact, Pacific Press reached agreement on a contract a few hours before Wasserman was to make his radio debut. The *Sun* pointed this out to him, and urged him to come home, but he insisted that he had signed a contract with CJOR and could not reverse his field.

His debut as a radio host became something of a media legend. The radio station had decided to introduce him with a fanfare worthy of the Second Coming. A roll of drums. A blast of trumpets. And then a doomsday voice, heavy with emotion: "And now, here he is! Vancouver's top reporter, bringing you comment and insights into the major stories of the day. Timely! Topical! Significant! For free, frank discussions of the salient issues, phone Wasserman. And now the lines are open . . ."

The reedy voice of a very old lady came on the telephone: "Oh, Mr. Wasserman," she wailed, "I'm having *such* a time with my corns. I'd be ever so grateful if you could suggest a remedy."

In due course it became evident that hot-line radio was not Jack's proper medium. He was, as somebody noted at the time, too *nice* a guy to compete with the blustering microphone behaviour of Webster and the rest. Eventually Wasserman returned to the *Sun* as a contract writer and embarked on a new career as a CBC television interviewer, which he did very well. The whole community was shocked when "Wass" collapsed and died while speaking at a Hotel Vancouver "roast" of the BC logger-politician, Gordon Gibson. In an unprecedented action, City Council designated a busy downtown corner as "Wasserman's Beat" and erected a street sign in his honour. His memorial service, in a Unitarian church, was attended by politicians, judges, night-club proprietors, journalists, artists, race-track touts, waiters, chorus girls, jockeys and even a religious fanatic who cried out that Wasserman wouldn't be dead if he had been a little kinder to the Pope in his column.

Access to the publisher's office by way of an "open door" policy, while good in theory, was not without its difficulties. Too often, staffers attempted to get me involved in some personal quarrel with their editors. A secretary implored me to fire a switch-board operator because "she had trenchmouth, and was endangering the health of the entire building". (I advised her to take it up with the Newspaper Guild.) A medical writer quit rather than tone down a series he had written on LSD. (I had asked him to lean more heavily on the perils of the hallucigen.) A delegation of angry women reporters demanded that I chastise columnist Paul St. Pierre because he used the phrase: "Sucking at the nation's tits." (I promised them we would give St. Pierre some spelling lessons.)

For years I wondered if it would ever be possible to create a happy newsroom, free of office politics. In the end I concluded (with supporting evidence from other papers) that it was an impossibility: that we were dealing with 175 disparate talents and

146

egos and that friction was a necessary concomitant of a lively newspaper.

Underlying all these factors was the publisher's responsibility to show a profit for his shareholders. In this respect the *Sun* was, if not unique, at least privileged. With the Vancouver afternoon field clear to itself, in a growth territory, it racked up astonishing revenues: in one year, $17 million in classified advertising alone. The only problem was to keep costs from going through the roof, which was not easy. Seven tough unions demanded healthy increases each year. Newsprint went from a pre-war $36 a ton to $325, then to $425. The cost of modern press units and a new computer system was staggering.

At the same time, it was absolutely essential to expand news-coverage and develop specialists — in science, medicine, education and government. When I went to the *Sun* in 1964, its newsroom budget was $1.5 million; when I left fourteen years later, it had grown to $6 million. Even so, that was only 10 per cent of gross revenue. The prospect for the 1980s was a dramatic rise in costs.

Indeed it is a strange industry altogether for the 1980s. Ask yourself: is there another business quite like it? Where the product may vary wildly, in size and content, from day to day, but always sells for a fixed price? Where, having gone through a sophisticated laser system straight out of NASA, it is handed over to a twelve-year-old boy with a frog in his pocket, who *throws* it at the customer?

It seems inevitable that publishers of the new decade will have to spend more and more time in the counting-house; that they will be recruited from the ranks of MBAs, chartered accountants and engineers. But there is a danger here, for this negates the Arthur Irwin precept (with which I agree) that "journalism is for journalists". What matters in creating the character of a newspaper is not the bottom line but the editorial line.

For example, one important attribute of a publisher is to know not only what to put *in* a newspaper but what to leave *out*. This, to a large degree, establishes the tone of the paper.

It is a curious fact, not much thought-about, that newspapers remain today one of the last bastions of media "respectability", while movies, literature and TV have all succumbed. To my knowledge only one Canadian newspaper (the *Globe and Mail*) has printed the basic four-letter word and it did so, it explained, because the quotation involved a prime minister and in a certain context was the only accurate way of reporting what was said.

Critics of newspapers have argued that they are guilty of a lack of taste (or sensitivity) in other directions — the exploitation of human grief, for instance, in news-pictures. Is it an invasion of privacy to publish a wire-photo of a wailing mother with a dead child in her arms? What purpose is served by a series of pictures of a Negro woman falling to her death from a blazing apartment roof? Is it necessary to show the Vietnamese officer blowing the head off a miscreant with a hand-gun?

The journalistic defence, of course, is that we live in an imperfect world. These things happen. It is the duty of newspapers to "hold the mirror up to life", to show society as it really is, rather than as we would *like* it to be.

A more serious charge against newspapers, in my view, is cynicism. A healthy *scepticism* is a positive asset to reporters but cynicism is different. It assumes that nothing in society is altruistic, that everyone is motivated by self-interest. It is reflected in churlish stories, sour front pages and an almost complete lack of optimism and/or good will.

Down through the years, one of my most persistent problems was to persuade editors to get a little "breeze" into the news columns and to concede that there were some good people left in the world. To be sure, I had encountered men who were scoundrels and cheats and bullies; I had also known some of integrity, generosity and compassion, who were worthy of support. I recall once asking for an editorial tribute, short but sincere, to a truly outstanding citizen whose good works were manifest throughout Vancouver. The first draft of the editorial submitted began: "Anyone can be a philanthropist if he has a lot of money to give away." I tossed it in the waste-basket and wrote the editorial myself.

It is, however, perhaps understandable if a reporter approaches his job with a chip on his shoulder. He has been conned in a hundred political speeches, handed self-serving press releases and defrauded by hyped-up "non-events". So, in the fullness of time, he abandons his girlish laughter and takes as his slogan the hostile phrase: "Show me." But in spite of his toughness — or

148

perhaps *because* of it — he remains one of the most useful persons in the country.

For both publisher and reporter Malcolm Muggeridge summed it up very well: "The only fun of journalism is that it puts you in contact with the eminent without being under the necessity to admire them or take them seriously. It is the ideal profession for those who find power fascinating and its exercise abhorrent."

# Chapter 15

"Some men spoil a good story by sticking to the facts."

— *Bob Edwards*

In his foreword to Mark Edgar Nichols' classic *CP — The Story of The Canadian Press,* the late Leonard W. Brockington wrote:

> It could be well argued that no single happening helped more than the founding of The Canadian Press to fashion the pattern of modern Canada, to harmonize our warring economies in a growing unity and to give shape and substance not only to our apprehension of ourselves but also to our knowledge of the world forces which govern our destinies.

In short, The Canadian Press, over long years and through the efforts of a thousand unknown, dedicated men and women, stitched the country together. As a non-profit co-operative, its mandate was simple: to exchange news between papers, to present that news in a calm, unbiased way, and to manage its affairs in a democratic "one paper — one vote" manner.

The CP Style Book, bible of the association, says: "CP's purpose is unbiased, fearless recording of a demonstrable fact. Accuracy is fundamental. Good taste is a dominant factor. Being reliable is more important than being fast. Straightforward writing . . . assures clarity."

Some of the news it gathers itself, some of it comes from outside by exchange arrangements, but most of it originates with the 109 newspapers in its membership. In every Canadian newsroom a small frame notice reminds members that they are required to "make a dupe" of each story to be examined by CP and, if deemed usable, to be fed into the wire. Thus, if each newsroom in Canada employs an average of ten reporters, then a nation-wide army of 1,000 or more reporters is at work daily in the interests of the national co-operative.

After sorting, re-writing and editing, The Canadian Press distributes this news flow to its members (75 per cent of whom depend on it totally for outside news) for display to an estimated 13.5 million newspaper readers in Canada. Thus CP head office on King Street in Toronto, with sixty editors and thirty communications men, is the "action central" of newsgathering in the nation. The service spends $18 million a year but makes no profit and declares no dividends. The annual budget is calculated and met by lumping the general charges — such as wire rental and salaries — and dividing them, city by city, on the basis of circulation. This leads to an inestimable benefit, the larger papers helping the smaller and the English-language helping the French, which are outnumbered on a ratio of about 8-1.

The Canadian Press is run by its general manager and directed by a nineteen-member board. Each member, regardless of size, has one vote. To ensure that large groups or chains like Thomson's or Southam's do not create an imbalance, three directors are appointed at large.

Today CP staff numbers 500 of whom more than half are members of the editorial side. Internationally, CP has contractual links with the Associated Press, Reuters and Agence France-Presse.

Across Canada there are eight bureaus — Halifax, Quebec, Montreal, Ottawa, Toronto, Winnipeg, Edmonton and Vancouver. Staff correspondents are stationed at St. John's, Saint John, Fredericton, Regina, Calgary and Victoria. Two staffers are maintained in New York, Washington and London. Obviously a large portion of CP's budget is for wire rentals across its 55,000-mile system. One-quarter of CP members receive a service known as Data-file which is a computer-to-computer delivery of the full CP report at an incredible 1,200 words a minute.

Since July of 1972 CP has moved into computerized editing and routing of news, resulting in important time-savings and faster deadlines. At the heart of the innovations — first of their kind in Canada — is a sort of combined typewriter and television set, known as a VDT or videodisplay terminal (which some staffers translate as "terminal VD"), linked to a storage-and-retrieval computer.

Though the newspapers and the electronic media continue to scramble aggressively for advertising dollars, they work together in the gathering and dissemination of news. This was made possible with the creation in 1953 of a new CP company called Broadcast News Ltd. which, for a negotiated fee, serves more than 340 private radio and TV stations and more than 100 cable TV outlets. "Voice reports" — on-the-spot transmissions from the field — are inserted into radio newscasts at about 100 stations. Another division, Press News, supplies copy to the Canadian Broadcasting Corporation.

For a quarter of a century, from 1945 to 1969, the architect and builder of CP was a man named Gillis Purcell. Because he believed it was a general manager's duty to stay in the background he was not widely known outside the craft. *Inside* the business, he was a legend in his lifetime: a demanding, ornery, stubborn taskmaster and at the same time a sensitive, thoughtful fellow. In the harsh judgement of Sydney Gruson, who rose from copy-boy at Canadian Press to vice-president of The New York *Times,* Purcell beat people down in order to indulge the satisfaction of building them up again. His most exasperating fault, according to I. Norman Smith of the Ottawa *Journal,* was that "he was damn near always right".

Purcell's philosophy on staff relations was summed up in a memo sent to a friend who was having problems with a fractious newsroom:

You mention staff troubles . . . and asked whether the *Star* and *Globe and Mail* were suffering from losing guys to PR and advertising — maybe because management is 'too tough' and advertising.

I'd take a close look at the people leaving before worrying about your guys being 'too tough'. They've got results over the years and it's better to change the material than try to change them. Just the same it is a fact that it's harder to find young guys who want to be blasted (never was easy) and old guys who won't cry when they're crabbed at. But I don't think there's any cure except maybe more pats on the back. If your supervisors quit supervising properly, you're sunk.

Like many another successful Canadian journalist, Purcell came out of the west. From the age of twelve he was educated at bilingual St. Boniface College, just across the Red River from his home in Winnipeg. His father was a printer and journalist who ended his career as King's Printer for the Province of Manitoba. To help pay his way through the University of Manitoba, the younger Purcell submitted feature stories and drawings to the Winnipeg *Free Press* and after graduation, found a job on the weekly Hanna (Alberta) *Herald* before moving on as a sports writer to the Windsor *Border Cities Star,* now known as the Windsor *Star.*

When Purcell was twenty-four, J. F.B. Livesay, then general manager of CP, offered him a job in Toronto, Winnipeg or Montreal. Purcell chose Winnipeg to be near his family. By 1934 he was definitely on his way as general superintendent of CP, the second-highest job in the organization, and in 1939, when Livesay retired, the general expectation was that the ambitious, hard-hitting young superintendent would be tapped as his successor. Instead, he was passed over in favour of J. A. McNeil, a veteran who was then managing editor of the Montreal *Gazette.* The formal explanation was that Purcell, at 35, was too young for such responsibilities. The actual reason, many contemporaries believed, was that a number of publishers in the network were reluctant to have a Roman Catholic in charge. "I'm a mick and I work at it," Purcell once remarked to a colleague. "But most of my friends are not Catholics."

With the declaration of war, Purcell was assigned to organize CP's coverage — which resulted in the Canadian agency scoring some notable world "scoops". It also resulted in a personal injury which was to pain him for the rest of his life and add to the growing Purcell legend.

In late 1939 Purcell went overseas with the Canadian Army First Division and in 1940 was appointed press officer under General Andrew McNaughton. In 1941, during an Air Force exercise in England, Purcell was helping with the filming of a parachute drop of food cannisters from a Lysander aircraft when one of the parachutes failed to open and the cannister ripped into Purcell's left leg. Standing nearby was Ross Munro, later to achieve fame as Canada's top war correspondent. To Munro's utter astonishment, the still-conscious Purcell had three requests: Would somebody please retrieve the shiny new Army boot which had adorned the mangled leg? Would Ross be sure to pick up the new copy of *Time* magazine he had been carrying? And would somebody please furnish a light for the cigarette dangling from his lips?

His leg was amputated, and later the next day Purcell was sitting up in bed, smoking a cigar and dictating memos to his staff. To cheer his wife Charlotte ("archy") in Toronto, Purcell composed fanciful dispatches about a one-legged sprinter named Purcell who was the sensation of Army track meets.

It soon became apparent that Purcell regarded the accident not as a calamity but as a challenge. "Never," he told friends, "worry about something you can't do anything about." Given a newsman's perfervid curiosity, he embarked on a study of prosthetics which would have done credit to any aspiring medical student. The first artificial limb he promptly christened "Barney". But when "Barney" was superseded by a more modern metal leg, full of valves, gears and squishing sounds, the original was consigned to the flames and duly immortalized at a ceremonial wake. One of the major problems was to ensure that the new legs (eventually there were a dozen) fitted the stump. Purcell and his friend Ralph Allen, the great war correspondent and *Maclean's* editor, resolved the problem in hilarious fashion, with a little help from Greg Clark. It was Greg's glorious conceit to have Purcell's stump and artificial leg tattooed with a trout and fly; when the two met, in perfect conjunction, the leg was on right.

Having scored notable beats at Dieppe and in the invasions of Normandy, Sicily and Italy, CP came out of the war with a vastly enhanced reputation and the earned respect of such rival news-gathering agencies as Associated Press, Reuters, and United Press International. Back in Toronto, Purcell was appointed general manager in 1945 and set about building the team which would solidify CP's position as one of the finest news services of the western world.

CP types were newsmen like no others. They worked terrible hours for modest pay ("We took out our pay in fun," said the boss) and such staff benefits as Purcell could wangle from the 109 publishers who were his bosses. To other journalists, CP staffers seemed more a cult than an organization, with Purcell as the resident guru. CP men hived off from the rest, drinking together and fishing together. And always at the centre of things, excoriating sloppiness with memos that curled the paper, rewarding excellence with congratulatory notes, was Gillis Purcell.

Lionel Tiger, the sociologist, described such relationships as "male bonding". Most of the CP men had been united in the camaraderie of war correspondence, and even developed a civvy-street "uniform" — polka-dot bow ties, tweed jackets with leather elbow-patches, baggy flannels. Yet, in spite of a common *persona,* the men around Purcell were distinct individuals. As his general superintendent Purcell had chosen Charlie Bruce, a gentle Maritimer who won a Governor-General's medal for poetry. It was a bit like placing a priest in charge of a foundry, but it worked.* To run the finances of CP, he depended on a quiet Newfoundlander named Harry Day. And to direct the expanding services of Broadcast News he tapped a one-time sports writer named Charlie Edwards, who was to become as famous — and as beloved — with the electronic media as Purcell was with newspapers.

They communed together in the jargon of initials. The two that made desks jump across the nation were GP. Charlie Edwards was CBE. John Dauphinee, the successor to Bruce (and ultimately, to Purcell) was simply JD. Before long, this attenuated code was expanded to include wives, children, and even in-laws. A visitor to Purcell's office on University Avenue was bemused one day when Purcell summoned his secretary, Mary Kibblewhite, and asked her to find an FFM.

"What the hell's that?" his guest inquired.

"A fleet-footed messenger," said Purcell. And in jig time a copyboy appeared at Purcell's door.

"Get us some water," he said. "We're going to have an SFO." Again, his visitor demanded an explanation. "A short fast one," grinned Purcell. His preference was for Mount Gay (Barbados) rum. With a full glass, and puffing contentedly on a select Havana

---

* Purcell once won an award for poetry himself. Under the pseudonym of "Steve Ford," he responded to a contest in *Maclean's* magazine for the best Canadian limerick on the notorious Gerda Munsinger and her affair with some Diefenbaker cabinet ministers. His prize-winner:

> There was a young lady of Munich
> Whose bosom distended her tunic,
> Her main undertaking
> Was cabinet making
> In fashions bilingue et unique.

cigar, he appeared oblivious to time. For hours he would discuss subjects as disparate as the art of Emily Carr and the latest chess moves of Bobby Fischer. It was a practice which did not endear him to the wives of the men with whom he was talking.

Purcell might easily have restricted himself to the role of administrator since his constituency ranged over 109 newspapers and it was his duty to know the problems and personnel of each. Always there was the delicate question of financial balance between small papers and large and the question of what the smaller papers could pay. From time to time there were threats to secede, and to set up an independent, minor-league service, but here Purcell exercised his diplomatic skills to achieve agreement. Such was the publishers' faith in their general manager that special assessments were approved and budgets gradually increased. By the time he left the job, Purcell commanded a staff of more than 400 and a news-gathering budget in excess of $6 million.

If administration was a necessary evil, the more important duty, in Purcell's view, was the actual content of the wire service itself. Thus he became, in fact, the national editor of CP. He was a stickler for accuracy and the Style Book, which he wrote, became the bible of the industry and was so widely admired that it was adopted, in large measure, by the Associated Press in the United States.

Wherever he went in Canada Purcell insisted on receiving the full file of CP copy. What one of his friends described as "GP's ganglia" extended into every corner of the nation. Sometimes GP would board a train, stand "Barney" up in a corner of his stateroom as a convenient ash-tray, and spend the next three days familiarizing himself with the file.

In recognition of *le fait français* Purcell was far ahead of his contemporaries. Having mastered the language himself, he insisted on Quebec regional meetings being conducted in French. His Montreal bureau chief, Bill Stewart, was flawless in French and enjoyed the complete confidence of his French-Canadian clients. As long ago as 1951 Purcell was able to push through a French-language service which was the only one in the world utilizing an automatic teletypesetter with all the suitable accents. And in 1966 he negotiated a contract with Agence France-Presse for the exclusive use of Canada's French-language dailies.

In view of the fact that nearly 90 per cent of CP's members were English, and would foot the bill for a service they could not use themselves, this was a far-sighted contribution to the cause of national understanding.

Looking ahead to the computer age, which would revolutionize the business, Canadian Press moved to high-speed teletypesetters across the nation. Transmission of pictures by wire-photo was extended to the west coast, making possible a speedy exchange of graphics which was to brighten Canadian newspapers immeasurably.

At the same time, human values were not neglected. One of the continuing irritants for Purcell was the penchant of his publishers for raiding CP staff and picking off the brightest talents. The only way to avoid this journalistic cannibalism was to pay wire-service people a bit more than "Toronto scale", which was the highest in the country. Nobody rejoiced more than GP when, one day, a former CP man, Rae Correlli, telephoned him from his new post at the Toronto *Star* to say: "Gil, I thought you'd get a kick out of this — we're trying to get *Star* scales up to the level of CP."

A pension plan which had been instituted in 1945 was reviewed and upgraded. In negotiation with "staff counsel" — a polite euphemism for company union — hours of work were shortened, and vacations extended, so that staff benefits at the wire service compared favourably with those of the member papers.

In 1969 Purcell reached mandatory retirement at 65. At an elegant banquet in the Royal York Hotel, attended by 200 of the nation's top publishers, editors and broadcasters, the guest of honour heard himself described as "a combination of Mack the Knife and Bishop Fulton J. Sheen" who nevertheless had "mellowed like an old chain saw". His retirement gift, appropriately enough, was a pair of Orvis fishing rods, with matched reels and lines.

Inevitably, Purcell was importuned to undertake a second career, perhaps in telecommunications, or in a top editorial post. Publishers urged him to write his memoirs. Four universities offered him honorary degrees. All of these were refused. The one honour he accepted was the Order of Canada. For the rest, he was content to go fishing with Greg Clark, Bruce West and other old pals; to root for the Winnipeg Blue Bombers; and to nurture his lifelong friendships with a correspondence of staggering dimensions.

This was achieved by means of what he called his "diplomatic pouch", delivered to CP headquarters in Toronto by an FFM. At least once or twice a week Purcell would scan Toronto newspapers and magazines for stories and columns which he thought would be of interest to his buddies in far-off places. These in turn would be topped by a succinct message and addressed to SK in Vancouver, INS in Ottawa, RM in Montreal or JB in Halifax. CP would do the rest. It was, of course, a reciprocal arrangement: the ganglia in the boondocks would respond in kind, or face the prospect of a chivvying note.

Purcell's insatiable curiosity had been reflected in the newsfile. As a chess nut, he was one of the first to urge Canadian papers to carry not only a general story on the big international matches, but a chart of the individual moves. A student of political cartooning, he insisted that the art form be included in National Newspaper Awards. As an amateur ornithologist, he became concerned with the plight of the whooping crane, an endangered species. When the count on the beautiful birds got down to 57, Purcell let his correspondents know that each egg hatched, as well as each death, should be recorded on the CP file, and the result was that Canadians were as well informed on this ongoing natural drama as they were on the World Series.

Nearing the end of his long and honourable career, Purcell suffered a final, grievous blow: his wife Charlotte ("archy") died suddenly, just when they were planning a retirement cruise together. To Steve Franklin of *Weekend* magazine, Purcell mused: "It's best not to get too bloody definite about what you're going to do, because maybe Somebody Else decides it anyway."

So Purcell goes on, uncomplaining, never backing down, never conceding out loud his love for his friends, his pride in his family. A very classy citizen.

# Chapter 16

"The sweetest music is the sound of the
30-second commercial at $30 a time."

*— Lord Thomson of Fleet*

One of the special pleasures of membership in The Canadian Press was the opportunity it afforded to meet publishers and editors from almost every city and town in Canada. Of all of them, the most dynamic — and controversial — was Roy Thomson.

I first met him in 1952 at a CP annual meeting in the old library on the mezzanine floor of the Royal York in Toronto. He sat in a high-backed chair in a corner of the room, surveying his fellow publishers with the encompassing glint of a dealer in a blackjack game. He was wearing a dark, heavy, double-breasted suit which accentuated his considerable girth. His eyes twinkled behind glasses which must surely have emerged from the same factory that produced Coca-Cola bottles.

In the afternoon "bull session", at which members were invited to sound off on any subject, one of the brethren was entering a long litany of publishing woes. At his modest Ontario daily, he averred, business was terrible. Circulation was down; advertising revenue was falling; unions were giving him fits; costs were soaring; the outlook for the industry was totally hopeless.

No sooner had he concluded this lugubrious recital than Thomson jumped up.

"Wanna sell?" he demanded.

The whole room erupted in laughter, albeit a bit uneasily. Already some apprehensions about the purpose and direction of the Thomson operation had arisen. To certain members of the Old Guard, the barber's son from Toronto was a mere upstart, with little more than a decade in the business; worse, he was a communicator of a lesser breed, a former salesman of *radio* time. They were appalled by his candid confession that he was in newspapering to make money and that, given a profitability factor, he would not be averse to owning every daily in the world.

Not that the metropolitan owners had much to worry about. Roy was not too interested in the high-cost, competitive markets of Montreal, Toronto and Vancouver; indeed, as we have seen, when he determined that the Vancouver *News-Herald* would never pay, he closed it down. Instead his pattern was to seek out dailies in smaller communities which could only support one newspaper, thus assuring a monopoly. Quite often these papers were losing money. Roy seemed prepared to gamble on growth. To that end, he installed modern presses and equipment, built spanking new offices, and generally established a presence in the community, usually with some proven advertising executive as publisher. On capital expenditures, he seemed generous; on operating budgets, his parsimony was famous.

I remember once calling on a Thomson publisher (whom I cannot identify, since he is still active) who had come up through the editorial side and had sold the family business to Roy. Renowned in the trade as a wit and *bon vivant,* this fellow appeared to be in a depressed and unhappy frame of mind as he showed me into his office.

"What's the matter, Joe?" I inquired.

"I'll tell you what's the matter," he said. "Some son-of-a-bitch from Toronto was in here this morning, asking me how much money I spent last month for binder-twine."

Thomson paid what was necessary for acquisitions, usually after careful research by his Canadian chiefs, St. Clair McCabe and Ian Macdonald. In fairness it must be added that Thomson insisted both parties to the deal must be satisfied with the terms.

It is true, as Thomson often boasted, that he "left his editors alone", trusting them to assess the needs of their respective communities. The people he sometimes referred to as "poets" could say what they liked — but they had to say it within the confines of peasant-like budgets. The sad result of Roy's tight-fisted editorial policy was that the Thomson group produced no distinguished newspaper in Canada, nor (except for Orillia's James Lamb) a nationally-known editor. In essence, his papers provided a training-ground for reporters, who would jump to the big-city dailies at the first opportunity.

What many Canadian newsmen resented was the curious disparity between the native operations and those overseas. At home, Thomson poured money like glue; abroad, he plunged millions of pounds into acquiring and improving such world-renowned dailies as the *Scotsman* and *The Times of London.* In addition (in 1964) he created the Thomson Foundation for the training of senior personnel from the new and developing countries of Africa and endowed it with seed money of $5 million — a generous gesture, but a little hard to justify to the impoverished Thomson journalists back home.

One explanation emanated from Georgina Murray Keddell, daughter of the famous "Ma" Murray of Lillooet, BC. In a signed piece for the Vancouver *Sun,* written after Roy's death, Georgina told of a 1937 dinner she attended in Timmins with Thomson and Gladstone ("Bill") Murray, who was visiting from England.

"How," asked Thomson, "would a man like me go about getting a knighthood?"

"Well, of course, there would be the question of money — a great deal of money," the surprised Murray replied. "You could build and equip a hospital, or subsidize a political party..."

According to Mrs. Keddell, this was the first enunciation of Thomson's long-range ambitions for a title. It's a long way from Timmins, Ontario, to Buckingham Palace, but Roy made it; it took him twenty-seven years.

The story of Thomson's meteoric rise has been told and retold — and nowhere more frankly than in his own remarkable autobiography *After I was Sixty.* Earlier resentment of the brash Canadian gave way to grudging respect and, eventually, to honest admiration, even in the highest places. His utter candour disarmed his sternest critics; with consummate showmanship, Roy reveled in putting them down.

Thomson liked to argue that Canadians succeeded in Britain because they were more willing to gamble, and to work harder, than their counterparts in the Old Country, and he was not above lecturing his colleagues on the virtues of aggressive salesmanship.

A classic example was related by Eric (later Sir Eric) Cheadle,

Thomson's deputy on a visit to Malaysia with the Commonwealth Press Union. One of his toughest jobs, Cheadle said, was to advise his boss on selection of his personal Christmas cards. One year, Lord Thomson decided that an ideal card would be a picture of the Queen Mother and himself with a regiment in Toronto of which he was Honorary Colonel, complete with sporran and kilt.

"Roy, that's in appalling taste," said Cheadle. "The Queen Mother will never permit it."

"What's the name of her private secretary?" asked Thomson, reaching for a telephone.

Cheadle listened with fascination — and horror — as Thomson made his pitch. "Hullo, how's the Queen Mother?" he began. "Remember that picture of the two of us in Toronto, full uniform? Like to use it as a Christmas card. Great PR. Shows the bonds of Commonwealth. Shows how democratic she is. Great lady. Canadians love her. They'll love her even more when they see her on that Christmas card."

"One moment, please," said the royal secretary. Then he returned to the line.

"The Queen Mother has no objection whatsoever," he said.

"There," said Roy to Cheadle, grinning. "You see? You Brits have got to learn a thing or two about selling."

The fact is that Roy Thomson remained a salesman until his dying day. This was made hilariously manifest the last time I saw him, in 1974, when he came to address the Men's Canadian Club of Vancouver. He was at the time at the peak of his power and fame, the owner of something like 140 newspapers, almost as many magazines, television and radio stations, hotels, aircraft, tourist agencies and (with J. Paul Getty) a sizeable hunk of the North Sea oil development off Scotland.

And what did this baron of the press choose as his subject for the day? The delights of one of his packaged weekend tours to Majorca!

The following day he was guest of honour at a private luncheon in the staid old Vancouver Club and during the course of the meal I asked him: "What are you going to say to this group?" To my astonishment and alarm, Roy reached into an inner pocket, removed a travel brochure, and said: "Same speech as yesterday." Like most private clubs, the Vancouver had a standing rule: no paper produced at the luncheon table. Indeed, it strongly inferred

162

that no true gentleman would discuss the crass considerations of the marketplace while at the Club table with friends. But Roy plunged blithely ahead, telling a few hairy stories en route, and — as usual — completely captivated his audience. At the end of the luncheon, his male secretary stood at the exit door and solemnly handed each departing guest two items: a brochure extolling the virtues of a sunny, $98 weekend in the Mediterranean and a facsimile front page of *The Times* for November 7, 1805 with a lead story on Admiral Nelson's death at Trafalgar.

When Thomson died in the summer of 1976 more than 1,000 persons turned out for a memorial service in London. There was no eulogy, but the dean of the cathedral offered "praise and thanksgiving for His servant Roy Thomson, a man of courage, honesty and loyalty..."

Roy left behind him a coterie of highly-trained and skilled executives. It appears today that expansion of the empire will be pursued with the same relentless drive and panache.

His son Kenneth, heir to the baronetcy as well as the communications kingdom, is more fond of Canada than of Britain. He has the business acumen and the pride of his father, but little of his flair; where Roy was extroverted and outgoing, Ken tends to be calm and self-effacing. Closest to his heart, one suspects, are his beautiful wife, Marilyn (a former "Miss Toronto") and their children; and an outstanding collection of ivory miniatures, fine paintings and antiques. Yet the affection of these two disparate personalities — the rough-and-ready Roy and the coolly elegant Ken — was a beautiful thing to behold. No matter how harsh the criticism of his father, Ken always defended him loyally. In a letter to a friend shortly after Roy's death, Ken wrote: "He was the finest father a son could have. We shall miss him terribly but the memory and the pride will certainly remain."

The sentiment was reciprocated by senior executives of the Thomson group, many of whom had been made wealthy by share participation. In the face of some spirited public criticism of the cheese-paring Canadian operation, a brilliant vice-president of the group, Margaret Hamilton, said: "I don't care what they say, I never want to work for a better man, or a better organization. I'm proud to be a part of it."

# Chapter 17

"I run the paper purely for the purpose of making propaganda."

— *Lord Beaverbrook*

Unlike the British, with their Beaverbrooks, Astors and Rothermeres, and the Americans with their Sulzbergers, Gannetts and Chandlers, Canada has had precious few charismatic publishers and only a handful of journalists known beyond the borders of our own country. Even these (Roy Thomson, Morley Safer), could be classified as "transplants".

One exception was John Bassett of Toronto, who for twenty years enlivened Canadian journalism as publisher of the Toronto *Telegram*. But in 1971 he closed down his newspaper, sold his circulation list to the Toronto *Star* for an outrageous $10 million and — horror of horrors — elected to spend all his time in the rival medium of television. Years later the wisdom of this act was still being debated in press clubs across the land; in a 1979 speech Clyde Gilmour was moved to describe his old boss as "El Foldo".

Ambitious, outspoken and opinionated, Bassett was inevitably a centre of controversy. A share of the criticism, no doubt, could be attributed to envy. He was better looking than appeared legal; he was tall (6' 4½") and the possessor of a booming voice and raffish vocabulary, the smile of a movie idol and the nimbleness of mind which bespeaks the born hustler. The trouble was, or so his press club critics contended, that he was a rich man's son, a playboy born to the purple. That this impression persisted, even though it was not true, was due largely to the fact that his father, a loquacious Irishman, was president and publisher of the Montreal *Gazette.* Many Canadians thought this meant that he *owned* the paper. He did not. His legacy to his son was some oddments of furniture and the Sherbrooke *Record,* a small-town daily in the Eastern Townships.

What his son John did inherit was an affinity for the rich and powerful, and a high-octane personality which permitted him to move at ease with the panjandrums of commerce. After fighting a good war in Italy and Northwest Europe, he accepted the Conservative nomination in the 1945 federal election, was defeated, and turned his attentions to the *Record.* But Sherbrooke, an eminently pleasant bivouac, was too small to hold the returning major; when his friend George McCullagh offered him a job in Toronto he accepted. After a brief stint as reporter on the *Globe and Mail* he fetched up as advertising manager of the *Telegram.* The next logical step was to acquire ownership of "the old lady of Bay Street", which he did with the aid of John and Signe Eaton, the two of them setting up an ownership trust in the names of four Eaton children and three Bassetts.

Bassett set out to convert the somewhat stodgy *Telegram* into a scrappy challenger to the dominant Toronto *Star.* He hired good people, paid them well, and instructed them to raise hell at every opportunity. It was, in fact, a newsman's paper and a rambunctious place at which to work. In subsequent post-mortems on the *Tely's* demise, critics faulted Bassett for over-staffing and profligate spending — not a common complaint in Canadian journalism.

Annual meetings of The Canadian Press were enlivened by Bassett's stentorian attacks on the shortcomings of the wire service. At one such gathering he bellowed that the *Tely* was getting so little use out of the wire that he was considering cancellation. Because it was the fourth largest daily in Canada, this constituted a serious threat. But the wily Gillis Purcell was ready for him. No sooner had Bassett finished his tirade than Purcell quietly produced a copy of that day's *Telegram.* "Let's take a look," he murmured. "Five CP stories on page one." Bassett joined in the burst of laughter and decided to stay in the fold.

While it is true that his brash interventions irritated a number of his colleagues, it is also true that his gung-ho spirit and genial irreverence won him a coterie of admirers. Over the years, we became firm friends. When Marilyn Bell came out to Victoria to swim the Straits we entered into joint sponsorship; from time to time we exchanged features and, eventually, even children. (This came about when John Sr. asked me to take on the staff of the Victoria *Times,* for training, his son Johnny F. Later Bassett reciprocated by hiring my daughter Kath as a summer trainee.)

In Toronto Bassett was moving relentlessly onwards and upwards. The *Tely* was going well and becoming, with the *Globe and Mail,* one of the major Tory voices in Canada. Whispers were abroad that the dynamic young publisher would offer himself as a candidate in the federal election of 1962. These rumours were confirmed by Bassett on one of our visits to Toronto. One night, after a party, we decided to repair to the apartment of the *Tely's* lawyer, Charles Dubin, for scrambled eggs and coffee. For some reason, Bassett and I chose to walk. It was a clear, crisp, moonlit night with the snow banked high on both sides of the road. As we walked, Bassett threw an arm around my shoulder and exclaimed: "Stukus, this is my town. They love me in Toronto. I'm going to run in Spadina and I'm going to be elected."

"Are you shooting for Prime Minister?" I asked.

"Why not?" he replied.

Once committed, Bassett threw himself into the campaign with immense zeal. One of his conceits was to have constructed a number of cardboard blow-ups of the candidate himself, hand outstretched and wall-to-wall smile personifying the Good Old Boy appeal. Each morning he would turn up at a different bus-stop in Spadina, offering a formidable combination of the cardboard man and the real, live, breathing candidate.

But as the countdown to election began in 1962, it became apparent that Bassett was out of synch with large segments of the voters. Spadina was, after all, an ethnic community — Italians, West Indians, Yugoslavs, Hungarians, Lithuanians, Chinese, Greeks and Portuguese. They found it hard to relate to the flawlessly-tailored young aristocrat, who made the initial mistake of touring his riding in a Rolls-Royce, Lincoln Continental or Thunderbird. On June 18, Bassett was defeated by 2,984 votes.

But he was a hard bird to keep in the cage. His political itch, he told friends, had been well and truly scratched. The *Tely* was planning splendid new premises on Front Street; Bassett was moving to acquire ownership of the Argonaut football club; Maple

Leaf Gardens of which he was a part-owner was providing elegant returns and seeking to expand the existing premises by moving out over Mutual Street.

This latter required some delicate negotiations with municipal and provincial governments, and showed up Bassett as a gut fighter. A back-bencher from the boondocks of Ontario mounted a lively opposition to the move, and it was defeated. Bassett reacted angrily. On a plane trip to Quebec City he inveighed against the bucolic legislator and told me: "He's finished."

"How?" I asked.

"I'll run that bum out of the country."

"Bass," I remonstrated, "you just can't *do* things like that."

"Like what?" he said.

"Use your newspaper to hound a guy who disagrees with you."

Bassett's eyes flashed. "What the hell's the point of having power if you don't use it?" he barked.

While the impression prevailed that Bassett was very close to the Jewish élite of Toronto, as the only Gentile member of the exclusive Primrose Club, it was not altogether true.

This was revealed in 1979 in a remarkable letter to the Toronto *Star* by Rabbi Reuben Slonim, commenting on an unauthorized biography of Bassett by Maggie Siggins, a former *Tely* reporter. Slonim had been hired by Bassett in 1955 as an editorial page writer and authority on Jewish affairs. In his letter Slonim wrote:

> From her description of the atmosphere on the *Telegram,* which Bassett bought in 1952 and presided over until its demise in 1971, one gets the impression that it was a bear pit, with everyone cantankerous and clawing at each other.
>
> We all had our difficult moments, but I also remember the inspiration of Bassett, who could lift us to see journalism as a responsible and meaningful profession, and the camaraderies and fellowship of editors and reporters . . . .
>
> In her book Ms. Siggins repeats from the common impression that Bassett hired me as an associate editor of the *Telegram* in order to gain support from the Jews as a means of increasing circulation among them. This sounds as though he manipulated me as he allegedly did others.
>
> The fact is that I consented to work for the *Telegram* to help transform its image through a change in standards and

policy. The paper, in the last half of the nineteenth century and during the period leading up to and including Hitler's Holocaust, was unrepentently anti-Semitic. In his recent book, *The Jews of Toronto,* historian Stephen Speisman documents this fact.

All through the Holocaust and its aftermath, 1933-1948, John Ross Robertson's newspaper could not muster an ounce of compassion for the plight of the Jews. To the contrary, it went out of its way to present the Jews as undesirables.

My purpose was to help the *Telegram* become an organ of integrity so that decent people would be attracted to it, including the Jews.

It is true that in 1955-57, the first two years of my association with the paper, I was starry-eyed about the State of Israel. But then I didn't know much about the Palestinians.

The *Telegram* allowed me to visit the Arab countries and, as a result, my judgement was deepened. From 1958 on, I wrote signed pieces in the *Telegram* which were critical of the Israeli government when I believed the criticism was justified. Whenever I disagreed with *Telegram* policy on Israel and the Jews — as the years went on that policy became cloyingly pro-Israel and unbelievable — Bassett accorded me the right to express my dissent in a signed piece.

The Jews of Toronto were clamoring that Bassett fire me, but he refused to do so. For at least fifteen years I was a hindrance to increasing circulation among the Jews. On only one occasion, when I sent a dispatch from Tel Aviv which the editors titled "The Agony of the Conquered Arabs," did Bassett, after the first edition, bury a story of mine in the inside pages.

Bassett doubtless failed to gain the support of the Jews partly because of me, yet he kept me on. That certainly reveals a side to his character which gets no treatment in the Siggins book. . . .

Bassett's sale of the *Telegram* rocked the newspaper world. The *Tely* was one of the oldest English-language dailies in Canada and had a circulation in excess of 200,000. To the casual reader it appeared fat and sassy. But directors knew of the considerable haemorrheage of advertising dollars to television and the startling escalation of publication costs. Only Bassett's son Johnny F. opposed the closure. The *Star's* offer of $10 million for the *Tely* circulation list was too good to resist. After all, the traditional rule of thumb pegged circulation value at $10 a head and this was five times that amount. Cynics could be forgiven for concluding that the *Star* had bought a clear evening field in Toronto.

A few key staffers, anticipating the sale, had drafted plans for a new daily. When managing editor Douglas Creighton, editor Peter Worthington and business manager Don Hunt announced that they would within seventy-two hours start publishing a new tabloid, to be called the Toronto *Sun,* there was widespread scepticism. Such perceptive operators as Roy Thomson, Clair Balfour, Dick Malone (and Bassett) predicted publicly that the new venture would not last a year.

They were wrong. To everyone's astonishment, the *Sun* was an almost overnight success, appealing to the "subway set" with a lively formula of sex, sports and provocative columns. With consummate skill, the paper managed to convey a "little guy" image, bucking the mighty *Star* and the prestigious *Globe and Mail.* It found its niche and exploited it shamelessly. After only eight years it decided to go public, ostensibly to finance expansion. This gave founders Creighton, Worthington and Hunt an opportunity to offload some of their original shares and make themselves near-millionaires. It was a newspaper success story without parallel in North America in the past twenty years with the possible exception of *Newsday.*

Bassett, in self-imposed retirement from the newspaper business but still active as chairman of CFTO, told friends that he wanted to ease off: play more tennis, ride horses, spend more time with Isabel, his talented second wife, and their new family. But from time to time the old lion would emerge from his den to chew up his adversaries and, if permitted, swallow them alive.

A 1979 bid to purchase CFCF-TV in Montreal, however, was denied. It would have made Bassett the most powerful operator of private television in the country. His emotional pitch to the CRTC was regarded by many as sheer show-biz: "I regard it as a chance to stand up . . . and say to all the world who care to listen that I believe in the future of the province of Quebec."

Corny? Perhaps. But people who knew Bassett well would regard it as an accurate reflection of his thinking: his affection for his home province of Quebec dates back more than half a century.

# Chapter 18

"The Press Gallery, of course, adds to my problems and to my pleasures."

*— Lester B. Pearson*

Today the "adversary system" decrees that press and politicians must operate at arm's length. This is a change in operating style and tone, and nowhere has the change been more vivid than in the Parliamentary Press Gallery in Ottawa. As Bruce Hutchison pointed out in his autobiography, *The Far Side of the Street,* once upon a time correspondents were frequently importuned to act as propagandists for the party supported by their paper. Half a century ago the renowned John W. Dafoe of the Winnipeg *Free Press* helped write Liberal Party policy and had no compunction in reminding Mackenzie King about the number of seats he (Dafoe) could deliver from the west.

The gallery at that time, of course, was much smaller than the two hundred men and women rampant today. The veterans toiled longer hours, for much less pay, and in retrospect (could it be sheer nostalgia?) they are remembered as giants — men like Ken Wilson, Grant Dexter, Bruce Hutchison, George Ferguson, Bob Farquhar, Torchy Anderson, John Marshall, Frank Flaherty, Hamish McGeachie and Blair Fraser.

Much later, in the 1960s, Peter Newman became famous as possessor of the greatest set of "leaks" in the gallery. No cabinet secrets were safe from him; a succession of prime ministers fumed as Newman weighed in with details of their arcane initiatives, always couched in arresting prose.

Today, only a few correspondents cling to a one-on-one relationship with cabinet ministers, rewarded with an occasional "scoop" for their fidelity. Indeed, the leading practitioners feel insulted if wooed by cabinet ministers with a special point of view to be propagated. They get their "leaks" from peripheral sources — the deputies and mandarins who wield the levers of power from the banquettes of the Chateau Grill. Hated by Diefenbaker (who when I once said a few nice things about him at a dinner, came to the podium with a twinkle in his eye and began his speech by saying: "This is the first time in my life I've ever been *Sun*-kissed"), held in contempt by Trudeau, the gallery nevertheless rejoices in the clean-hands approach of independent reportage.

Of the four prime ministers I came to know in twenty-eight years of newspaper publishing, the one with the keenest understanding of the press' role was Lester B. ("Mike") Pearson. Indeed, in the first volume of his memoirs the late prime minister made it clear that he actively *cultivated* journalists throughout his career:

> I suppose no Ambassador spent more time at the National Press Club than I did. This was an agreeable and useful activity, for it was a good place to find out what was going on, who was going up, or who was going out. It was quite as valuable a source of information, and rumour, as my colleagues in the diplomatic corps, or even my friends in government departments.

This approach, of course, defied the rules of the "arm's length" relationship which had grown up, over the years, between the press and public men. The simple explanation is that most newsmen found Mike Pearson irresistible. He was close to Bruce Hutchison, Blair Fraser, Michael Barkway, Gillis Purcell, Grant Dexter and a dozen others. In fact, I knew only one Ottawa correspondent who confessed that he "couldn't stand the man" (a feeling which, I have reason to believe, was warmly reciprocated).

Mr. Pearson was a civil servant, a deputy in External Affairs, when I first met him at a Biltmore hotel reception in 1946. Observing the ease and graciousness with which he moved among his guests, his infectious grin and jaunty manner, I became an instant fan, and in ensuing years, we became good friends. In 1963 he appointed me to the Canada Council, which required half a dozen trips a year to Ottawa. Although no advance notice of these visits was recorded, the Prime Minister somehow managed to "keep in touch"; on the last day of each conference, a secretary would appear with a scribbled message: "The Prime Minister would like you to drop by 24 Sussex for a bit of lunch or a drink."

On one such visit I decided to test his allegedly encyclopaedic knowledge of baseball. As an old sports editor and a baseball buff, I had been intrigued by stories of his love of the game. One of the most famous television clips of the time had shown Mr. Pearson brushing off a cabinet minister so that he could follow a World Series game in progress. The Prime Minister had been a semi-pro infielder in his younger days ("good field, no hit") and it was said that two of his most cherished honours were a lifetime pass to Yankee Stadium and Honorary Presidency of the Montreal Expos.

For a while we talked politics. Then, during a lull in the conversation, I went (as the sports writers say) with my high, hard one:

"Mr. Prime Minister," I said, "are you aware that one of your constituents struck out Joe Di Maggio more often than any other pitcher in the Big Leagues?"

Mike's face broke into a broad grin and his head began to bob from side to side, like a prize-fighter sparring with an opponent. (Mike was one of the all-time great head-bobbers. He telegraphed his most important pitches.)

"Oh, Shtu," he said, with that faint lisp which characterized his speech. "You are referring to Phil Marchildon of PEN-E-tang-uish-SHENE. Phil was a great ball player. In 1942, he was 17-14 with the As. The following year he went into the Air Force but it didn't seem to hurt him too badly; in 1947 he won nineteen and lost nine. His ERA was 3.22. In 1949 he developed a sore arm and was traded to Boston. Never did much after that. The amazing thing about Phil, though, was that he was a good hitter. Pitchers aren't supposed to hit but in 1947 his average was .276 . . ."

This statistical recital brought me close to tears of laughter and

I held up a restraining hand. But the Prime Minister plowed doggedly on: he had found an enjoyable turf and was not about to quit it for the mundane affairs of Canada.

"Oh yes, Shtu," he continued, "Phil was great, but another of his contemporaries was even greater. This was Dick Fowler, a Toronto boy whose ten years in the majors almost exactly spanned the same era as Phil's. You'll remember that Fowler pitched a no-hit game against St. Louis in the fall of 1945, after he came out of service. But that's not all. He won fifteen games both in 1948 and 1949, with an ERA of 3.7 both years. Not quite as good a hitter as Phil but he was .227 in 1947, not bad for a pitcher."

By this time I was ready to collapse on the floor. "All right, Prime Minister," I protested. "I believe! I believe!"

An amusing sequel to this conversation occurred not long after when Jim Bouton, the Yankee pitcher, published a book called *Ball Four*. Bouton, an irreverent spirit, had produced a semi-diary which detailed not only the sins of the baseball moujiks, but the nocturnal activities of his teammates. This was a raunchy story and hardly the kind of thing one would recommend to a former prime minister. But knowing Mike's love of baseball, I took a deep breath and fired off a copy to Carleton University, where Mike had been installed as Chancellor.

I did not have to wait long for a response. On Carleton note-paper, the Chancellor replied:

Dear Stu. I am more than grateful to you for brightening my life with Jim Bouton's book. I have been deep in the fasci-nating, mystifying and, at times misleading, last two volumes based on Mackenzie King's diaries. Then your gift came and I was able, with good conscience, to abandon Mr. King's spiritual and personal politics for real sound literature! Thank you very much indeed. Mike.

Behind this genial exterior, of course, there lay the spirit of a man of considerable fibre. He had shown this at an election meeting in Vancouver in 1963, when he literally shouted down a band of heckling communists; and again in Winnipeg, when he defended his Maple Leaf flag against a crowd of hostile Legion-naires. But nowhere was it more apparent than in his response to De Gaulle's famous *"Québec libre"* speech, which the Prime

Minister found "totally unacceptable". What made him livid with rage was the attempt to compare De Gaulle's *Chemin de Roi* procession through Quebec with the Allied liberation of Paris from the Nazis.

As everyone recalls, the Prime Minister went on national television to denounce this outrage, reminding his listeners that "Quebec is free — all Canadians are free." What may not be so well known is that De Gaulle (and France) have not to this day apologized for, or explained, their non-appearance at a State dinner planned by Governor-General Roland Michener for the next night in Ottawa. Mr. Pearson told the story one sunny afternoon on the terrace at 24 Sussex.

"The telephone rang at about six o'clock," the Prime Minister recalled. "It was Roly Michener, across the street. He wanted to know if Maryon and I had any plans for dinner. I told him we were free. 'In that case,' he said, 'come on over. We've got the table set for forty-eight places.' So Maryon and I went across the street and the four of us sat down to this elegant dinner. I'm afraid we didn't do it justice. Not a word from the French embassy. Not a note, not a wire, not a telephone call. De Gaulle, after hearing my broadcast just packed up and went home. An amazing performance."

The passage of the years brought us closer together. In 1966, the Prime Minister asked me to act as a one-man mediator in a dispute involving the "Seven Days" television programme. While the results of this informal commission were inconclusive and unsatisfactory to me (since both sides to the quarrel had acted very badly) they at least had the effect of averting a national strike, for which the Prime Minister expressed his gratitude.

It was in February of 1966 that I received a most astonishing telephone call from the Prime Minister, one which demonstrated his ability to take a light-hearted approach to essentially serious matters.

"I have two questions I want to ask you," he said. "The first is important and the second only trivial."

The important question, he said, had to do with Vancouver's bid for a franchise in the National Hockey League. An original submission had been turned down because of inadequate facilities. The Prime Minister was being asked to contribute $2 million of public money to the building of a coliseum but this was a delicate matter, as any city or town in Canada might demand similar support.

We talked about the climate of hockey on the Pacific Coast, dating back to the days of the Patricks. I ventured the opinion that Vancouver was a sure-fire franchise.

"Well," the Prime Minister said, "we may be able to help. Possibly a Coliseum could be justified if it was built to accomodate agricultural fairs and merchandise marts, as well as an arena. I confess I don't like the idea of the whole six hockey franchises going out of Canada. But there's not much point in moving on it unless there's a group in Vancouver willing to back it."

I assured him that there was considerable enthusiasm for the project. (In due course, a $6 million Coliseum was built, with one-third of the money coming from Ottawa — not without some criticism from the hustings.)

The Prime Minister paused. "And now to the trivial matter. I would like to have you in the Senate."

A day or so later I was in Ottawa and went to 24 Sussex to discuss the invitation. While I was honoured, I felt that the offer was unworkable in terms of newspaper independence from politicians: the *Sun* had to be free to belabour Mr. Pearson and his party, which it frequently did. Nevertheless, I was flattered that the offer came from a man whom I considered one of the world's great statesmen.

The burdens of office were bearing heavily on Mike. The petty scandals which plagued the Liberal party in the early 60s were anathema to the Prime Minister. He was less than enthusiastic about the media's penchant for describing the era as "the Diefenbaker-Pearson years", which not only linked him with a man he did not like, but accorded him second billing. He was anxious to get out.

He was persuaded to stay through the Expo year of 1967, which many have described in retrospect as Canada's finest hour. But in December he announced his intention of retiring (he was seventy-one) at the leadership convention scheduled for Ottawa the following April.

The day before the convention we lunched together, alone, at 24 Sussex Drive. Before lunch we had a gin and tonic in the small library off the entrance hall, a cosy retreat adorned with pictures

176

of Dwight Eisenhower, Dean Acheson, Pandit Nehru and Vincent Massey, his old wartime boss. Over lunch (soup, steak and kidney pie on rice, baked apple), we talked about a variety of things, from the recent Press Gallery dinner — the Prime Minister deplored the fact that Galleryites had to get bombed before they went into their act — to Lou Rasminsky's dollar-devaluation crisis, and of course the impending leadership contest. Contrary to what has been written and spoken elsewhere, I got the distinct impression that he was leaning to the new Quebec meteorite, Pierre Elliott Trudeau. The Prime Minister, of course, had been scrupulously careful to remain neutral, not publicly endorsing any of the seven Cabinet colleagues vying for his job. But there was admiration in his voice when he said: "Pierre has great ability, and a lot of fibre. He can do almost anything. The best thing that could happen to him would be broad support across Canada — and a bit of opposition in Quebec."

The vote-counting four days later was fraught with drama and fierce political in-fighting. But the vignette many delegates recalled years later was that of Mike and Maryon on the platform, hands clasped and smiling through tears as 10,000 partisans sang a farewell "Auld Lang Syne".

The subsequent sad news of Mike's cancer was brought back to the Coast by Bruce Hutchison. Unhappy rumours were confirmed when it was announced in July of 1970 that he was going into hospital to have an eye removed. I wanted to send him a get-well telegram and debated a bit about the tone. Knowing Mike, I concluded that a sombre statement about a serious operation would only depress him; what was called for in my opinion (rightly or wrongly) was the kind of carefree approach we had enjoyed during our twenty-five years of friendship. So I wired him: "Delighted to hear your operation a success. Know you will make the public forget Admiral Nelson, Moishe Dyan and the Hathaway shirt man. Love, Stu."

Within a few days, I received a reply: "Dear Stu, Your message was delightful but I am sorry to have to disappoint you as I will not be wearing a black patch but will have a beautiful new eye, complete with veins painted on. Many thanks for your thoughtfulness and warm regards."

Dear Mike. I wept at his funeral.

Not only for my friend. For my country.

# Chapter 19

"As bad as the press is, and it can be awful
at times, it is the only shield we have against
encroaching government control of what
we can read, what we can talk about, what
we can think."

— *Dennis Braithwaite*


Perhaps the most serious knock on the press of Canada is that
it is dull. But in all the fundamental criteria — freedom, honesty
and independence — it can take pride of place with the press of
any nation in the world. Canada's press is free in the sense that
it can (and does) write what it thinks about government, at any
level. It is honest in the sense that readers cannot buy their way
into the news columns — and perhaps what is more important,
cannot buy their way *out* of them. It is independent of political
parties as newspapers were not, half a century ago. There are not
many nations in the world enjoying such freedoms.

In the middle 1950s Bill Cowles, the highly-respected publisher
of two Spokane dailies, began to look north to Canada for support
of the Inter-American Press Association, a freedom-fighting organization of some 500 newspapers in the United States, Central
and South America. Among those he approached was Max Bell,
who agreed to put his newspapers into the organization and
asked me to represent our group. In due course Southam's signed
on and eventually some sixty-five Canadian dailies (and newsprint
suppliers as associates) became members.

It proved to be a fascinating and educative assignment. To
begin with, the IAPA met in exotic corners of the Western Hemisphere such as Rio, Lima, Tobago, Montego Bay, Cancun and
Acapulco. More importantly, it brought us into direct contact with

some genuine heroes of the press, like Dr. Alberto Gainza Paz, whose paper (*La Prensa*) in Buenos Aires was stolen from him by Juan Peron; Pedro Beltran, who became Premier of Peru and straightened out its finances but was later deprived of his newspaper by another junta; and Pedro Joaquin Chamorro, the courageous editor who was ambushed and gunned down by political rivals in Nicaragua.

For a variety of reasons, Canadians never pulled their weight in this organization. One explanation was the very obvious one that there were just too many journalistic organizations: a man could make a career out of attending conventions to the detriment of his home-office duties. In Canada there is a lingering bond with the Commonwealth Press Union. There is also the Federation of International Journalists; the International Press Institute (the IAPA, as it were, on a global scale); the American Newspaper Publishers Association of New York, and its corresponding structures in Canada. All were worthy, as all were time-consuming. Our relationships with IAPA were a bit like Canada's relationship to the Organization of American States; we were prepared to act as observers but scarcely ready to get down into the pit and fight.

Thus, as a member of the Freedom of the Press Committee of IAPA, and in due course a director, I found myself in the unhappy role of "token Canadian" at its meetings. It was no trick to be elected a director: the other countries were anxious to have Canada involved and voted me into office in spite of a hit-and-miss attendance record. My duties were the essence of simplicity, and consisted of an eight-word annual report:

"There is freedom of the press in Canada."

In many respects I found these moving words — particularly in comparison with the reports of Latin American members, where tales of killings, destruction of presses, seizures by dictators, censorship, and control by means of newsprint licences were commonplace.

But in the late 1970s a subtle shift in North American reports became evident. At Trinidad in the spring of 1979 I was able to report again that "there is freedom of the press in Canada", but was compelled to add that interventions by the courts in our country were the source of serious and mounting concern.

In the space of six months three judicial rulings against newspapers appeared to impair, if not impede, the free functioning

179

of the press. In Victoria, political cartoonist Bob Bierman was found guilty of libelling a provincial cabinet minister and fined $3,500 — the first such ruling in newspaper history. (Happily, this judgement was overturned by Chief Justice Nathan T. Nemetz and four of his brethren on the BC Court of Appeals, in a unanimous verdict.) In Vancouver, the *Sun* was fined $5,000 for a mild, four-paragraph editorial slapping Simma Holt on the wrist for her work with a prison reform committee touring California. More seriously, a Saskatchewan daily was ordered by the Supreme Court of Canada to pay $25,000 to a local lawyer-alderman on the grounds that he had been libelled in a letter-to-the-editor.

Of even greater gravity was a charge against Toronto *Sun* publisher Douglas Creighton and editor Peter Worthington under the Official Secrets Act, on the strength of a column by Worthington about Russian espionage in Canada. Conviction on this charge would have sent both men to jail for long terms. Happily, the charges were dismissed.

Earlier in the year, the Vancouver *Sun* had found itself involved in a bizarre series of events which had to be challenged. I came out to the newsroom one day, shortly after noon, to find about half the staff standing around, bemused, while two strangers rifled the desks of reporters, seizing notebooks, story dupes and lists of contacts. I asked the managing editor what the hell was going on. He told me that the Combines Investigation Branch in Ottawa had secured a warrant from a provincial court judge to search our rooms for information. Our in-house lawyer had done a spot investigation and advised that, in his opinion, the warrant was valid.

The whole notion seemed outrageous to me. What the Combines people were seeking, it developed, were some pictures, and some reporters' notes, on a union dispute in Prince Rupert, far to the north. We had not been charged with anything. What we were being asked, in effect, was to provide the research which the Ottawa authorities had been unable to dig up on their own.

This did not appear to me to be the duty of a free and independent press. Within a few days we appealed to the Supreme Court of British Columbia and were upheld by Chief Justice Nathan T. Nemetz, a one-time labour lawyer who numbered among his early clients the American Newspaper Guild. In due course Mr. Justice Nemetz' decision reached Ottawa, where Justice

Minister Ron Basford upheld the verdict and said that such raids on newspapers were not consistent with the free-press traditions of Canada.

This, interestingly enough, is in direct contradiction to the view of the United States Supreme Court, which has ruled that newspapers and broadcast stations are subject to unannounced searches of their files. Federal courts have also upheld the right of the government to obtain access to the private telephone records of newspapers and newsmen.

What many American editors regard as a dangerous drift to court controls was dramatized by the case of Myron A. Farber, who spent almost two months in jail for refusing to turn over his files to a trial judge in New Jersey. The New York *Times,* for whom Farber worked, paid fines of $5,000 a day, to a total of $285,000 before Farber was released.

Not to put too fine a point on it, some of the most influential publishers and editors in the United States are convinced that the present Supreme Court is militantly hostile to the press and resolved to bring it "into line". Further credence to this view was lent by its 1979 decision by a vote of 6 to 3 that journalists can be compelled to answer questions about their "state of mind" in libel cases brought by public figures. This landmark decision, which overturned a federal appeals court ruling, stemmed from an action arising out of a "Sixty Minutes" television show produced by Barry Lando, a former Vancouver reporter.

The notion that any free citizen of the United States should have to define what was on his mind, or why he asked certain questions, sent a shudder through newsrooms. To many, the ruling sounded positively Orwellian: "Why did you use this adjective, and not another?" "What caused you to pick up on this fact but refrain from using these others?" "What are your own political beliefs? Did they influence your thinking on this sequence?" "Did you oppose the Viet Nam War?" and so on . . .

In writing for the majority Supreme Court decision, Judge Byron ("Whizzer") White, the old football star, argued that the press already enjoys a great deal of protection against libel suits. Ever since the landmark New York *Times vs Sullivan* case in 1964, public officials must prove "actual malice". Thus, wrote White, the Sullivan judgement made it essential to focus on the newsmen's state of mind. In dissent, Justices William Brennan and

Thurgood Marshall said that they did not know how a journalist could be prevented from thinking. They feared that journalists would be intimidated; would not wish to discuss stories openly, even with their editors and colleagues in the newsroom.

Before 1970, very few reporters were subpoenad to explain their actions. At the end of the decade, they were being summoned at the rate of more than 100 a year.

The practical effect of these First Amendment (freedom of the press) decisions was hard to assess. "The big boys can look after themselves," said lawyer Fred Abrams, who acted for CBS in the Lando trial. But he wondered if smaller papers could afford to fight such cases. At a subsequent meeting of the American Newspaper Publishers Association, president Allen Neuhharth said it was exploring ways to help small newspapers fight costly court battles to protect press freedom, presumably by a subsidized insurance program.

In spite of these provocations, it is quite evident that the press in Canada, the United States and Britain is infinitely better off than in the non-democratic countries. Surveys by the International Press Institute and the IAPA indicated that only 25 per cent of the world's press is free. And the emergent countries of the Third World have recently sought intercession from a UNESCO commission whose recommendations, Western newsmen fear, would result in government control of news and opinion. In the words of German Ornes, president of IAPA, the 146 nations represented at the UNESCO conference in Paris "opened the door to direct or indirect official control of the media".

Some attempts to water down UNESCO's declaration on the mass media were successful but the result was a document that tried to please everybody and pleased very few. The most glaring omission in UNESCO's Interim Report (written by members of its Secretariat) is any recognition of the fact that there are two diametrically-opposed theories concerning the role of the press: one that the State must control the press if the press is to serve the interests of the people; the other that the press must be free from State control if it is to serve the interests of the people. Reconciliation of these opposing views seems a long way off; in the meantime, many western publishers and editors believe that the best way to proceed is by closer contact between journalists, rather than governments. Some have suggested setting up an

182

International Communications Fund, on a non-ideological basis, to train media people, award scholarships, establish travel grants, and assist in setting up printing and electronic equipment and working toward a more even flow of national and international news.

The jolting fact of life in Canada, though, is that a majority of Canadians do not believe in freedom of the press. A survey taken by the 1970 Davey Commission elicited the disturbing statistic that 51 per cent of respondents believed that newspapers should be subject to some form of control.

Do they really believe that? Have they thought it through? Do they believe that newspapers published by governments, or directed by bureaucracies, would permit the same free-wheeling discussion as the existing dailies and not insist upon a numbing adherence to the party line? Do they really want to see restraints upon the new breed of journalist — the highly-educated specialist writing about medicine, space technology, religion and education, and the investigative reporter, digging into stories which might take three to six months to reach print. This type of copy was not designed to please the politicians or jurists — or, for that matter, rascals with a lot to hide. Inevitably, enemies are made.

What, actually, does "freedom of the press" mean? Essentially, it seems to me, it guarantees the right to criticize (or praise) governments at all levels; the right to dissent; and the right to choose its own content, including the right to publish unpopular opinions. These functions must be exercised within the parameters of fair comment: taste, libel and obscenity. But whose taste? Here again we fall back on the juridical definition: "In keeping with current community standards."

The question of choice of content is one which arose in an action fought over three years between the *Sun* and the Gay Alliance Towards Equality. The *Sun,* a decade before, had supported editorially the "consenting adults" legislation which Pierre Trudeau had immortalized with his line about "the state having no business in the bedrooms of the nation". But when the Gay Alliance sought to advertise in the classified columns of the *Sun,* the newspaper turned down the business. The advertisement, seeking subscribers to the magazine *Gay Tide,* appeared innocuous enough; the publication itself was lurid in the extreme, featuring articles on (among other things) the methods of recruiting "luminous young boys". The *Sun* rejected the ads on the grounds of taste, pointing out that the Canadian newspaper industry had, in a recent year, refused some $6 million in advertising which it regarded as offensive — and arguing that a newspaper could not be compelled to print *any* copy — editorial or advertising — which did not meet its standards.

The Gay Alliance took its protest to the British Columbia Human Rights Commission, and won, on the grounds that the newspaper's refusal to print the classified ad. was discriminatory. The *Sun's* appeal to a judge of the Supreme Court of British Columbia was dismissed. It promptly went to the BC Court of Appeal and was sustained, the decision of the Rights Commission overturned. The Gay Alliance, pledging an all-out fight, appealed to the Supreme Court of Canada.

By now, the case was being watched with keen interest by newspapers across Canada and in many areas of the United States. That the Supreme Court recognized a complex problem was indicated by the length of time it took in arriving at a decision. Nine months after it was seized of the case, it brought down its verdict — 6-3 in favour of dismissing the Gay Alliance action, with costs.

Somewhat unexpectedly, Mr. Justice Martland cited Chief Justice Burger of the Supreme Court of the United States:

A newspaper is more than a passive receptacle or conduit of news, comment, and advertising. The choice of material to go into a newspaper, and the decisions made as to limitations on the size and content of the paper, and treatment of public issues and public officials — whether fair or unfair — constitute the exercise of editorial control and judgement. It has yet to be demonstrated how governmental regulations of this crucial process can be exercised consistent with First Amendment guarantees (freedom of speech and of the press) as they have evolved at this time.

Martland J. concluded the Supreme Court judgement with these words:

The case in question here deals with the refusal by a newspaper to publish a classified advertisement, but it raises larger issues, which would include the whole field of newspaper advertising and letters to the editor. A newspaper exists for the purpose of disseminating information and for the expression of its views on a wide variety of issues. Revenues are derived from the sale of its newspapers and from advertising. It is true that its advertising facilities are made available, at a price, to the general public. But *Sun* reserved to itself the right to revise, edit, classify or reject any advertisement submitted to it for publication and this reservation was displayed daily at the head of its classified advertisement section.

The law has recognized the freedom of the press to propagate its views and ideas on any issue and to select the material which it publishes. As a corollary to that a newspaper also has the right to refuse to publish material which runs contrary to the view which it expresses. A newspaper published by a religious organization does not have to publish an advertisement advocating atheistic doctrine. A newspaper supporting certain political views does not have to publish an advertisement advancing contrary views. In fact, the judgements of Duff, C. J. Davis, J., and Cannon, J., in the *Alberta Press Case,* previously mentioned, suggest that provincial legislation to compel such publication may be unconstitutional.

In my opinion the service which is customarily available to the public in the case of a newspaper which accepts advertising is a service subject to the right of the newspaper to control the content of such advertising. In the present case, the *Sun* had adopted a position on the controversial subject of homosexuality. It did not wish to accept an advertisement seeking subscription to a publication which propagates the views of the Alliance. Such refusal was not based upon any personal characteristic of the person seeking to place that advertisement, but upon the content of the advertisement itself.

Section 3 of the Act does not purport to dictate the nature and scope of a service which must be offered to the public. In the case of a newspaper, the nature and scope of the service which it offers, including advertising service, is determined by the newspaper itself. What S 3 does is to provide that a service which is offered to the public is to be available to all persons seeking to use it and the newspaper cannot deny the service which it offers to any particular member of the public unless reasonable cause exists for so doing.

In my opinion the Board erred in law in considering that S 3 was applicable in the circumstances of this case. I would dismiss the appeal with costs.

Thus was inscribed in law the basic principle that a newspaper could regulate its own content. This, coupled with the earlier decision barring raids by government agencies on reporters' files, represented a major victory for a free press. With the added knowledge that all parties in Ottawa are pledged to a meaningful Freedom of Information Act, it appeared that Canadian newspapers could enter the 1980s with a strengthened recognition of their rights as well as their duties.

# Chapter 20

"A little more self-analysis and a little less self-admiration would not hurt our business."

— *James Reston*

The most powerful newspaper publisher in Canada in the two decades 1958-1978 was also one of the least known to the public: Richard Sankey Malone, head of FP Publications Ltd. I once suggested to David Macdonald, an associate editor of *Reader's Digest,* that Malone's considerable journalistic clout made him a natural subject for a profile in the magazine. Macdonald agreed, but could not sell the notion to his editors. "They feel," he said, "that the only people interested in newspaper publishers are other newspaper publishers." Maybe. I found Malone, through two decades, not only interesting but unique; a complex, lonely, proud, domineering and insecure human being, and about the only person I found difficult to get along with, in more than forty years in the business.

To the working press, he was almost invariably known as "Malone", and in a curiously pejorative way. Clair Balfour, president of Southam's, was commonly known as "Clair", and Lord Thomson of Fleet as "Roy", but the man at the head of FP Publications Ltd. was known solely by his last name.

Bruce Hutchison once described him in a column as "handsome", and it is true that he possesses a certain rakish elegance. He always reminded me of one of those ageing juveniles in a Noël Coward play who bursts through the French doors with a racquet under his arm, crying: "Tennis, anyone?" Not to imply

187

that he was jaunty. In fact, he was cool long before the hip society imparted to that word a different connotation. When talking about money, a fine coating of permafrost seemed to form over his steel-grey eyes.

His speech was punctuated by many "Ahhs!" and "mmms", and was to a large extent impossible to comprehend. This puzzled me, until I realized that the Muriel cigar drooping beneath his military moustache so stifled every phrase that he sounded like Jacques Cousteau, gargling through a snorkel. In dress, he affected British tweeds, brown suede shoes and a carelessly-adjusted pocket foulard. These accoutrements were mostly souvenirs of his annual, two-week summer holiday in England, a country to which he remained passionately devoted. Like Viscount Bennett, he seemed to find there a lifestyle and an acceptance more congenial than that in his native Canada.

A great name-dropper, Malone managed to suggest to Canadian colleagues that his social schedule in the UK was totally geared to the nobs and toffs of Debrett's. His conversation at such times sounded a bit like the dialogue from a Noël Coward play. "Dear old Winnie. Had me down to Chartwell with The Beaver. Poor old boy — he's getting a bit potty." And one year he returned to Canada with jovial reminiscences of a man he called, simply, "Sonny". This last one baffled me and I made bold enough to question Malone. He looked at me with the disdain and hauteur Jeeves manifested towards Bertie Wooster.

"Sonny, you know," he replied. "Sonny Blandford, Princess Margaret's ex. Stood next to him at the gaming tables. Blew a packet, the crazy boy."

Along the way, Malone allowed that he had had "useful talks" on his vacation with the Home Secretary, the Chancellor of the Exchequer, the foreign minister at Brussels, and Gavin Astor. They were all deeply concerned about inflation, immigration, relations with Rhodesia, the Common Market, NATO, the dwindling gold reserves and other riotous holiday topics. From time to time, one of these moujiks would sell Malone a bad book, which would be serialized and pumped into the FP chain back home, to the utter distress of local editors.

For social reasons—as an unattached man Malone was much in demand at Winnipeg and Toronto dinner tables—he returned from these overseas sallies with a remarkable fund of stories, which he appeared to have conned by rote. One concerned the night a ghost had entered his bedroom at the Savoy Hotel in London, and stayed through a spirited conversation. (Fortunately, the ghost turned out to be a hell of a listener.) Another brought the startling revelation that a study of the inscriptions on the Ten Commandments proved that Jesus was left-handed. I sat with Malone one afternoon when he recited this dubious yarn to the ageing Vancouver lumber tycoon, H. R. MacMillan. Mr. MacMillan fell asleep.

Nevertheless this complex man Malone, who drove a Rolls-Royce and self-consciously parked it behind a delivery truck in the company garage, was master of a newspaper empire hitherto unknown in Canada. Until hit by devastating strikes in Montreal, Ottawa and Vancouver in the late 1970s, his papers had a total circulation in excess of 1.1 million, larger than Southam (1 million) and Thomson (450,000). They dominated the market in Montreal (the *Star*), Winnipeg (the *Free Press*) and Vancouver (the *Sun*) and, in terms of prestige if not circulation, in Toronto (the *Globe and Mail*). The group owned both the *Times* and *Colonist* in Victoria, which were booming until hit by a six-month strike in 1974. The Lethbridge *Herald* thrived in southern Alberta. In Ottawa the *Journal,* until it became hobbled with labour troubles, ran a spirited race with the Southam's *Citizen.* Alone among FP papers, the Calgary *Albertan* was clobbered by Southam's *Herald,* but managed to keep afloat with valuable printing contracts and suburban "shopper" inserts. In total — adding in the *Free Press Weekly* and some successful commercial printing operations — the group by 1973 was grossing $150 million a year and showing a net profit of $18 million.

How did "The Brigadier" emerge in command of this imposing group? His friends attributed it to genius ("the infinite capacity for taking pains"), a relentless dedication and singleness of purpose. More irreverent observers called it a stroke of extraordinary luck.

A man whose ultimate fate in life seemed destined to be that of an aide, Malone just happened to be on the spot when his various bosses died. First there was Victor Sifton, whom he had served as general manager of the Winnipeg *Free Press.* Sifton died of a heart attack in 1961, aged sixty-three, and his paper passed to his son John. John had a genuine talent for the mechanical side of newspapers but was really more interested in jumping horses. He developed lung cancer and died in 1969 at age forty-three.

Suddenly Malone found himself in command of the Winnipeg situation, publisher of the *Free Press* and an executor of the family estate. In this capacity he not only voted about 25 per cent of the parent company shares but looked after the financial affairs of the daughters who had survived.

Not long after, in 1972, Max Bell died and the process was repeated: Malone voted the Bell shares in FP, was named an executor of the Bell Foundation (some $20 million left for educational, medical, religious and sports charities, particularly in the west) and tended to the finances of the survivors.

Three deaths in eleven years. Three principals. And with no sons equipped to carry on the family tradition, who better to step into the vacuum than General Manager R. S. Malone? Thus, although he held only about 7.5 per cent of the stock in the parent company — while the Howard Webster and Derek Price interests of Montreal had approximately 25 per cent each — Malone found himself in day-to-day command of the powerful group.

He had come a long way. Born September 18, 1909 in Owen Sound, Malone was briefly exposed to education at Ridley College, one of the staunchest old-school-tie institutions in the country, and was just eighteen when he turned up for work as a reporter with the Toronto *Star*. In the depression years he went west to work for the Sifton-owned Regina *Leader-Post* and Saskatoon *Star-Phoenix,* doing all the menial jobs from bossing the carrier boys to webbing up a press. (James Cooper, publisher of the *Globe and Mail,* in his retirement assessment of Malone said he was "the most knowledgeable man on newspaper affairs I have ever met.") In 1936, Malone moved to the Winnipeg *Free Press* and began his long association with the Siftons. At the outbreak of World War II, he went from reserve to active service and before long was functioning as an aide to the Defence Minister of Canada, the Hon. James L. Ralston.

By any standards, Malone had an interesting war. He came out of it a Brigadier. He set up the Canadian Army's public relations branch and founded *The Maple Leaf,* the Army's overseas paper. As a combat brigade major he landed in Sicily on D-Day and suffered back injuries when his Jeep struck a land mine. He was credited with being the first Allied officer to accept the surrender of an Italian general. He was in Paris the day it was liberated and on the deck of *USS Missouri* on the Pacific when the top-hatted Japanese dignitaries signed the surrender papers.

The assignment which gave him his greatest cachet — and fund of stories — came in the latter days of the war when he served as Canadian liaison officer with the temperamental, prickly General Montgomery. In 1946, Malone wrote what literary critic Robert Fulford described as a "curious, stiff-necked little book" about his war called *Missing From The Record,* in which he detailed the frustrations of Canadian officers in dealing with Montgomery. (Malone consistently leaned to a defence of Monty.)

*Missing From The Record* is replete with sentences like this: "While it is certain that some exceptions will be taken to portions of this book it will be appreciated that in dealing with many highly controversial incidents it is impossible to please everyone." Fulford commented: "A man who had a dashing, exciting war managed to make his account of it sound like an inter-office memo."

Malone did not, however, underestimate his own contribution. A reviewer for the *Globe and Mail* wrote in 1946: "This book leaves you with the impression that Col. Dick Malone was something of a magician who strolled the upper channels of policy, solving military-political problems with a tap of his wand. . ."

Something of the same attitude carried over into Malone's peacetime journalistic career. Dedicated to one of the most earthy, free-swinging, irreverent callings in the world, he has always seemed *above* its raffish eccentrics, a banker embarrassed by the belly-dancers imported for the annual staff party.

When the *Globe and Mail* joined FP in 1966, it made the Winnipeg-based group the largest in the country. Because there had been spirited bidding for the paper — including one serious offer from the United States — there was considerable public interest in the news.

Robert Fulford went along to interview Malone for the Toronto *Star* and described him as ". . . the sort of man who — after four decades in the business — goes out of his way to invite bad publicity by insulting newspapermen. For instance, the other day he instructed me: 'Now look, I've given you a straight story. You write it straight or I'll get on to Ralph' — meaning Ralph Allen, the managing editor of the *Star*. Malone apparently resents any questions about the future of the *Globe*. He seems to have the idea that the subject is unimportant, even routine, as if Canada's leading morning newspaper . . . changed hands every few weeks or so."

It is difficult to resist the view that Malone was a bully — a man who had to gratify some inner daemon by pushing other people around. He once telephoned me in Palm Desert to chew me out for taking a holiday. When, in a burst of righteous indignation, I asked him if he wanted my resignation, he backed down. But on my return to Vancouver I found myself summoned to Winnipeg for a further dusting. There ensued a spirited slanging match which became a bit one-sided when Malone called up, as reinforcement, the ailing John Sifton. Sifton had had an operation for lung cancer and could scarcely speak. The whole scene depressed me. I thought it was a chintzy thing for Malone to do, and refused to quarrel with Sifton. On my return to Vancouver, Max Bell telephoned me from California. I was on the point of quitting, and told him so. "Aw, forget it," he said, cheerfully. "Remember — you've got a friend at court."

At about the same time, Malone's marriage blew up and a court battle ensued in Winnipeg over custody of the three children. To the dismay of a great many persons, Malone turned up in court with a little black book which revealed the number of times his wife had been drunk — names, places, parties. This, incidentally, was surprising news to most newspaper executives who had met the woman at a number of conventions and had found her not only sober, but chic, intelligent, and an ornament of the meetings. Malone's production of the liquid log was not, in the opinion of many Winnipeggers, the action of a gentleman. Some long-standing friendships were dissolved as a result.

Some years later in discussing the matter with me, Malone said: "It's too bad, really. She's a nice little girl. But can you imagine what she said to me? She said: 'Dick, you *drove* me to drink!' "

"So what else is new, Dick?" I asked. "You drive *me* to drink." Malone laughed edgily.

There was another factor: what *Time* magazine described as Malone's "parsimonious" nature. Max Bell, who didn't often criticize his general manager, mildly pointed out one day that Malone didn't provide his family with a first-class house until after the marriage foundered. While he drove a Rolls-Royce, he boasted that it was second-hand and was purchased at bargain-basement rates. This penchant for tossing nickels around as though they were dollars was deeply ingrained in Malone. On the wall of Col. Victor Sifton's office at the *Free Press* was a framed letter from his father, Sir Clifford Sifton, the main thrust of which was contained in the sentence: "In times of prosperity, prepare for trouble." This became Malone's guiding gospel and creed.

A man who more or less lived on aircraft (and kept the affairs of FP on the back of his ticket), he invariably travelled economy class. This resulted in some embarrassment one night when Malone, Howard Webster and I were flying west for a meeting and Malone discovered that his companions were booked into the first-class section while he was back aft. With great grumblings, he decided at the last minute to get his ticket switched. As he boarded the plane, Malone waved his ticket at us and said: "This is costing $14 more, Ottawa to Winnipeg. I hope it's worth it." In the same thrifty spirit, Malone insisted on a twice-year check of newsprint waste and a review of free copies which newspapers traditionally gave to police and fire officials (because we depended on them frequently for news tips), advertising agencies, which liked to check reproduction of their ads, and even newsroom personnel.

A classic example of Malone's parsimony occurred on one of his visits to Victoria in the 1950s. We were starting to make decent profits and some modest raises for non-contract staffers were indicated. I had prepared a list of about a dozen people, with increases ranging from $2.50 a week to $15. Malone picked up the list from my desk and began to read it. "What's this?" he demanded. I told him. "Mmm," he murmured, taking a pencil from his pocket. Systematically, he went down the list — of people he didn't know — striking out the intended increases and substituting his own estimates. One concerned an editorial secretary down for a raise of $2.50. Malone struck it out and wrote in the margin: "$1.75." To me, this was almost as funny as it was pitiable. I put his revised list aside and proceeded, as was my mandate, to make the raises.

To be sure, someone in the national organization had to watch the pennies and Malone could not be faulted on that score. In this role, he performed a valuable function for then-president

Max Bell. Bell could be off at the Derby in England or in Ireland with his horses or playing golf at Pebble Beach with the certain knowledge that someone back home was minding the store.

Malone's judgements on business matters were quixotic — some highly successful and some disasters. He brought the Montreal *Star,* after long negotiations, into the FP fold and gave the group a strong base in French Canada; and he scored a genuine coup when he acquired the Toronto *Telegram* plant and equipment for approximately the same price as he realized from sale of the *Globe and Mail* building on King Street in Toronto. But he also muffed a cablevision deal in Vancouver — because he neglected to put his deal in writing — which cost the company about $3.5 million in paper profits in less than a month. He resisted when his Vancouver executives urged him to buy Spectacolor, a new process which provided living colour on one side of a pre-printed newsprint roll, but they wore him down. Malone's judgement proved correct. The rich sheet was costly, wasteful, and infrequently used.

In many respects, he was a mass of contradictions — an arch-conservative at the head of a famous Liberal newspaper; a soldier who painted (in a style worthy of any Moir's chocolate box); a writer of stupefying solemnity; an executive who mistrusted reporters; a robust scrapper who could still address an opponent as "old dear".

Among his early decrees was one to the effect that no FP executives should accept directorships in corporations outside the newspaper business. It was a sound decision, rendered meaningless a few months later when Malone joined the board of Monarch Life and became one of its most active members.

In 1974 the Brigadier removed himself, and the head office of FP, to Toronto, where he also named himself Publisher and Editor-in-Chief of the *Globe and Mail.* This caused some old-timers to recall the remark of Travers Coleman, the waggish CPR public relations man, when Col. Victor Sifton took the same titles for himself at the *Free Press*: "The greatest appointment since the Emperor Caligula made his horse a pro-consul of Rome."

# Chapter 21

"The great editors of the past had usually
been autocrats ... but with respect for those
who worked with them. They listened, discussed and were prepared to argue. They
recognized that the voice of a newspaper
was more than one man's voice. They ruled
as the first among equals."

— *Lord Northcliffe*

When in the summer of 1973 the Montreal *Star* amalgamated
with the FP group, *Time* magazine seized on the opportunity to
do a short take-out on Malone. It published four fat paragraphs
and a picture of Malone staring soberly at something off-camera
and clutching the inevitable Muriel cigar. The caption under the
picture read: "No penchant for interfering." The horse-laughs
engendered by this statement were enough to rock the Fordham
University seismograph to an 8.2 reading on the Richter scale.
A great many FP employees — too many, in fact — felt that they
had to wire Malone before going to the bathroom.

Malone wanted regular reports not only on newsprint waste,
but on vacation schedules and circulation figures, as well as
monthly statements of expense for each department. On a visit
to Victoria, he demanded that an addressograph machine be
moved from one corner of the office to another. He advised
Lethbridge that its contribution to a Red Cross drive (the request
was for $2,500) should not exceed $500, only to be cut off by
Howard Webster who, tiring of debate, said he would make up
the difference out of his own pocket. In a historic memo to all
points, Malone asked to be advised when his executives planned
to be away from their desks for more than two days. On another
occasion, he asked the *Sun* if it would pick up one-third of a

$350 charge to send a medical reporter to a convention in Philadelphia. In view of the fact that his company was at the time doing more than $150 million gross business, this intervention seemed a bit remote for a busy president.

In addition to overseeing the group's nine newspapers, Malone insisted on appointing London and Washington bureau chiefs, and paying them subsistence salaries. A *Sun* man who was being paid $14,000 a year and scoring substantial news-beats, found himself well in arrears of journeyman Washington reporters. When the New York *Times* and the Washington *Post* offered him jobs at $25,000, he resisted temptation and stayed on the promise of a top editorial post in Canada later on.

Not all had the same faith, or endurance. An outstanding loss was Shane MacKay of Winnipeg. After two years as *Free Press* correspondent in Ottawa and Washington he resigned to become editor of *Reader's Digest* in Canada, returning to the *Free Press* as editor in 1959. Eight years later he quit this prestigious post to become a vice-president of International Nickel in Toronto. Malone explained that MacKay left "because of the money". But to friends MacKay confided: "I had to leave. It was a one-man show, with no future."

The roster of FP alumni who tried, but gave up in despair, was impressive. Anthony Westell, Jack Cahill and Stan McDowell, all first-rate journalists, went to the Toronto *Star*. Ian Macdonald and Mike Gillan joined the federal government service. Duart Farquharson, son of the famous managing editor who built the *Globe and Mail,* Bob Farquharson, shifted over to Southam. Don Peacock, who had done a book on Trudeau, found the shoestring budget at the *Albertan* intolerable and shipped off to Canada House in London as information officer. These eight men would have adorned any newspaper staff in the country.

Of particular concern to me was Malone's mishandling of negotiations which would have brought Bob Elson to FP as chief of the Washington bureau. Nearing retirement with Time, Inc., after a brilliant career, Elson advised me that he wanted to stay on in journalism and would be happy with a desk in Washington. As a long-time participant in Time's profit-sharing plan, he wasn't too much concerned about money. It seemed like a perfect set-up and I reported it to Malone with enthusiasm. At first, Malone reacted positively to the idea. But then, as an exchange of letters got under way, he blew it. He could not resist telling Elson how he should do the job. His task, Malone said, would be "to give us the Canadian news from Washington". Elson, not unnaturally, saw it in broader perspective. He had been in Washington for many years and was one of the most respected men in the business. He had headed up the *Time-Life* bureau in London. He had roamed the world for *Fortune*. While Canadian news was important, it was in limited supply in Washington; what was needed was a broad overview of world events as seen through the eyes of a man who was both Canadian and American. (Elson was born in Cleveland, raised in Vancouver.) Eventually, Elson decided not to move. "Sorry, Stu," he told me. "It just wouldn't work."

Nobody disputed Malone's right, as president of the company, to hire whom he wished. The tragedy was that his low opinion of journalists was only surpassed by his authority. Indeed, there was strong evidence to indicate that Malone didn't *want* strong personalities around him. As the papers in the chain had grown from five to nine and the problems of the Sifton and Bell estates proliferated, Malone's pace became increasingly frenetic. Clark Davey, former managing editor of the *Globe and Mail,* once said of his publisher: "There is no such a person as Dick Malone. He's an airline ticket." En route Malone would scrawl notes on the back of an envelope; this would become the agenda for his meetings with executives at the next stop. When fellow directors urged him to hire an assistant, Malone concurred but refused to do anything about it. It was apparent that he was incapable of delegating authority.

What was lacking throughout FP was a spirit of team-work, of men and women pulling together in a worthwhile mission behind a leader who could inspire the troops. In the first fifteen years of the group's existence I can recall exactly three occasions when publishers and general managers of various cities were called to Winnipeg or Ottawa to break bread and discuss common problems. No incentives by way of scholarships or prizes were offered to young talent in the organization, to help build a logical line of succession.

When the job of publisher of the Victoria *Times* came open, Malone appointed Arthur Irwin, who was seventy and had not been active in newspapers for more than a quarter-century. A brilliant man, Irwin had edited *Maclean's* magazine in its "golden era" and had gone into the National Film Board as director and thence to the foreign service, where he had represented Canada with distinction in Australia, South America and Mexico.

On his retirement, friends gave Irwin a dinner at the Union Club in Victoria. This shy, diffident man, possessed of a glacial intellect, made a pointed speech in which he urged FP to remember that "... journalism is for journalists."

Malone, who was present, seemed not to hear. He had hired three young men as junior executives on whom, he said, he was "pinning his hopes for the future". One was his son Richard who became publisher of the Winnipeg *Free Press*. A second was Bruce Rudd, a Ridley old boy, who became publisher of the Calgary *Albertan*. A third was Dennis Ashworth, who quit and went back to Halifax. All three were lawyers. Malone believed that he could make newspapermen of them by "putting them through the drill". This meant putting them on a circulation truck for a couple of months; sending them out to sell classified advertising for a few weeks; and having them assist on the news side until they had published a few stories or written an editorial.

To be sure, Malone professed a hands-off attitude and insisted that he would give his publishers "every support and backing". To insiders, he confessed that there were two papers he would not tamper with — the *Globe and Mail* and the *Sun*. As an old Army man, he considered it good policy to reinforce success and cut losses; both the *Globe* and the *Sun* were eminently successful.

The *Sun* had an added advantage: geographically, it was further away from head office than most papers in the group and hence less susceptible to interference. Not that Malone could resist the attempt. He frequently called our house, at strange hours.* A few weeks after FP took over control of the *Sun,* Malone's disposition to meddle became vividly apparent when I was faced with a top-level shift in editorial appointments. The man in charge of the *Sun's* editorial pages at the time was Paul St. Pierre. A gifted

---

\* This prompted my daughter Kathryn to compose a little jingle, which she sang to the tune of Harry Belafonte's calypso "Mary Ann":

> All day, all night Dick Malone
> Call me daddy on de tely-phone
> Why can't he leave us alone?
> Goddam! Sumbitch! Dick Malone!

writer, St. Pierre had decided that he wanted to be an administrator and, ideally, to proceed onwards and upwards to the position of publisher of one of FP's papers. The only thing wrong with this scenario was that St. Pierre was a poor administrator; a prickly personality who had difficulty in getting along with his staff. From time to time, insurrections were threatened.

Before very long, I found I was spending an hour to ninety minutes each morning, wrangling with St. Pierre about fine editorial points. He was tough, unyielding, strongly cynical and disputative. It soon became apparent that he would have to move. I relieved St. Pierre of his editorial-page duties and turned him loose as a columnist, free to roam the country as he pleased and write the wryly humorous kind of copy at which he had few equals.

This, of course, created a vacancy as editor of the editorial pages. But there was a competent successor waiting — Cliff MacKay, a rangy, laconic man with Mount Rushmore features who had, in all his career, worked for only one newspaper. His knowledge of civic affairs was encyclopaedic, and he had moved progressively up the ladder at the *Sun* until in 1944 he became editor.

In 1960 Cromie had shifted him to the business pages, in which capacity he had performed in his usual stalwart style and quickly won the confidence of financial readers with carefully-researched columns and factual analyses. But in yet another shake-up MacKay was bounced again and found himself back on the city hall beat, where he had first made his name thirty years earlier.

Observing all this from Victoria, I was appalled at the treatment meted out to so capable an employee. But it was a notion of mine that the true test of a man was how he reacted to adversity. MacKay was outstanding: in spite of two cruel set-backs, he was performing nobly at his diminished duties and was widely respected as a kind of "elder statesman" of municipal affairs.

I called him at city hall and said: "Cliff, how would you like your old job back?"

"I'll be right down," he replied. And he was.

Although the terms of the Sun-Southam agreement clearly specified that it was the publisher's prerogative to make all appointments in editorial, advertising, circulation and promotion, I decided to telephone Malone and advise him, as a courtesy.

Malone listened for a moment and then said: "Tell you what you do, Stu, make him acting editor. You never know how these things are going to work out."

"But Dick," I said, "Cliff MacKay held this job for sixteen years before Cromie bust him. It would be an insult to list him as 'acting'."

And Malone replied: "Tell you what you do, Stu. Give him three to six months and then if he seems satisfactory put him on the mast-head."

"Dick," I replied, "the appointment is already made. I have offered the job to MacKay. He has accepted. I have advised Bruce Hutchison. He is happy."

"Tell you what you do, Stu, " said Malone. "Just hold your fire. It will all work out."

"Dick," I said, with growing exasperation, "Cliff's name is already up on the mast-head."

"Tell you what you do, Stu . . ."

Suddenly, it dawned on me: This guy *wasn't even listening* to what I was telling him. *Tell you what you do, Stu.* A broken record. The most splendid example of the doctrine of uninterruptability since Harry Luce.

A few weeks later, Malone tackled me on the *Sun's* use of news pictures. He felt that they were much too large and that, in fact, no page one picture should be wider than three columns. Anything else, he argued, was "cheating the public" by depriving them of news stories, in cold type. This was an extremely sensitive area for a newspaper which had, in fact, won an international reputation for its bold and dramatic play of pictures. Photographers across the country sought jobs at the paper, realizing that their work would get more imaginative use in its columns than anywhere else. Also, the pictures were developed by the "wet engraving" process, which produced sharper tones and more distinctive lines. By contrast, the *Free Press,* the *Times* and the *Colonist* reproduced pictures by a cheap process called Klischograph, which tended to make pictures look as though they had been chewed up by ravenous moths.

Inevitably, Malone's overtures had to be rebuffed. They erupted anew when the *Sun* came out one day with an eight-column picture on top of page one, reporting on a pair of young American skiers who had elected to be joined in holy matrimony on the shining snows of Garibaldi mountain, near Vancouver. It was a joyous, happy picture, given considerable photographic clout by the generous framing of snow-capped peaks in the background. "Snow-capped," of course, could also be translated as "white space," which is all a newspaper has to sell. Malone was incensed and called me angrily to demand that we eschew publishing pictures of "crazy American kids getting married on a mountain". The white space, he estimated, could have become three or four columns of hard news. Sure. And the *Sun* could have become the Winnipeg *Free Press.*

About this time, help arrived from an unexpected source. The president of Gannett newspapers, the largest chain in the US, was a photographic buff named Vincent Jones. From time to time his people conducted a survey of picture-play in various North American newspapers — a survey which consistently showed the *Sun* in the top half-dozen papers on the continent. In the fall of 1970 — six years after Malone had begun his campaign to trim back *Sun* pictures — Jones wrote to me: "So far as I am concerned, the Vancouver *Sun,* day in and day out, does the best job of handling pictures of any newspaper I have seen — and I have seen a lot of them at one time or another . . ."

I sent a letter to Malone, enclosing Jones' comments, and saying:

> I thought the picture of the New York couple getting married on a nearby glacier was fascinating, and just right for a Saturday weekend illustration. As you know, one of the most persistent complaints we get in newspapers today is against the steady flow of gloomy and depressing news of the world: riots, murders, floods, hurricanes, etc. Such pictures provide a welcome 'change of pace' for our readers and serve as an antidote to the grim fodder of the news columns.
>
> Another thing you will appreciate is that snow is *news* in our area. I know it is not in other parts of Canada, but our frequent use of scenics provides a reminder to our readers how lucky they are to live in these balmy climes. Our readers love it. . . .
>
> In contrast with the *Sun's* sharp, imaginative pictures I am enclosing tear-sheets of recent copies of the Victoria *Times,*

the *Colonist,* and the *Free Press* . . . I think the readers of those important papers deserve a better break. . . . I am sure it would be folly to tamper with techniques which have proved such a big winner in this area.

Malone did not reply.

# Chapter 22

"The job of an editor is to march down the
hill after the battle and shoot the wounded."

— *Murray Kempton*

At six o'clock on a certain November morning in 1977 I was
awakened in my Harbour Castle hotel room in Toronto by a clap
of thunder. Sullen skies, illuminated by bolts of lightning, indicated a stormy Ontario day.

The lake-front electricity was appropriate. A mile away, at the
Front Street offices of the *Globe and Mail,* a thunderhead of
another dimension was gathering which would reverberate through
the newsrooms of Canada. For at 10 a.m. Derek Price, former
publisher and principal shareholder of the Montreal *Star,* was to
lay before FP directors a twelve-page manifesto demanding that
the company elect a new president.

He was not alone in this sentiment. A gradual dissatisfaction
with the operation of the company had been building. While the
profits of Southam and Thomson were rising, and new acquisitions were strengthening their respective bases, FP's profits were
declining. Howard Webster, a principal shareholder, had quit the
board, though not his chairmanship of the *Globe and Mail.* It
was becoming embarrassingly evident that a multi-million-dollar
enterprise, in an era of technological revolution and expansion,
could not be run on an *ad hoc* basis "from the back of an airline
ticket".

Copies of the document had already been provided to the
meeting. In a tense atmosphere, chairman Joe Sedgewick said:

"Now we have this letter from Derek. Would you care to speak to it?" Price looked straight ahead and murmured: "I don't think I have anything to add. The paper speaks for itself."

The case had been stated in quiet tones. But Price's message was clear: Malone must step down, or the *Star* group would have to reconsider its position in the FP galaxy. Malone, at 68, had discussed with a few associates the possibilities of retirement; he had backed an earlier request for a "search committee" to find a successor. But little had happened and he appeared content to hang on, hinting that he might accept a position as chairman of the board (the classic corporate gambit) or even, under pressure, stay on as publisher of the *Globe and Mail.*

Dispassionate Malone-watchers understood. The newspapers were his life, love, and power-base. He had few hobbies beyond the occasional game of croquet, a bit of skating, and reading military history. He kept in touch with his son Richard in Winnipeg by telephone and was the adoring father of an only daughter, Deirdre, in Toronto. He lived alone in a handsome old house on Dunvegan Road, tended to by a white-haired housekeeper he had brought with him from Winnipeg. There was little to persuade him to relinquish the presidency. Price's memo irritated him. "Those *Star* fellows have never been on the team," he fussed. "Derek thinks he can find some hot-shot on Bay Street or St. James. What we need is someone who knows something about the newspaper business."

But the anti-Malone forces were not to be denied. Eight weeks later, on January 24, 1978 their decision was announced at a 10 a.m. meeting in the board room of the *Globe and Mail*—not a large room, all smoked mirrors and leather chairs, but a room pervaded with the soothing ambience of power and money. The fatal cut was delivered, in clean and surgical slices, by a cherubic Toronto lawyer named Purdy Crawford. As head of the "search committee" Mr. Crawford read from a six-page report. Some eighty contenders for the job as president of FP had been considered. These had been winnowed down to six, who had been personally interviewed. The final choice was a fifty-year-old Toronto management consultant named George N. M. Currie. It was the unanimous recommendation of the committee that he be offered the post.

Midway through the report there was a paragraph which surprised me. The affairs of the company would be directed, for at least a year, by an executive committee consisting of Currie, the new president, Derek Price of Montreal and Stuart Keate of Vancouver. The first I had heard of this was in a conversation the day before when FP director David Ferguson had spelled out the background of this new initiative to me: "George Currie has never been in newspapers," he said. "Derek is a former publisher and the largest single shareholder in FP. You are the only journalist on the board. The two of you can advise the president and ease the transition.

On the 24th I had arrived at the *Globe and Mail* offices at 9:45, fifteen minutes before the meeting was due to start. Malone immediately asked to see me in his office. It was clear that he was unhappy about the turn of events. He deplored the fact that the search committee could not produce a newspaperman. He knew Currie (a Ridley old boy) and professed to like him, but he had had some negative reports on his career as a business-management expert and thought he was the wrong choice. He intended to "say his piece" at the meeting and urged me to "speak up". He, Malone, was going to press for Bruce Rudd (another Ridley old boy) as president. If he was not acceptable in this role, Malone intended to back him as publisher of the Vancouver *Sun* when I retired, probably at the end of the year.

This brief conversation placed me in an extremely difficult position. I did not know Currie and could scarcely comment on his qualifications. On the other hand, I could not support Rudd as president of the company. I felt — and told Malone — that Rudd was in exactly the right spot as general manager. He had been my assistant in Vancouver for five years. Trained as a lawyer, he had shown some talent for labour negotiations but had only limited experience on the editorial side and was not in my opinion qualified to direct the affairs of one of Canada's largest metropolitan dailies, let alone an entire group. But Malone managed to introduce one more caveat. What, he asked, was the position of the shareholders and particularly the majority owners? Did this recommendation have the blessing of Howard Webster in Montreal? When Crawford, Price, Joe Sedgewick (chairman of the board and Webster's lawyer) and David Ferguson all reported that Webster was in favour, Malone's last redoubt was demolished.

The final, approving motion was carried with only Malone

dissenting. Later, in his office, he was surprisingly philosophical. "I don't like it, but we'll try to make it work," he mused. He would stay as publisher of the *Globe and Mail* for an indefinite period.

But new president Currie obviously had other plans. Within five months he announced the appointment as publisher of the *Globe and Mail* of a forty-one-year-old Irishman named A. Roy Megarry, who had been vice-president of corporate development with the Torstar Corporation. A special meeting of the FP board was called and met for the first time at new company headquarters in the Royal Trust Tower in Toronto. Around the table were Malone (who would assume the post of chairman of the board); lawyers Joe Sedgewick, Don McGavin and Purdy Crawford; Derek Price, David Ferguson and myself.

George Currie opened the meeting by reading a four-page, single-spaced letter outlining his negotiations with Roy Megarry. He detailed Megarry's background and told the meeting that the Toronto *Star* was greatly upset at the prospect of losing him. He was, in effect, a number two man to Beland Honderich at the *Star* and a hard-hitting, talented young executive. After some tough negotiating, Megarry had agreed to come over to FP and had initialled the letter of agreement.

Malone was sizzling. When Currie had finished, Malone asked to "make a few comments" and read from six pages of long-hand notes which he had prepared since receipt of the black-spot letter. Malone elected to take the high road, objecting to Megarry's appointment on principle. He was not a journalist and it was terribly wrong to impose on the *Globe and Mail,* "Canada's National Newspaper", a man with so little experience in the field. Furthermore, Malone argued, the present board had not been properly briefed. Most of those at the meeting had not met Megarry (true), nor received the president's letter in time for careful study.

Also, there was the board of the *Globe and Mail* to consider. What would they say? Jim Cooper, who had retired as publisher when Malone acceded to the office, and had presided over the highly-regarded "Report on Business" could hardly approve a non-newspaperman, and Malone had no doubt that editor Dic Doyle and managing editor Clark Davey would be "shaken" by the news. Montreal *Star* publisher Bill Goodson, he said, was an aspirant for the Toronto job and would have his nose out of joint. Other top contenders like Assistant Publisher Colin McCullough and Bruce Rudd would probably seek employment elsewhere.

These strong arguments were followed by an impassioned brief from Don McGavin, who said he was stunned that this mighty newspaper should be placed in the hands of a veritable novice. With unconscious irony, he exclaimed: "Why, *Globe and Mail* editors rub shoulders with deputy ministers in Ottawa. Would this man have easy entrée to the deputy ministers? I doubt it." Since the *Globe and Mail* not infrequently hosted the Prime Minister, and members of his Cabinet, at luncheon conferences in their boardroom, this question appeared academic. Finally, McGavin made a motion to the effect that the agreement with Megarry be rescinded. Malone seconded the motion.

It was, of course, doomed to fail. As a member of the executive committee, I was asked to comment. I told the meeting that I had not met Megarry, regretted the fact that he was not a journalist, but was prepared to accept the evaluation of him by Currie and Price as a "hard-hitting, talented young executive" whose appointment was a calculated risk, but one worth taking. More importantly, I said, the motion before the meeting must fail because its passage would leave the president in a "totally untenable position". He had made a deal, Megarry had initialled it, and it could not be rescinded. I concluded by saying: "It seems to me there is only one course of action open. Dick has to swallow hard, endorse the president's initiatives, and issue a statement wishing Megarry well."

The motion to rescind Megarry's appointment was defeated by a vote of six to two. Malone, to his credit, murmured: "I'll do my best to make the transition easy. But I don't approve the action and want my objections in the minutes."

A press release the next day announced the turnover date as September 1, two months hence. Malone would continue as chairman of the board. In due course he moved his office, his *Globe and Mail* secretary, and twelve filing cabinets to the new FP offices. Like an old soldier, he had apparently resolved to "lay me down and bleed awhile, and rise to fight again . . ."

The eruptions he had forecast did not materialize. President Currie moved quickly to bring together new publisher Megarry and the proud *Globe* editors, Doyle and Davey. They received

Megarry cordially and promised their new boss co-operation. Later, Currie arranged to take Megarry to lunch with Don McGavin, after which McGavin pronounced himself as "greatly relieved" at the decision.

Within a matter of weeks of his appointment it had become clear that the top priority of Currie, the "business doctor", was to impose some management systems and structures on the haphazard FP organization. One of his first acts was to hire away from Eaton's, as director of personnel, forty-six-year-old John Egan, with a mandate to review pensions and salaries across the chain (some of them were miserable); establish organizational charts at each paper; advise the president on appointments to senior positions; and advise on all aspects of labour relations.

Ted Bolwell, an aggressive Aussie, was sent off on a tour of all papers to discuss with publishers a much-needed overhaul of bureau appointments, notably in Ottawa where the *Globe and Mail* wanted to stand alone and there was much duplication of effort and under-utilization of talent. Before long Bolwell was named as editorial director of the chain, to advise the president and ensure maximum flow of copy between papers. A new design editor, Keith Branscombe, was appointed to introduce face-lifts where needed, starting with the Winnipeg *Free Press*. Consulting firms were engaged to make in-depth studies of Ottawa, Calgary and Winnipeg. A chartered accountant, Ken Wheeler, was hired as Controller of the Corporation to prepare budgets and a system of reviewing capital expenditures instituted.

The parent company itself was divided, for tax considerations and more uniform reporting, into FP (Eastern) and FP (Western). This last became possible when shares of *Sun* Publishing in Vancouver were redeemed (at $69 a share) and control passed from Vancouver to Toronto. The meeting approving this structure was not without heartbreak: two veteran shareholders deplored the loss to BC of a company rooted in the western tradition, no matter how fair (or *unfair,* as one argued) the pay-off.

"Winds of change" began to blow throughout the organization. In Victoria, veteran Reuter's chief and *Times* publisher Stuart Underhill announced his retirement and was succeeded by Colin McCullough. In Vancouver, Bruce Hutchison, now 77, accepted a new title as "Editor emeritus" and Frank Rutter was recalled from London to take charge of the editorial pages. In Ottawa, the strike-weary Lou Lalonde stepped aside in favour of Ray Morris, who had been president of commercial printing operations of the Toronto *Star*. Lalonde moved to Toronto as a special consultant to the president.

Meanwhile Roy Megarry was justifying the faith expressed in him by the selection committee. Working around the clock, lunching with editors, getting to know his staff, Megarry infused the paper with a gung-ho spirit which was reflected in increased circulation and lineage. The highly successful "Report on Business" was expanded to six days a week. New sections were added on sports, entertainment, outdoors activities, fashions and the arts. An additional 800 "honour boxes" were created in Toronto to meet the inner-city challenges of the Toronto *Sun*.

It soon became apparent that Megarry represented one of the "new breed" of publishers. In an early interview, he described himself as an "operations-oriented financial manager". Later he said, "I'm going to be looking for any and every means of recycling the data base we have at the *Globe and Mail*." The *Globe*, he said, was well along in the development of an electronic "morgue" — a newspaper's system of filing stories and editorials.

Towards the end of 1979 Megarry announced a plan to transmit the *Globe's* first edition by satellite to Calgary, for faster regional distribution. The hope was that existing circulation in the West (6,000 of the *Globe* and 16,000 of the "Report on Business") could be expanded to 50,000. Executive editor Cam Smith estimated the cost at about $1 million, half of which would be needed to operate earth stations and to pay for transmission time. Megarry was quoted as saying: "I hope there's something more here than dollars. It's much more than solving the telecommunications problem, much more than solving the post office problem — it goes right to the heart and essence of the newspaper. It really is going to usher in a new era for the *Globe*. For the first time in our history, the circulation will be truly national."

Give Megarry marks for enterprise, and boldness. But the record does not inspire optimism. The classic experience in North America was the New York *Times'* bid to establish a western daily edition out of San Francisco. For all its treasure and talent, the *Times* could not significantly penetrate the market and abandoned the enterprise. The paper failed for reasons both practical and sentimental. Start-up costs invariably exceed early projections.

And sheer excellence is no guarantee of acceptance. The record shows that, given a choice between a home-town newspaper and one originating 3,000 miles away, the vast majority of readers will remain loyal to the home-grown sheet. Indeed, one wonders if Megarry and Smith have fully considered the degree of resistance by western Canadians to *any* product of Toronto. Even if their target of 50,000 copies is achieved, it will represent only about 15 per cent of the circulation of Vancouver's dailies.

Nevertheless, a newspaper can never stand still. The *Globe* situation reminded me of Ted Reeve's immortal quatrain:

*Pierre had a dog team, the pride of the Bay*
*The lead dog got sore so he gave him away.*
*But the team kept running as though they had wings*
*The second dog had a new outlook on things.*

# Chapter 23

> "There is something intensely personal and intimate about one's love for one's news-paper. When a newspaper is ill, her sons are unhappy; and when she dies, they grieve, and they receive the sincere sympathy of the sons of all other newspapers. Then almost everyone gets drunk, and there is a wake."
>
> — *Gene Fowler*

Not long after George Currie took over as president of FP, we had a heart-to-heart talk about my position at the Vancouver *Sun.* At best it was short-term. I was a few months away from retirement age of 65. Letha was urging me to get out. The daily round of problems were taking on a sense of *déjà vu* which I found increasingly irksome.

In addition, I was not well. On a trip to Toronto I had tripped on some steps and opened up my forehead for nineteen stitches. A few months later, returning to the Pacific Press plant after lunch, I suddenly felt my feet "slapping" and my knees weak. *If I can only make it to the elevator,* I thought, *I'll be okay.*

I made it to the door and collapsed in a heap. The staff nurse suddenly materialized and helped me to the first-aid office. A doctor checked me over and could find nothing wrong. Nevertheless, I made an appointment the next day with the company doctor, Nairn Knott. As we were preparing for a check-over, he asked me for a medical card. I fumbled for the wallet in my hip pocket. When, after a couple of minutes, I was still fumbling and could not execute this simple act, Nairn looked at me quizzically and said: "Hey — what's all this? I'm sending you to a neurologist."

Exhaustive tests were inconclusive. I had the circulation system, two doctors averred, of "a twenty-year-old boy". In compliance with the doctors' wishes, I cut my weight back to 196 pounds, reduced my consumption of cigars from about six to two a day, and took to drinking only a glass of wine, or Perrier water, with meals. Nevertheless, the "spinny" attacks continued. About once a week — usually after climbing a flight of stairs, or getting up suddenly — I felt an uncontrollable dizziness, usually lasting only twenty seconds or so. Twice I collapsed — once at home and again in a downtown restaurant.

The doctors concluded that I was suffering from a "very mild" form of Parkinsonism. There was no known cure for the disease, but it could be controlled by regular use of a drug called Sinemet. None of this was conveyed to my principals, or staff, although I had no doubt that news of the elevator collapse had whipped through the building. But it did confirm my resolve to retire at the earliest convenient moment.

In the end, it was agreed that I would take normal retirement at 65 but stay on until the end of 1978 to assist my successor in the transition. At Currie's request, I joined the search for a candidate and in due course submitted the names of ten men whom I believed should be considered for the job. The ideal, of course, was to find someone we could "promote from within". But after several months of searching, and interviews, it came down to three men from other parts of Canada: Clark Davey, Ted Bolwell and Shane MacKay.

Davey was the outstanding, hard-hitting managing editor of the *Globe and Mail.* Bolwell had held important posts on the *Globe and Mail* (from which he had once been fired), the Toronto *Star, Time* magazine, the New York *Times* and, most recently, the New York *Post.* MacKay was the former Winnipeg *Free Press* editor who had left the business to join Inco as a vice-president. I had nominated all three and was certain that any one of them would do an elegant job in Vancouver.

When Bolwell decided that he wanted to remain in Toronto, it left only Davey and MacKay. Currie chose Davey on the not unreasonable grounds that he had been intimately involved with the *Globe and Mail* as managing editor for the past fifteen years while MacKay — despite his unquestioned talents — had been

212

out of the business for almost a decade. Arrangements were made for Davey to fly out to Vancouver toward the end of October.

Clark Davey was inheriting a going concern. *Sun* circulation had climbed back to a healthy 252,000 and was still growing. Marketing director, John Toogood, reported that the month of October was the greatest, in terms of revenue and profits, in the history of the newspaper. Our budget indicated a before-tax profit of $13.5 million on the year which, while a million or so below the previous year, was by far the greatest in the FP group and among the first three or four (the Toronto *Star*, Edmonton *Journal*, and Hamilton *Spectator*) in Canada.

But ominous labour clouds were gathering. Pacific Press, disturbed by restrictive practices and feather-bedding in the press-room and mailing departments, had demanded some relief in contract language which would stop the haemorrheage in over-time charges, estimated to cost an extra $800,000.

Pressmen were joined by the Newspaper Guild, involving about 850 workers in the newsroom, clerical, business-office, advertising and maintenance staffs, on the issue of "exclusions". This involved a company demand for certain department heads — sports, womens', photographic and some columnists — to be released from the Guild and recognized for what they were: second-level management people who operated budgets and had a good deal to say about hirings and firings. The pressmen argued that they had negotiated manning practices in past contracts and were not prepared to discuss them. Guild officers told their members (quite incorrectly) that management was insisting on removing as many as 200 persons from their authority with the aim of creating an inside "scab staff" which would be capable of producing a paper without union participation. At no time had this been considered by management; while they were capable of producing a paper, it was recognized that it would be impossible to get it out past the picket-lines of pressmen, mailers and delivery people, some of whom were affiliated with the tough Teamsters Union.

In essence, it was the same problem which was wracking the New York *Times*, St. Louis *Post-Dispatch*, Montreal *Star* and Toronto *Star*. In 90 per cent of North American papers new language had been accepted which would phase out restrictive practices over a period of years, mainly by attrition. The New York *Times* won such concessions, prompting executive editor A. M. ("Abe") Rosenthal to observe: "This is the last big strike, at least round here. There's nothing we can't do now. ... It was a necessary strike. We had to stop the feather-bedding; we waited too long as it was.... The government can't close us down ... but these people could. That won't happen again."

In order to soften the blow, and the inevitable reductions, Pacific Press guaranteed that no regular staffer would lose his job. What he had amounted to tenure up to normal retirement. As a "sweetener", the company placed on the table a bonus averaging $5,000, payable immediately, for each press and mailing-room employee. The response of the unions was: "Our contracts are not for sale."

On October 31, I gathered the newsroom staff, announced my retirement as publisher, and introduced Clark Davey. At 9:45 the next morning the staff walked out. The company countered with a formal notice of lock-out, which meant simply that it would not be obliged to pay people who were prepared to enter the plant with no prospect of working. The whole initiative was sickening. I was convinced that the great majority of workers had little appreciation of the nature of the dispute although one of them, a courageous environmental reporter named Moira Farrow, stood up before TV cameras and said "This is all nonsense. We're being asked to subsidize overtime for the pressmen."

That something was wrong was evident in the fact that this was the fifth strike in ten years — one a wildcat lasting less than a day but another, in 1970, stretching out for three months. In that one, we had lost about 25,000 circulation as readers turned to TV and radio for their news. Like Sisyphus, we had over the next eight years rolled the rock back to the top of the hill only to have it slip and come crashing down on us once more.

Two days after the strike the unions came out with their own thrice-weekly paper, the *Express*. But this time public attitudes were vastly different than in 1970. For one thing, subscribers wondered how it was possible for the unions to produce a paper while denying that right to management. If reporters worked for $175 a week at the *Express* as opposed to the $400-a-week scale at the *Sun*, were they not in effect producing a "scab" newspaper?

In the general public revulsion against recurring strikes, and widespread resentment of bully-boy tactics, readers tended to sympathize with the established dailies. The Board of Trade, in a spontaneous gesture, urged its members not to buy the strike paper. Department store and theatre advertisers elected to stay out of the *Express*. But the strikers had chosen their ground carefully. By November 15, commitments for the rich Christmas advertising trade had gone aglimmering. With that deadline past, the prospects for early settlement were minimal.

In news terms, and corporate terms, it was simultaneously the best of times and the worst of times. The last six weeks of 1978 brought a flood of news unprecedented in recent history. A civic election (which remains unreported in detail to this day); a conference of first ministers; the mass suicides and killings in Guyana; a judges' scandal which had rocked Vancouver to its foundations; the death of a new Pope after only thirty-four days in office, and the election of a successor; liberalization in China, and recognition of the People's Republic by the United States; bloody upheavals in Iran and Nicaragua.

In addition, editors recalled a lesson from the strike of 1970. What concerned readers most — more than the federal bye-elections, more than Middle East peace initiatives — was the simple day-to-day record of births, deaths and marriages. A man who asked an old friend "How's your wife?" was embarrassed to learn that she had died a week before. Arrangements were made with funeral directors for a complete list of obituaries to be published free in the classified columns at strike's end.

While Clark Davey found himself in the unique and unpleasant position of a "phantom publisher", George Currie in Toronto was up to his armpits in alligators and doubtless wondering why he had entered such a lunatic business. Before the end of his first year the company was in deep trouble in Montreal, Ottawa, Winnipeg and Vancouver. Montreal pressmen had walked out on June 14; the Ottawa *Journal* was reeling from the after-effects of a violent and bitter strike; and in Winnipeg Southam's *Tribune* was spending millions of dollars to take a run at the *Free Press,* and making some not-inconsiderable gains.

Newspaper-watchers seemed to detect a new spirit of animosity between the two leading groups, and an apparent willingness to fight it out to the bitter end. In Ottawa, the *Journal* had a written agreement that the papers would stand fast, together, against the assaults of the unions. To the intense surprise and dismay of Malone, the *Citizen* announced one day that it was prepared to sign a unilateral contract.

In Montreal there appeared to be developing a turn-around reminiscent of the Vancouver strike of 1946. Up until the day Montreal *Star* pressmen walked out, the morning *Gazette* was suffering. Its circulation had dwindled to 110,000 (vs. the *Star's* 165,000) and, with Quebec's new language laws threatening the very existence of English newspapers, it was freely predicted that the *Gazette* would go under. But, with the *Star* shut down, the *Gazette's* fortunes began to improve. Circulation climbed to 150,000, to 200,000 and even to 225,000 for special editions.

Six months after the *Star* was closed the *Gazette* wrote a contract for 200 craft employees which could only be regarded as a "sweetheart" deal, designed to solidify its stronghold. It gave pressmen a 35 per cent increase over the ensuing thirty months, raising their salaries to $473 a week ($24,596 a year, exclusive of overtime) for a four-day, 32-hour work week.

A similar arm's length atmosphere had descended on the respective head offices of Southam and FP in Toronto. As fellow engineering graduates of McGill and card-carrying alumni of the Old-Boy network, Gordon Fisher of Southam and George Currie of FP had been friends. Now their relationship was described by intimates as "formal".

The 1970 injunctions of the Davey Commission — which deplored the fact that the three majors were engorging the little fellows — had been largely ignored. FP proceeded with its amalgamation with the Montreal *Star*. Southam's swallowed up a number of smaller papers, including the Owen Sound *Sun-Times,* the Sault *Star,* the Prince George *Citizen* and the larger Windsor *Star*. A court order for the break-up of five Irving papers in New Brunswick was appealed, and the appeal was won.

If the 1970s represented a time of expansion, it appeared to many newspaper analysts that the 1980s, faced with the exigencies of higher costs and depleting equipment, could easily result in contraction or merger. This view was given credence by Gordon Fisher in a somewhat surprising speech to the Montreal Society of Financial Analysts. The *Gazette,* capitalizing on the misfortunes of the *Star,* was going well. But Fisher told his audience that the

*Gazette* might be forced to close within a few years or merge at least part of its operations with its rival, the *Star*.

"It is logical to say that it will not be possible to publish two profitable English-language newspapers in Montreal," Fisher observed. "Given the competition between [Southam and FP] both in Montreal and across Canada they might find it prudent to talk to one another, within the law and when the pressure is great enough."

The strike at the Montreal *Star* finally came to an end in mid-February of 1979. The paper had been shut down for eight months, the longest strike in its history. It returned with a flourish, running 200,000 copies, heavily promoted via radio, TV, trade paper advertising and even lapel stickers.

Newspaper watchers expected some lively competition; they were hardly prepared for the flat-out war which rapidly developed. The *Star* could not conceal its glee that four *Gazette* staffers left the Southam paper, at the peak of its prosperity, to join a paper reeling from a long shut-down. Within a week the skirmishing had escalated into a full-scale newspaper war. When the *Gazette* announced that it would publish an afternoon edition, to compete head-to-head with its rival, the *Star* angrily responded with plans for a *morning* edition, and managed to beat the *Gazette* onto the street by a few hours. Bemused Montrealers thus found themselves with a choice of *four* English-language dailies, with direct competition in both the morning and afternoon fields.

It couldn't last. In the event, the *Star* blinked first, suspending publication of its morning edition after a few weeks as costly and insignificant in terms of circulation. But the greatest shock was yet to come. On September 25, and virtually without warning, the *Star* announced that it was going out of business.

The death of *any* newspaper is normally a cause for distress. But news of the *Star's* demise shook the communications world of Canada. The newspaper, after all, had been publishing for 111 years and had established clear dominance over the *Gazette* in its field. It provided a crucial and respected voice in the French-English debate now wracking the province. It had also been a substantial money-maker ($5.7 million in 1976), with the McConnell wealth behind it.

Within a few days of the announcement, it became evident that former president Bill Goodson was going to carry the can. David Perks, Treasurer of FP said on radio that they should have settled with the pressmen "before the *Gazette*" and that Goodson's hard-nosed stance was a mistake. (Goodson replied that he had kept his company fully-informed of his negotiations.) At any rate, losses of $17.5 million since the start of the strike had become "a threat to the whole FP group" and could no longer be tolerated.

In an interview which appeared in the *Gazette,* FP president George Currie conceded that "a serious miscalculation was made on our part".

"And you are responsible for it?"

"No question. I accept responsibility for the closing of the Montreal *Star.*"

"Does that hurt?"

"It hurts a lot."

Later, in an appearance on "Front Page Challenge", *Star* managing editor Ray Heard attributed the demise of his paper to "conceit and arrogance on both sides — management and labour".

A small but important caveat was appended to all press releases: the *Gazette* needed those new presses at the *Star* and perhaps a deal could be worked out, with two papers produced from a common plant and FP in a minority partnership position. Public pronouncements from the rival camps crackled with electricity. Bill 101 had made the future of English-language newspapers problematical in Quebec, to say the least, and the departure of an estimated 80,000 Anglos was evidence of a declining market. But the *Gazette,* with the field all to itself, was confident that it could maintain 200,000 circulation and show a profit. The ultimate irony was the prophecy of a French-Canadian publisher, Pierre Peladeau, that he could produce a successful English-language tabloid to succeed the *Star.*

Three situations across Canada seemed to invite mergers. In Ottawa, Winnipeg and Calgary the two major chains were clashing head-to-head, with FP fighting back strongly.

In Ottawa, the *Citizen* was running away from the strike-plagued *Journal.* But in an effort to recover, FP moved the able Art Wood from the deceased Montreal *Star* to the *Journal* as publisher. By May of 1980, Wood was able to tell his readers of a 25 per cent growth in circulation over the past seven months.

By moving to the morning field, and brightening his columns with the work of Allan Fotheringham, Doug Small and other talents, Wood had increased the sale from 57,846 in September 1979 to an average of 72,381 in April 1980.

In Winnipeg, Southam's *Tribune* had been spending millions to challenge the lead of the *Free Press*. But the *Free Press* lashed back, re-designed its paper, broadened its coverage, and maintained a healthy lead over its aggressive rival.

In Calgary, the Southam's *Herald* was almost 3 to 1 ahead of the *Albertan,* which had shown some improvement, and a higher degree of acceptance, by going to a tabloid but suffered an ancient press and was at best a marginal operation.

Production from a common plant undoubtedly made economic sense in each of these constituencies. But would it be a good or a bad thing for the reader? Opinions vary. Advocates of the joint-operation system point out that weaker papers can be "carried" by the stronger; that wire services and bureaus can be expanded to give broader choice of news and columns to their members; that staffers can enjoy more "upward mobility" by progression through the chain; that special talents and ideas can be exchanged between papers, to the greater glory of all (as when Allan Fotheringham became a national columnist for the FP group in 1979); and that, given clear dominance in a morning or evening field, papers can forget about "scoops" and produce more responsible and reflective sheets.

This argument, persuasively set forth by such whopping chains as Thomson, and Gannett in the United States, of course ignores the benefit of direct, head-to-head competition — which purists regard as the essence of the business. Nor does it fire the blood of winners to realize that the profits they rack up will go to subsidize the losers.

To be sure, newspapers produced out of a common building could compete vigorously; it all depended on how much freedom local publishers were granted by head offices in Toronto. The Thomsons, for instance, liked to say that their papers enjoyed local autonomy and in the editorial sense this was probably true — but what did it matter if a rigid budget structure, imposed on every paper, prevented the publisher from making necessary improvements? Clair Balfour, president of Southam and once a publisher himself (of the Hamilton *Spectator*) knew enough to institute a hands-off policy. To a large extent, his papers were free. Malone, as we have seen, felt he had to inject his own views on everything from reportorial assignments to Red Cross contributions.

In my own lifetime, I had worked for three different kinds of newspaper apparatus: the privately-owned (Vancouver *News-Herald* and Toronto *Star*); the one-owner, two-papers-in-one-plant concept (Victoria *Times* and *Colonist*); and the Pacific Press, Siamese-twin structure where rival papers worked out of a common building, with the partners sharing profits. In retrospect, I would have to conclude that the direct, head-to-head competition was the most rewarding. The sharp-pencil boys, the accountants, tax-men, lawyers, and worshippers of the bottom line, would disagree. But surely Toronto provides living proof that competition works. There, readers have a choice between three papers, all of them profitable. Each has a distinct character; the person who subscribes to all three gets such a torrent of information (and gossip) that he enjoys the ultimate luxury of making up his own mind on the affairs of the day. It is difficult to think of another North American city, save perhaps New York, which is as well served by its press.

# Chapter 24

"I do lack my father's compulsive drive. I must force myself to develop in his direction. That includes expanding the business."

— *Lord Kenneth Thomson*

In 1979, as we have seen, the FP group of newspapers was in serious trouble. For most of its young life, from 1958 to 1978, FP had racked up healthy profits. Now the new president, George Currie, had to tell his shareholders that 1979 would, for the first time, be a year of losses.

This statement did not escape the attention of other newspaper owners in Canada. For months, there had been rumours of deals with Southam; indeed, some informal talks had been held between Currie and Gordon Fisher, but the Montreal situation had not been tidied up (the *Gazette* had yet to take over the *Star*'s facilities) and the two giants seemed far apart on possible mergers in Ottawa, Winnipeg and Calgary.

Suddenly, on the eve of the new decade, there erupted a flurry of FP take-over bids which rocked the industry and promised to change its face forever. For thirty-seven days of back-room wheeling and dealing there were exposed some towering aspirations, conflicts and cross-currents with four families and estates divided in their assessment of the property.

First into the game was a group headed by Conrad Black, celebrated "boy wonder" of Argus Corporation, who had declaimed at a recent Couchiching conference that Canada's journalists were "over-paid, under-worked, lazy and incompetent". Among his partners in the $102 million bid were George Gardiner, a financial whiz who had until recently been a director of FP and was a long-time trustee of the Max Bell Foundation, which held 22.5 per cent of the shares; John Bassett, whose apparent interest in getting back into newspapers was no surprise to his friends; and Fred Eaton, personable president of the department store family. Black's offer did not excite shareholders, at least one of whom argued that the *Globe and Mail* and Vancouver *Sun* were together worth more than $100 million.

Three weeks later, Howard Webster of Montreal, a previous owner of the *Globe and Mail* who had brought it into the FP fold in 1965, and held 22.5 per cent of the shares, offered $109 million with a deadline at year's end. On that date, Black stepped up his offer to $119 million and Webster's original overture lapsed.

But the fun was just beginning. Two days into the new year, Lord Kenneth Thomson entered the fray with a bid of $139 million. A week later, Howard Webster tossed in another blue chip, raising the ante to $149 million. While an industry looked on in fascination, Ken Thomson promptly called Webster and raised him $10 million, to a total of $159 million. Each protagonist had set a deadline for January 11, the next day.

Closing time had been set at 5 p.m. Forty minutes before expiry, Webster weighed in with what proved to be his last offer: $163.3 million. But Ken Thomson and his group, gathered in the office of Roland Michener, former Governor-General of Canada and a trustee of the Bell estate, immediately bumped their bid to $164.7 million.

The shareholders accepted. The ball game was over. Ken Thomson had acquired 54 per cent of the voting shares in FP and 79 per cent of the equity. Only Howard Webster and the estate of John W. Sifton in Winnipeg had not tendered their shares. June Sifton, John's widow, protested that the family shares were held in trust for her fifteen-year-old son, Victor John Sifton; he was to receive the shares at age twenty-five, provided he was physically and mentally equipped to step into the business at that time. She rejected Richard Malone's advice to sell out to Thomson and attempted by court order to block the transaction.

The Manitoba Court of Appeal, however, denied June Sifton's petition, ruling that there was "not the slightest bit of evidence" that the trustees were acting contrary to Victor's interests. Indeed, they seemed to think that an eventual after-tax inheritance of $12 to $15 million was enough to give almost any red-blooded Canadian boy a leg-up in life.

Malone, with 7.5 per cent of the shares, held a strong balance-of-power position between the contending factions, and it was not surprising (even though his early loyalties were to FP) that he came down on the side of the Thomsons. At one stage in his career, he had been offered a top spot in the organization by Roy Thomson and for years had been a friend of Thomson senior executive St. Clair McCabe, whose tough style of operating was very close to his own. Furthermore, he had for some years been at loggerheads with Howard Webster. It was, in essence, a personality conflict. Howard was a hands-off operator; shy, but also a two-fisted drinker, and the man who brought a major league baseball franchise (the Blue Jays) to Toronto.

There were 1,448 voting shares (of which Malone held only 112) and 1,949,426 equity shares outstanding: Thomson's final offer was $2,000 for each voting share and $77 for the equity. This offer was accepted by the Max Bell Foundation, the McConnell family of Montreal, Dick Malone, the equity shareholders of the Sifton estate in Winnipeg, and four Bell children. At first, Webster held out. No one could question his pride in ownership of the *Globe and Mail*. On the night of the take-over he visited the home of a friend in Toronto, began to talk about the day's events but broke down and wept. Three months later he abandoned his minority position and sold his shares (for $34 million) to Thomson. This sale ended a unique newspaper career: while a journalistic non-pro, Webster had built what many Canadians consider to be the finest newspaper in the country.

The man who confounded the pundits, and emerged as one of the most powerful men in Canada, was the soft-spoken Ken Thomson. Alone among newspaper-watchers, Gillis Purcell had predicted twenty years ago that Ken "would be tough". My own assessment of the man couldn't have been more wrong. I had pegged Ken as a gentle aesthete, a man who would probably retire early from the hurly-burly of business. But in two lightning strokes, in late 1979 and early 1980, Thomson invested more than $800 million in Canada — $640 million to win the "Store Wars" and acquire control of The Bay, and $165 million for the FP newspapers. No doubt he was influenced by the gung-ho people around him — people like St. Clair McCabe and Margaret Hamilton, and his brilliant legal aide, John Tory. But in the end, the decision was Thomson's and he resolved it with the aplomb of a Vegas croupier.

Overlooked in the general brouhaha over the newspaper bidding was the probability that Thomson had made a very shrewd buy. Thomson, after all, had acquired a circulation of 800,000 (or about $170 a customer); dominance of the market in Winnipeg and Vancouver; a "flagship" in the *Globe and Mail;* and monopoly situations in Victoria and Lethbridge. (By contrast the late Sam Newhouse had in recent years paid $300 million for Booth Newspapers Inc. which had 500,000 subscribers, or $600 a head.)

Addition of the FP group to existing Thomson holdings of forty-nine dailies and weeklies in Canada gave Ken Thomson almost half the newspapers in Canada and a total circulation of 1.3 million, a shade ahead of Southam.

Reaction at the *Globe and Mail,* according to *Star* reporter John Picton, was "almost total silence". The majority of staff appeared disappointed that Howard Webster had not succeeded in his bid. But they were prepared to adopt a wait-and-see attitude. For years, Thomsons had boasted that they left editors alone to enunciate policy and this was demonstrably true. But it begged the question: if a Thomson editor said he needed $2 million to cover the news, and was told that he could have only $1 million, was he being interfered with editorially? And yet the dollars were undeniably there; Roy Thomson's policy of buying small-town monopoly newspapers in growth communities was paying off handsomely. In the nine months ending in September of 1979 they had returned an after-tax profit of $43 million and the stock continued to climb on the Toronto Exchange.

On the face of it, the further acquisition of eight dailies (four of them majors) would seem almost unconscionable. Why would anyone want to own fifty-seven newspapers in one country? Pondering this admittedly academic question, it seemed to me that a maximum of ten would be about right: one for each province. Roy Thomson had once told an interviewer that he would be quite happy to own every newspaper in the free world. We all thought at the time that Roy was joking. When his son Ken told the annual meeting of Thomson Newspapers in the spring of

1980 that he was interested in further Canadian acquisitions, we began to wonder.

The materialistic answer to the question can be summed up in one word: profits. The idealistic answer is that a crusading owner saw an opportunity to revive and invigorate a quality press, and was willing to risk millions to bring it about.

Fortunately for all concerned, Ken Thomson is a decent and honourable man who would not abuse his power. But he cannot live for ever. Who, twenty years down the road, would succeed him? Could he assume, in the inevitable play of checks and balances, that the Canadian people would reject any attempt to insinuate a single Group-think point of view? For now, though, apprehensive Canadian newsmen can take heart from the Thomsons' performance with the London *Times*. There, in the face of monstrous union provocations and grinding losses, they poured millions of pounds into "The Thunderer" and kept alive the world's most prestigious newspaper. Both *père et fils* had treated the paper as a sacred trust and in so doing had won the admiration of journalists and readers around the world.

But the harsh fact remains that, as Canada enters the 1980s, the number of newspaper groups in the country has been reduced from three to two, both centred in Toronto. A terrible burden of responsibility had been imposed on two men, Lord Kenneth Thomson and Gordon Fisher.

Their mandate — to inform an audience of some ten million Canadians in an objective and even-handed manner — leaves them with a formidable duty. Perhaps as great as a Prime Minister, or even more — for newspapers always outlive the politicians.

For a few weeks the merged companies operated with two boards, Thomson and FP. It was obvious that this situation could not last. On April 2, 1980 — almost precisely two years to the day since George Currie's assumption of the presidency of FP — Ken Thomson announced a merger in which Currie would "step down". At the same time, it was announced that Richard S. Malone would serve Thomson as an interim consultant in integrating the two companies. He thus became one of the first men in history to serve as both corpse and undertaker.

Within a few weeks the "Currie Team" was dissolved. Gone were personnel officer John Egan, financial vice-president David

Perks and editorial director Ted Bolwell. Egan issued a statement to the press in which he said that they had been fairly dealt with and that the Thomson people had been "decent, generous and understanding". Star columnist Allan Fotheringham left to join Southam.

But insiders knew that there was some residual bitterness. Bolwell returned from a flying visit to Australia, where he had gone to see his ailing father, to be told that his job was "redundant". He had, in about a year, assembled in FP News Service one of the finest collections of editorial talent in Canada — precisely what Thomson's did not have, and sorely needed. Its fate was uncertain. But to describe the hyperthyroid Bolwell as "redundant" was a bit like calling Sophia Loren "winsome".

That Thomson's intended to pursue a hard-line policy on editorial costs became starkly evident in August of 1980 when it was announced that the Victoria *Times* and Victoria *Daily Colonist* would be merged into a single morning-evening combination. This meant a loss of more than fifty jobs, twenty of them on the news side. The *Colonist,* founded in 1858, was the oldest daily of continuous publication on the Pacific Coast; the *Times* dated from 1886. While both dailies had suffered grievous labour problems with the arrival of automation in the 1970s, they had recovered. As they entered the new decade they were once again fraught with advertising and making a profit. But now another editorial voice would be lost — and in a capital city, where disparate opinions were crucial. The obvious question arose: was this merger really necessary? How could it be justified, except in terms of maximization of profits?

A few weeks earlier the Thomson group had off-loaded the Calgary *Albertan* to Douglas Creighton of the Toronto *Sun,* thus divesting itself of its most consistent loser. The *Albertan* was never much of a newspaper, paying meagre wages and operating with as few staff as possible. Its historical significance was that it had given Max Bell his start as a classified advertising manager in the hungry thirties and had provided an unlikely base camp on his ascent towards the merger that created FP Publications Ltd.

But if Victoria and Calgary were merely volcanic hiccups, a major belch was impending. On a "Black Wednesday" late in August 1980, without warning, Thomson's shut down the Ottawa *Journal* and FP News Service; Southam's gave up on the Winnipeg

*Tribune* and (for $40 million) bought out Thomson's half-interest in Pacific Press, represented by the Vancouver *Sun*. Students of newspapers could not recall as sweeping an upheaval in the history of Canada's press. Close to 1,000 people lost their jobs. While disclaiming any back-room wheeling and dealing, the principals conceded that these moves had cleared the way for monopoly operations in two important capitals.

Indeed this "rationalization of the market", as the accountants and analysts described it, left Canada's 109 dailies with only four head-to-head competitions: in Toronto, in Edmonton and Calgary (where the cheeky Toronto *Sun* hoped to repeat its remarkable home-town success), and in St. John's, Newfoundland.

Some newspaper columnists, like Mike Valpy and Charles Lynch in Ottawa, were moved to compose reflective pieces on their craft, in which they wondered whether they were part of a "dodo" industry or at least representative of a vanishing breed. Many others simply took Gene Fowler's advice, went out and got drunk.

The distress which pervaded newsrooms across Canada, however, would not go away. The government announced the establishment of a Royal Commission to look into the new arrangements, but whatever its recommendations, newspaper staffs seemed set for a rough ride. The warning light for the eighties appeared to read: *attachez vos ceintures*!

# Epilogue

In a farewell visit to my office at the *Sun,* at the end of 1978, I set about gathering the accumulated bric-a-brac of fifteen years as publisher. At the door of the newsroom, I turned for a last look. Curiously, I could not feel sad. Forty-five years had raced by, the bad patches forgotten, the good ones remembered.

And journalism, for all its wild fluctuations, for all its infinite jest and variety, *had* been good to me. It had enabled me to roam the world (at someone else's expense) from the High Arctic to Russia to Malaysia; to dine with royalty and to introduce Sir Roger Bannister and his family to the delights of a drive-in hamburger heaven; to play golf for dimes with Bing Crosby and Bob Hope (Hope watched me tee off at Shaughnessy and exclaimed: "With a swing like yours, you should be the playing pro from Disneyland"); to sit on the New York Yankees' bench and chat with Casey Stengel; to number among my friends such disparate personalities as Jimmy McLarnin, the welterweight boxing champion, and Homer Thompson, the world-ranking archaeologist.

It was also a great time to be alive, and in Canada. In my own lifetime, I had witnessed the advent of supersonic aircraft, of radar, television, polio vaccine, an alphabet of nuclear bombs from A to H; of Man on the Moon, satellite broadcasting, direct dialling, newspapers printed by computer, bubble gum and the no-slice golf ball.

In Canada we had survived three major wars and emerged from the bleak depression days as one of the most dynamic and affluent societies on earth. We imposed on the world no territorial ambitions; we looked to the health of our citizens and treated our old people well; we opened our borders to refugees in generous numbers.

To be sure, there had been frustrations and reverses and heart-break along the way. But in retrospect most of it was fun.

In some respects it could be argued that I was leaving at precisely the right moment. When I started in the craft, some of our veteran reporters were still writing their stories in long-hand. Now, forty-five years later, we were totally into electronics: the newsroom looked like NASA control in Houston, with about 100 video screens and black cables snaking across the floor.

I thought of that dreadful day when we had a numbing crash of the entire computer system and all the stories disappeared from their screens — indeed, from the host receivers. In the elevator, I met one of our electronic whizkids and asked him what happened.

He replied — and I quote — "Our infrastructure suffered an improbable interface."

As an editorial boffin, I wasn't disposed to let him get away with it. So I fixed him with a flinty stare and murmured: "Surely you are guilty of an elliptical solecism?"

Wordlessly, we stepped off the elevator.

There, in microcosm, was the problem of Pacific Press. We spoke to each other but in strange, incomprehensible terms.

It was clearly time to go.

## Index

230

232

238